w/

# BLACK
# HATS

A NOVEL
OF
WYATT EARP
&
AL CAPONE

WILLIAM MORROW
*An Imprint of* HarperCollins*Publishers*

# BLACK
# HATS

## PATRICK
## CULHANE

BLACK HATS. Copyright © 2007 by Max Allan Collins. All rights reserved. Printed in the United States of America. No part of this book may be used or reproduced in any manner whatsoever without written permission except in the case of brief quotations embodied in critical articles and reviews. For information address HarperCollins Publishers, 10 East 53rd Street, New York, NY 10022.

HarperCollins books may be purchased for educational, business, or sales promotional use. For information please write: Special Markets Department, HarperCollins Publishers, 10 East 53rd Street, New York, NY 10022.

FIRST EDITION

*Designed by Susan Yang*

Library of Congress Cataloging-in-Publication Data

Culhane, Patrick, 1948–
    Black hats : a novel of Wyatt Earp and Al Capone / Patrick Culhane. — 1st ed.
      p. cm.
    ISBN: 978-0-06-089253-1
    ISBN-10: 0-06-089253-6
    1. Earp, Wyatt, 1848–1929—Fiction. 2. Private investigators—New York (State)—New York—Fiction. 3. Capone, Al, 1899–1947—Fiction. 4. Gangsters—New York (State)—New York—Fiction. 5. Mafia—New York (State)—New York—Fiction. I. Title.

PS3553.O4753B55 2007
813'.6—dc22

                      2006048611

07 08 09 10 11 WBC/RRD 10 9 8 7 6 5 4 3 2 1

# FOR STEVE LACKEY—

who fired the first shot

*This is funny.*
—Doc Holliday's last words

---

*There are those who would say it all breaks even*

*because the rich get ice in the summer*

*while the poor get it in the winter....*
—Last words written by Bat Masterson

---

*Suppose, suppose....*
—Wyatt Earp's last words

# ONE

# PLAY POKER*

*gambler lingo for:* get serious

APRIL, 1920

# One

THE NIGHT THOSE BASTARDS SHOT VIRGIL, IT WAS
storming like this.

Sky darker than the inside of your fist, rain
slanting in from the east, slashing at will, unseen
till lightning gave it away.

Wyatt Earp, not in particular reflective, found
his memory bestirred by weather, most often. And
back in Tombstone, what? Almost forty years ago?
That craven crowd had ambushed Virgil, a marshal making his midnight rounds, maimed him,
ruined his left arm forever with their buckshot and
cowardice.

Now Wyatt was doing the ambushing, and his
nightly rounds were hardly marshal's work. He
did have a badge in his wallet, a private detective's star courtesy of his friends at the Los Angeles Police Department, for whom he occasionally
did jobs.

Not this job, though.

Lowman's Motor Court on North San Fernando Road consisted of a dozen pink adobe cabins, six facing six across a graveled courtyard, where tiny pools glimmered in the sky's occasional shouts of white. The other night—this was Wednesday, that had been Monday—when Wyatt had stopped here, the foothills of the green Verdugo Mountains had conspired with a blazing orange sunset to provide a majestic backdrop for this sordid little assignation village.

Tonight the hills were just shapes, dark shoulders that couldn't be bothered to shrug in this downpour. Wyatt knew how they felt.

A damned domestic case.

Wasn't exactly dignified work for a man, was it? City of Angels coppers, at least, always gave him real jobs to do—hauling back wanted men from Mexico, sub rosa; putting the boot to claim-jumpers in the wilds of San Bernardino County. Hell, getting an investigative operator's license had been only to please Police Commissioner Lewis. Wyatt had never had no intention of hanging out a shingle and becoming a goddamned bedroom dick.

But word had gotten round that Wyatt Earp himself, the Grand Old (for Lord's sake!) Lion of Tombstone, was doing detective work; and the occasional client would find him at his rented bungalow on Seventeenth Street.

Not that this job came from the "occasional" client. This was the kind of thankless task that he would do only for a friend. He'd had very few real friends in his life, but when one came around asking a favor, Wyatt Earp was not the kind to say no.

He stood beneath a palm tree, the tree swaying, Wyatt not. He'd positioned himself between that tropical excuse for vegetation and the teal Model T that William S. had loaned him—Wyatt had learned to drive ages ago but had never owned an auto—hands in the pockets of a black rain slicker and wearing a wide-brimmed black Stetson that funneled the sluice nicely. Slender, six one, with Apache cheekbones, unblinking sky-blue eyes and snow-white hair with a well-trimmed matching mustache, Wyatt Earp might have been fifty-five. But he was seventy.

In this weather, a man like Earp—legendary lawman, gambler, buffalo hunter, prospector, Indian fighter, survivor of more bloody encounters than even the Wild West might be expected to throw at a body—should darn sure feel that moisture in his joints, be well and truly plagued by phantom pulsing pains from all those wounds.

Had he ever been wounded.

Wyatt Berry Stapp Earp—who had shot it out with drunken cowboys and notorious outlaws, gone toe-to-toe with the Clantons and McLaurys at the gunfight near the O.K. Corral, been through countless Indian raids and rode posses against cattle rustlers and tracked stagecoach bandits, whose brothers Virgil and Morgan had been shot down in the streets of Tombstone—had thus far in his lifetime suffered not a single bullet wound.

That time with Curly Bill Brocious, Wyatt wading across that stream with his damned fool cartridge belt slipping down around his knees and turning him into a waddling duck of a man, answering Bill's shotgun with a sixgun, that time? That time he'd come close to a cropper, skirts of his coat shot all to pieces, pretty well riddled to shreds. And a horse had died. Also Curly Bill.

Wyatt had never been one to wear a gun unless he was on marshaling duty, or maybe carting a big sum—the latter leading to that embarrassment when a police captain on security detail disarmed the former frontier marshal going into the ring to referee the Fitzsimmons/Sharkey bout in '96.

This bounty huntering for the Los Angeles blue boys, however, had him hauling the long-barreled Colt .45 out of mothballs. The ungainly old girl cleaned up good; she'd been a gift in Dodge City days from a dime-novel writer, an eccentric who'd pumped Wyatt for info, then never wrote a damned word about him!

Anyway, Wyatt had always prized the weapon, especially the way he could sight down that ten-inch barrel; but it was awkward as hell in a shoulder-rig. So, tonight, he carried her in a stiff-leather holster on his left hip, cross-draw, border-style—like Doc used to.

Something near a smile worked at the line of his mouth, summoned by the thought of his deceased gambler friend. Most people, back then, had hated Doc Holliday, mean drunken consumptive that he was. But Holliday's dark sense of humor had always tickled Wyatt.

*You'd be hurting in this wetness, Doc,* Wyatt said to his friend, in his mind. *Coughing like a schoolgirl getting her first taste of whiskey.*

*I like the rain, thank you very much, Wyatt,* Holliday might well have drawled back in his Southern gentleman's way. *And what would you know of schoolgirls, or whiskey for that matter?*

The lights were still out in cottage number four. Wyatt found the notion distasteful of interrupting the couple, *in flagrante delicto.* He would wait for them to finish. It was the Christian thing to do.

Just over a week ago he'd gone to Bill Hart's home in rural West Hollywood. For a movie star's diggings, the place was modest, a ranch-style ramble with some horses in a corral and a barn no bigger than Wyatt's bungalow. The former deputy marshal and the current Western film star sat in Hart's study where the walls were lined with books about the old days and authentic artifacts from back then were displayed in glass cases as if something precious—six shooters and buffalo guns and assorted Sioux Indian junk.

Flames whipcracked in the big stone fireplace over which hung a Remington painting of a Blackfoot war party on horseback. This unseasonably chill April day in California almost justified the fire, and Wyatt couldn't blame his actor friend for indulging himself. Big comfortable leather chairs with rough-wood arms angled toward the warmth.

The deeply tanned Hart—Wyatt had a card player's pallor—possessed the long narrow face and craggy hawkish features of the gunfighters and Indians he so often portrayed. An inch taller than Wyatt and just as muscularly trim, William S. Hart struck a handsome figure on the silver screen, but Hart was no young leading man, and would never see fifty again.

Still, Bill was a hell of a horseman, and made the only of these so-called "Western" pictures Wyatt could sit through.

Nonetheless, Hart was not his only actor friend here in Hollywood—he and Tom Mix associated, too. But that silly-ass nonsense Mixie dished out in those gaudy childish white-hat outfits, Wyatt wouldn't waste his time on, though Tom was an even better rider than Hart. Not that stunt riding had anything to do with anything except Buffalo Bill Wild West Show bunkum . . . whereas Bill Hart's Old West rang damned near true—good guys threw down liquor, fought with fists more than guns, gambled, chewed (and spat) tobacco, and the clothes were nothing fancy, except on the saloon girls.

Of course Wyatt was always willing to go to a film set as a paid consultant, and had done so for Mix as well as Hart. This was a lean enough time that Wyatt Earp could scarce refuse offers from either the LAPD or Hollywood.

Right now Hart wore an orange, green, white and black plaid shirt and denim trousers with turquoise-buckled wide leather belt and tooled brown-leather boots, while Wyatt wore a white shirt with black suspenders and no tie, gray slacks and black Oxfords.

Hart's gray-blue eyes under heavy black brows seemed to look inward; the hard lines and sharp angles of his face were heightened by the reflection of the fireplace that provided the study's only light.

Melodrama was the stock-in-trade of a fellow like Hart, so Wyatt couldn't hold the theatrics against him.

"I am a fool with women," Hart said.

"Not a small society," Wyatt said.

Hart's eyes found his friend's. "I don't mean to say that I . . . dally freely."

Wyatt managed not to smile. Of all the actors he'd known— and he'd known many, from Eddie Foy playing the Commy-Kew in Dodge to Charlie Chaplin losing at faro to him last month in a private, slightly rigged game—Wyatt had never known any of these hams to be such a puritan as Bill. Little drinking, no wild parties, with stud poker the star's only vice.

But not his only failing: Hart had a habit of falling in love with his leading ladies, and had asked his latest one to marry him.

"I am having second thoughts," Hart admitted.

"Better now than later."

"I . . . I hate to listen to gossipmongers. You know how malicious the rumor mill can be in this town."

Wyatt nodded.

"So the bad things that are being said about Millie, I should really ignore, but . . . Wyatt, is it ungracious of me to question her sincerity?"

"No."

"When we had dinner last night, at Musso and Frank's, I suggested, perhaps, that we should spend more time together before we formally announce our engagement . . . you know, away from the set and the seductive hurly-burly of filmmaking."

"Yeah. Hurly-burly can get away from you."

His nostrils and eyes flared. "And do you know how she reacted?"

"No."

"She covered her hand protectively—the one with the diamond ring I gave her! As if I might snatch it away! And she said that if I embarrassed her, if I thought I could make a public fool of her, we would just see what the lawyers and the reporters thought about it."

"Sweet gal."

Hart swallowed. Sighed heavily. Gestured more dramatically than he allowed himself on screen. "I assured her that alienating her affections was the last thing on my mind, and in my heart."

"That settled her down?"

"Yes. Yes, it seemed to."

". . . How much did the ring set you back?"

"Three thousand."

Hart had said three thousand like three bucks.

Wyatt shifted squeakily in the leather chair. "Bill, what can I do for you?"

"I'd, uh . . . like you to find a graceful way out of this entanglement."

Wyatt nodded. "Have you looked into her past at all?"

He shook his head. "She's from Chicago, she says. Told me money was no concern—her father was in the meatpacking business."

"Well," Wyatt said with a lift of an eyebrow, "that covers a lot of territory. He could own a stockyard or a plant. Or he could be the dub who mops the slaughterhouse floor."

Hart turned to the fire, its flickery dancing reflections making a mocking movie screen out of his long mournful mug. "I don't want to hurt her, or embarrass her."

Wyatt said nothing. The lay of it said the twist intended to do just those things to Hart.

Hart's gaze went back to Wyatt, painfully earnest. "Use a . . . a delicate touch."

Wyatt nearly reminded Hart that as a lawman in Wichita, Dodge City and Tombstone, pistol-whipping troublemakers from behind had been about as delicate as Marshal Earp was known for.

But instead he leaned forward, the fire a little too warm on his face, and said, "Could cost a few hundred. I need twenty-five a day, and information from the cops can run higher than an old warhorse like me."

Hart waved it off.

"All right." Wyatt sat back and folded his arms. "Then if money is no object . . ."

"It isn't."

". . . I have a suggestion."

"Go right ahead. By all means."

The actor had approved the strategy, and now, several days later, Wyatt—standing between a palm tree and a Ford car, rain-drops pearling the parchment of his impassive visage—prepared to put his plan into motion, as the light in the window of cabin four finally winked on.

He strode quietly across the graveled courtyard, avoiding puddles. His black "fish" (as Tombstone lingo had dubbed rain slickers, so long ago) had metal snaps and these he undid as the slanting wet trailed him, and the white flashes of lightning did their best to betray him.

For a few seconds he stood on the stoop beneath the overhang outside the cabin door. The path of the rain was such that the overhang provided scant protection, but at least with his back to the spatter of liquid bullets, he could get the lengthwise folded manila envelope from out of his waistband, and the room key out of his pants pocket, in a dry way.

The envelope was in his left hand and the key—which had cost him (or, anyway, Bill Hart) a finif from the motel's night clerk—was in his right.

Wyatt worked the key in the lock and pushed the door open— a thunderclap accompanied him, but the two in bed would have probably sat up in surprise even without it.

"Stay put," Wyatt said, shutting the door behind him, keeping his back to it, "and just listen."

Rain pelted the window behind the curtains, echoed by moisture dripping from Wyatt to the hardwood floor.

The room was nothing special, walls of pale pebbly plaster, with a framed print of desert landscape, heavy on the cactus, over the double bed. A dark-wood chest of drawers at Wyatt's right, no mirror, and a pair of nightstands, both with yellow-shaded lamps, one on, one off. Bathroom door open, just past the bedroom area, the sink in sight, the stool not. One of those motel rooms with space enough to walk around either side of the bed, and that was about it.

Millie had been curled up facing the wall, her back to her agent, Phil Gross, who was propped up with pillows against the headboard, smoking a cigar and reading *Variety*—or anyway, had been. The paper had dropped to his lap, partially covering his red-and-white-checkered shorts; he also wore an athletic t-shirt and black socks with garters. The cigar drooped in his mouth like an uninterested pecker.

Wyatt's pecker managed not to be interested in Millie—he was, after all, a professional—but he could have hardly blamed it, had it perked. Millie, like Gross, was atop the covers and she wore only a lacy off-white chemise that didn't hide much of her peaches-and-cream complexion and a full figure that a screen vamp such as Theda Bara might well envy.

No wonder Bill had cast her.

Gross was less attractive than his cabin co-star, but Wyatt figured the feller wasn't bad for an agent—not tall but muscular in his upper torso, with masculine, regular features and dark hair, mussed from recent attention. Hairy arms and legs.

All of this Wyatt took in, in half a second or so.

"Who the fuck are you supposed to be?" Gross said, eyes traveling from the floor to Wyatt's Stetson. "Wild Bill Hickok?"

"No. Wyatt Earp."

Gross, who was still on his back on the bed, raised his eyebrows and the cigar finally tumbled from his lips. He brushed it off of him, sparking, onto the floor.

Millie, not a particularly modest girl, was grabbing on to Gross's nearest arm, stealing glances at Wyatt as if afraid to allow her eyes to light on him longer than a second.

She was saying, "That's that gunslinger! That friend of Bill's from Tombstone!"

Wyatt took a step forward. He held up the manila folder. "Take a look at these."

He tossed the folder onto the bed.

Gross snatched it up and withdrew the photos. Millie sat on

her legs, pretty knees winking at Wyatt as she crowded near her agent, taking in the photos like a kid Sunday morning reading the color funnies. Full breasts under the chemise bobbled, like they were trying to get a look, too.

"These are . . ." Gross looked up, mildly surprised. His tone was dismissive. "We're just getting out of the car. Going into one of these cabins."

"And out," Millie added, frowning in concentration.

Wyatt said, "I don't do bedroom photography. But those indicate what's going on here." He took one more step, nearing the foot of the bed. He was still dripping. "Those tell the story."

Millie snatched the photos up and sat like an Indian and studied them some more. Gross, thoughtful, got off the bed, one of his bare feet crushing the forgotten cigar. He was three paces from Wyatt.

"*What* story do they tell, Gramps?"

Gross was maybe thirty, thirty-two. Five nine, five ten. A solid, fairly muscular specimen. Probably played handball, tennis; maybe even boxed a bit.

"You know what story, son. You're shaking down Bill Hart, who never did a damn thing to this girl but put her in the motion pictures."

Thunder shook the sky and the windows.

"These won't hold up in court," Gross said, gesturing to the pictures Millie was going over, as if studying her next script. "I'm Miss Morrison's agent, after all. We might have been having a private business conference, for all those pictures indicate."

Wyatt granted him a nod. "Might seem that way to a court. Won't to your wife."

Gross's eyes tightened. He took a step forward.

Wyatt raised a hand. "Stay put. Here's what's what. You intended to bilk Bill Hart. This child would marry and divorce him, and he would pay through the nose. Plus, her name value in the flickers would benefit from the press."

"Divorce never benefits—"

Wyatt held the hand up again. "I'm sure she'd have a tale to tell on the witness stand that would curl the hair. How Bill beat her, or maybe forced perversions upon her. She's a good actress. She could sell that."

Millie smiled up at Wyatt, as if to say "thanks," caught herself and remembered to frown at him, which she did.

"Now here's the deal," Wyatt said. His words were affable but spoken in a deliberate fashion. "You get the negatives of those photos . . . and our word we won't go public."

Gross sneered. "*Your* word?"

Wyatt didn't care for the man's tone, but he merely said, "If Miss Morrison does not hold Mr. Hart to his proposal of marriage, we would have no reason to embarrass her . . . or you, Mr. Gross."

The agent thought about that.

Wyatt said to the actress, "And Mr. Hart says you may keep the diamond as a memento."

Her eyes flashed. "Really? Do I . . . *have* to keep it?"

"Yours to do with as you will. At your discretion."

The agent stepped forward—two paces. He was less than an arm's length from Wyatt now, and smelled of pomade.

"Listen, Mr. Earp," Gross said, smiling now. If a snake could smile, that was how. "You know and I know that William S. Hart is worth a lot more than that diamond."

"Yes he is. But you and Miss Morrison are worth considerable less."

The agent's eyes widened and his teeth bared and he grabbed Wyatt by the rain slicker and slammed him against the door.

"Listen, old man," Gross said, and the pomade scent was overpowered by the Sen-Sen on his breath, "you can't intimidate me. This is blackmail, and you can tell that fart Hart that if he so much as—"

What happened next was so fast, the agent didn't see it happen—but he felt it. He surely felt it.

The long-barreled .45 came out from under the fish, Wyatt's right hand jerking it from the holster on his left hip, and the side of the gun met the side of the agent's head with a sickening *whump*.

Wyatt saw the man's eyes roll back like slot-machine horseshoes and the agent, right side of his face bloody, dropped at the foot of the bed in an ungainly pile of flesh and underwear.

Millie's eyes were almost as wide as her mouth; the actress was still sitting like an Indian, with knees cuter than a teddy bear, and the photos were in her lap and hands.

"Can you reason with him?" Wyatt asked her.

She nodded. "I . . . I . . . I . . ."

"You what, child?"

"I never . . . never *saw* one that big before."

She meant the gun.

Wyatt put it away.

"You can keep those," he said, meaning the photos.

Down on the floor, Gross was stirring.

Wyatt knelt to him. The man was conscious enough to understand the words Wyatt had for him, which were these: "You know how to settle the matter with Mr. Hart. That's one thing. This is another. If you ever put your hands on my person again, Mr. Gross, you will have to settle with me."

The agent swallowed; then he swallowed again. "You'll have no problem with me, Mr. Earp. Tell Hart . . . tell Hart his terms are fine."

Wyatt stood. "Nice doing business with you." He tipped his Stetson to the girl in the chemise on the bed. He couldn't resist adding, "Ma'am," and he stepped back out into the storm.

# Two

WHEN THE BLACK TAXICAB ROLLED UP TO THE curb in front of Wyatt Earp's rented bungalow, the woman rider spoke to the driver as she paid him from the back seat. Then the cabbie came around and held open the door for her and even tipped his cap. The tip must have been good, because the driver returned to his post behind the wheel and waited for her while she made her way up the sidewalk toward the porch where Wyatt sat in a hard chair with a book in his lap and a dog at his feet.

She was dressed appropriately for the cool sunny April afternoon, and very modern—white straw hat, coral silk dress with white polka dots and kimono-style sleeves and waist cinched with a satin sash, black purse fig-leafed before her. White stockings. White shoes.

She was tall enough to carry it off, slender

enough, too; but too old by half. Sixty if she was a day. He was just wondering what kind of damn dress-up party this was when he recognized her, half-way up the walk.

The little spitz pooch sat up and, furry tail a blur, studied their approaching visitor with the one eye he had left after fighting two cornered rats at the Happy Days copper mine two summers ago. The pooch's name was Earpie, and that the animal wasn't growling was a good sign . . .

. . . or would have been, if Wyatt hadn't felt like growling himself.

"Kate," he said.

Not greeting her so much as identifying her, out loud.

And she halted.

She should have looked foolish in that get-up, but she was clearly well-preserved, the long oval of her face still smooth and glowing. Hell, she had always had a way about her. . . .

"Wyatt," she said, in that musical voice corrupted by an accent that she always claimed was Hungarian; did sort of sound like a mouthful of goulash. "May I send the taxi away?"

"No one's stopping you."

"I'd like to talk to you."

"You already are."

She turned and nodded to the taxi and the driver nodded back and rumbled off hurriedly, knowing no fares would likely be found in this modest residential neighborhood with its stucco-and-frame bungalows and indifferently mowed grass and old men sitting on porches.

When she reached the two wooden steps, Wyatt finally rose. Earpie's furry tail was twitching, tongue lolling, eyes bright—eye bright, anyway.

Wyatt said, "Sit yourself," and gestured to the rocker, which was his wife's.

As if Kate knew that, she asked, "Oh, is Sadie home?"

"She's gone for the afternoon. Shopping."

Gambling was more like it. Off to San Bernardino on the Big Red Car, for some backroom poker game at one hotel or another. But that was nobody's business.

"Pity," Kate said. "Be awfully nice to see her."

Wyatt figured seeing Sadie again was about the last thing Kate would have wanted—the two women had never got along—and knew damned well this old gal in young silk was just trying to be sociable.

Coquettishly, Kate climbed the two steps, gathered her dress and lowered herself into the rocker, setting her purse on the wood slats beside her. Wyatt returned to his hard chair, angling it toward his guest.

"I'm surprised you recognized me," she said.

Hard not to. "Big-Nosed" Kate Elder, the common-law bride of Doc Holliday, had distinctive features, albeit not the big beezer one might expect. She'd also been called "Nosey" Kate, which was more accurate. She liked to stick her nose in, where it had no call to be.

True, her nose was noticeable, long not big, her eyes crowding it some; but most considered her pretty, in her day—the eyes were dark blue and sparkled (still were, still did), her mouth a small girlish bud (thinner lips now). Damn, her face was smooth for her age.

In the 1880s, she'd had a lot of dark, lustrous hair; and even six decades along, no signs of white were apparent, or henna coloring either, for that matter—she had it pinned up in back, but he'd seen it flow.

She was settling her hands in her lap. "After all, it has been a while."

"Twenty-five years," he said. "Rock Creek, Colorado. You were married to that blacksmith—George something-or-'tother. What became of him?"

"I divorced him. He drank too much."

Wyatt was too much of a gentleman to point out that Kate had a leaning toward that ilk.

"You're reading a book," she said, as he set the thick little red-bound volume on the porch railing.

"You needn't sound so surprised."

"What is it?"

"*Hamlet.* Friend of mine suggested it."

Bill Hart.

This seemed to amuse her. "What do you think of it?"

"This Hamlet feller is a talkative man. Wouldn't have lasted long in Kansas."

"Most likely not." She glanced toward the house, revealing little white teeth that seemed to still be the original articles. "What a quaint little place. How charming."

"Not hardly. It's a rental."

The living room turned into the bedroom when a Murphy bed came down, the kitchen was a sink and a stove in a corner behind a pull curtain, the bathroom tiny enough to make a crowd out of a sink, toilet and shower. Not much better than a cheap motel room. Like out at Lowman's Motor Court.

"Just temporary," he assured his guest.

Wyatt's fortunes would turn; they always did.

"I heard that you and Sadie were working a mine out Vidal way," Kate said, in a friendly if strained small-talk fashion. "That you work the mine and prospect around the Colorado River, winter months, and spend the rest of the year here in Los Angeles."

His eyes searched the supposed innocence of her facial expression. "How is it you know that, Kate?"

"Well, your diggings are near Parker, Arizona, aren't they?"

He nodded.

"And I live in Dos Cabezos; in fact, I've spent many, many years in Arizona . . . where it's no secret who I am, or that is, used to be. People ask me about you. People tell me about you. What you're up to. They assume we're friends."

"People assume lots of fool things, don't they, Kate?"

She glanced down, noticing the spitz who was sitting at her side, staring at her with that bright eye of his, apparently hoping for affection, heavy tail fanning. Kate rocked forward and scratched him around his ears and his collar.

She gave Wyatt a glance that was a little too friendly. "I heard you're doing detective work again. Like in the Wells Fargo days."

He sighed. "Some," he granted.

"I thought perhaps you might do a job for me."

Earpie was on his hind legs now, paws at the nice silk dress.

"Earpie," Wyatt said sternly.

The dog looked over at its master who gave him hard eyes, and then the animal hung its head and returned to his place and curled up at Wyatt's feet. Sullenly, but the dog did it.

Kate laughed. "So, Wyatt—everybody still jumps when you bark."

Sadie didn't, but he didn't point that out.

"Even Doc jumped at your command," she said, trying to sound light but bitterness edging in.

"I couldn't make the funeral," he said.

Funny to be making an apology over something that happened thirty years ago. Sort of just came out.

She gave him a sharp, surprised look that immediately softened. "You couldn't have got there in time, and I couldn't afford the ice. Anyway . . . you and Doc had your goodbyes, year or so prior, I understand."

Wyatt had been in Denver, to gamble, staying with Sadie at the Windsor Hotel. Doc had heard the Wyatt Earps were in town and came looking for his old compadre. The two men had sat and talked in the lobby, but Doc did more coughing than speaking. His dapper friend had always been slender, but now was a skeletal apparition.

"Can't last much longer," Doc had said. His eyes were sunken, his cheeks, too; but the mustache was perfectly trimmed. "Wanted to see you one more time, Wyatt."

". . . Strange."

"What is?"

"If you hadn't saved my tail in Dodge that time, I wouldn't be sitting here. And, Doc—I have no damn way to repay the favor."

Doc's eyes were moist; the sickness, surely. "You have repaid me myriad times, Wyatt. With your friendship."

Suddenly Doc embraced him, startling Wyatt.

Then the notorious gunfighter got to his wobbly feet and managed a half-bow. "I will see you again, but not too soon, I hope . . . considering where I'm bound."

And Doc moved away quickly if feebly. Next thing he knew, Wyatt had needed to dry his eyes with a hanky, feeling like a goddamned woman.

And this goddamned woman in the coral dress, for all her faults—and she had considerable—had loved that man, too. Of course, oftentimes Big-Nosed Kate had expressed her abiding affection by hounding Doc and trading drunken blows with him, shaking a gun at him while he shook a knife at her, and vice versa. Never had two people walked the line between love and hate more unsteadily than Doc and Kate.

In a way, Wyatt's brother James bore the blame for bringing the two of them together, Doc Holliday and Kate Elder.

Saloonkeeper James and his wife Bessie ran prostitutes on the side, in those days, and Kate had been one of their soiled doves, a pretty sassy thing in her twenties when James and Bessie brought her (and a wagonful of other wenches) to Fort Griffin; and Doc, working the gaming tables, took to Kate right away, smart, good-looking, well-educated lass that she was, with that clumsy, graceful European accent of hers.

Kate had proved her mettle to Doc the night things got out of hand at Shannsey's Saloon. Doc was playing poker with a local gambler, Ed Bailey, and Bailey started fiddling with the deadwood, the discards. Doc called Ed on it, Ed jerked a sixgun, and Doc slashed a blade across the cheater's brisket.

Ed seemed to be dying (he survived but didn't look he would), and the town marshal held Doc under house arrest at the Planter's Hotel. Hearing of this later, Wyatt figured Doc had been betrayed by the marshal, because jail would have been safer, and the hotel gave a local lynch mob an easy avenue to the prisoner.

But spunky Kate had set fire to a nearby shed, and while the vigilantes transmogrified into a fire brigade, the pretty little whore waltzed into the hotel, drew down on the deputy sitting guard, and escorted Doc out to the waiting ponies.

Or so the story went, as Doc had so often grandiosely told it. Kate once denied the rescue, calling it a fairy tale; but Wyatt believed Doc. After all, if Doc said up was up, Kate would call it down.

"If you live in Arizona," Wyatt said to his guest, who was gently rocking now, "what are you doing in Los Angeles?"

"Perhaps I came to call on you."

"Just to see me."

"To see you about doing a detective job."

"All the detectives in Arizona busy?"

Her small mouth twitched a smile, but her eyes were nervous. "This isn't a job that . . . just . . . just *any* detective could do."

"Takes a Los Angeles one, then. Something out here?"

"Something . . . something in New York."

Wyatt didn't know what to say to that.

She sat forward, her hands clasped prayerfully tight in her lap. The smile disappeared but the nervous eyes remained. When she leaned closer, lines around her eyes and on her upper lip showed. Still, a smooth mug for an old gal, though.

"Doc and I . . . you know that we were together, at the hotel in Glenwood Springs, those last six months . . . ?"

Wyatt nodded, and took any edge off his words. "I know that you were at his side. That you nursed him. That you comforted him, and for that I am damned grateful."

She averted his gaze, nodded back, rather absently; then said, "Thank you," very softly.

Then she sat in silence, for an eternity—perhaps thirty seconds. The spitz was snoring. Traffic noise thrummed, and down the block a neighbor was playing "Avalon" on the piano, badly.

Wyatt arched an eyebrow. "Kate?" he prompted.

She swallowed. "I did more than just . . . comfort Doc, Wyatt. I . . . *we* . . . had a son."

Wyatt blinked. "The hell you say."

"Doc never knew it. He had no interest in having any children with me or anybody else; he considered himself some kind of . . . dark soul, a strain of the Holliday blood best not continued."

That sounded like Doc's line of bull.

"I was expecting his child, at the time he passed," she said. "You know we were married, don't you?"

"Yes," he said.

He knew she claimed it. Doc denied it, of course. God had not invented the subject Kate and Doc agreed upon.

Despite his assurance, her response was defensive: "My son is *not* illegitimate! I want you clear on that. I had a rough start in life, lost my parents to influenza back in Davenport, Iowa; left the foster home for a riverboat and wound up earning my keep on my back, just *sixteen*, Wyatt Earp! Sixteen and soft, pleasuring hard men like you!"

"Those are distant days," he said, thinking that last sounded a mite rehearsed. "Nobody need be judged."

Indeed Wyatt had been one of her customers—hell, she was his brother's wife's worker, using the last name Earp at the time!— but that had been before Doc, and their friendship, and Doc's doings with Kate, for that matter.

She touched her forehead, where the wide-brimmed bonnet shaded the skin. "I'm . . . I'm sorry, Wyatt. I haven't spoken to anyone of John. Anyone from the old days."

"John? You mean . . . Doc?"

"I mean John. John *Junior*."

Wyatt's eyes narrowed and he sat forward. "Was that the blue-eyed child with you, in Rock Creek? I thought that was that feller *George's* boy."

She nodded, then immediately contradicted it with a head shake. "George took the boy on when he took me on; Johnny was part of the package. Probably had to do with why the drunken bastard beat me so."

"Under what name was the boy raised?"

"My maiden name—real name, Haroney. There's a birth certificate says John Henry Holliday, Jr., but it's tucked away, and is neither here nor there. Anyways, George refused to lend the boy his name. He . . . he hit *Johnny*, too. Would get lickered up and, when I wasn't handy, take all his worldly woes out on my young boy. That was partly why I left the man."

Doc Holliday's son.

Wyatt had been with Sadie for many years, and their marriage had been a good one, but childless. At times Wyatt—whose family had been large, five brothers, two sisters—found his and Sadie's life limited; but their nomadic bent had always been aided by the lack of offspring. Footloose and fancy free, he was. Even today. At seventy.

"He's a good boy, Wyatt. Good man. You see, I've fared well. About twenty years ago, I became housekeeper to a rich widower. We grew . . . close. We've never married, but I live with him, I care for him. I have all the comforts a woman could ever crave."

"Happy for you, Kate."

A tiny smile pursed the lips, near a kiss. "My . . . my benefactor's name is John—like Doc . . . like our son. And he took to my boy from the start. Saw to it that he got the kind of upbringing a young man needs."

"Well, that's just fine, Kate."

Even with the smile, and such positive words, her gloom was apparent.

She went on: "My son was very bright, like his father. Always first in his class. And my other John, my . . . *benefactor* John, he put my son through dental school, in Denver."

"Ha! Junior's a dentist, too?"

She managed a small smile. "Wyatt, it's my fault. He always

wanted to know about his real father; and I told him his papa was a Southern gentleman, an educated man, a professional man . . . a doctor of dentistry. And even from childhood, my boy wanted to follow in his father's footsteps."

"Well, I think that would please Doc."

In the bonnet brim's shade, her forehead clenched, and finally she showed some wrinkles worthy of her age.

"Wyatt, Johnny never knew his father was Doc Holliday. I told him of an imaginary Dr. John Haroney, who *was* Doc, in a way . . . but a Doc who never caught tuberculosis, who never turned to gambling and drink and . . . and women like me. Who wielded only dental tools and not knives and sixguns and shotguns. A Doc stripped of his faults but overflowing with his merits."

Wyatt, frowning, said, "A boy has a right to know who his daddy was."

Her eyes tensed. "I know. I know. And . . . and he *does*, now."

". . . Someone told him?"

"I did, Wyatt." Her expression grew grave now. "I finally did."

He grunted a thoughtful, "Hmmph," then asked, "What changed your mind?"

She swallowed hard and then she reached down for the black purse, brought it to her lap, snapped it open and fished out a big white hanky with no lace at all. Purely functional.

And its function, right now, was for her to bust out crying in.

Wyatt watched, uncomfortably, while she bawled; down the block the neighbor on the piano was mangling "Look for the Silver Lining," and Earpie had stirred from his slumber to look up sympathetically at their weeping guest. Stealthily the spitz crept away from Wyatt and curled up near Kate's feet, careful to keep his tail out from under the rockers—that lesson had long since been learned.

Finally, as the waterworks were letting up, Wyatt asked if she wanted a glass of lemonade or maybe something harder.

She shook her head, the bonnet flopping a bit. "Wyatt, I'm sorry for losing my . . . my composure."

For a foreign-born, Kate sure knew some four-dollar words.

"You see, two years ago Johnny was married to a lovely girl named Prudence. He had a dental practice in Bisbee, and he met her there—her father owns a big hardware store, downtown. Very well off. Very well-to-do, for Bisbee. The girl studied out east, some fancy female school, and came home and met Johnny at a local dance at the First Methodist Church."

"The Methodists are holding dances now? Times have changed."

"It was a square dance at a social. Nothing sinful, Wyatt Earp. But that's where they met. And they bought a nice little house with a big yard and a picket fence."

"A white one?"

"Now you're teasing. But it *was* white, the fence, and so was the house. Prudence was a slip of a thing, pretty as a pansy patch, but not strong. Last summer . . . last summer . . ."

She raised the hanky again but managed not to start the bawling back up. Just blew her nose, in a fairly ladylike manner, apologized for it, and went on.

"Last summer, Prudence died in childbirth. The little girl died, too."

Wyatt drew in a breath. "I'm sorry."

"Johnny took it hard, as you might expect," she said, and commenced to telling him how.

But Wyatt wasn't listening. His mind carried him to a place he rarely visited, and never cared to, which was the bedside of his own young bride, Urilla. He was twenty-two and she was twenty, a beautiful slender dark-haired thing with a teasing smile and serious brown eyes. Lamar, Missouri, where he took his first lawman job. Where Urilla's father owned the hotel, and where he and Urilla had their own little house and their own picket fence.

Until, a year after they were married, more or less, the typhoid took her in childbirth, and their baby son.

"Wyatt? Wyatt, are you listening?"

"Yes. Yes. Hit your Johnny hard, this loss."

Kate was staring into nothing. "He began drinking. He'd never so much as touched a drop before, and now . . . now he was living in saloons, drinking till he got tossed in the street. He . . . he closed up his practice. Everyone figured it would be just till he got past the grieving; but months went by, and his father-in-law got a hold of me and said I should come and be with my boy. To get him over this terrible rough patch."

"And you went to him."

"I did." She closed her eyes. "And I made a terrible, terrible mistake."

"You told him he was Doc's boy."

"I . . . I told him." Her eyes remained closed. "I told Johnny that drink had ruined his father. That his father had been a brilliant man, an intellect, a gifted dentist, who gave in to his demons when the world didn't go his way."

"Kate, Doc was dying. He was too sick to practice his medicine and, God, woman, *you* drank him glass for glass."

Her eyes popped open. "Do you think I don't *know* that! I didn't want that boy going down my road, either . . . at least, not the first leg of it. I managed to come back from that dark place, Wyatt. I wanted to keep him from going there at all!"

Wyatt sighed. Then he asked, "And how did your Johnny react to this news about his true heritage?"

Her smile had little to do with the usual reasons for smiling. "It gave him a new purpose. He told me, bitter as coffee grounds, that he would do precisely what I had dreamed of him doing—he would follow in his father's footsteps! And he sold his house and took all of his savings and he began to gamble."

Wyatt laughed humorlessly. "And lost it all."

Her eyes flashed. "No! Would that he had—perhaps this terrible episode would be over." She shook her head despairingly. "He's as brilliant as his father, he can hold the odds in his mind, he can read the character of those sitting with him, he can win with the best of them."

"Well, I'll be damned." He resisted saying, *Doc would be right proud.*

"More than likely you *will* be damned, Wyatt Earp, but I refuse to let my Johnny be." She sat forward, her expression dreadful earnest. "If you will go out there, and talk reason to him . . . discourage him from the saloon life, the gambler's life. . . . He's heard the stories—who hasn't? He knows that you and his father were fast friends. That you faced down death, side by side. He may listen to you."

"Is . . . is this the New York job?"

"It is." She snapped the purse open again and withdrew a thick bank-banded wad of cash.

Both Wyatt's eyebrows went up.

Her smile had something feral in it. "I thought that might perk you up—five hundred dollars, Wyatt. Plus I'll pay for the train, and your hotel, and you can keep an expense account on meals and incidentals."

Trying to think past all that money, Wyatt managed, "What the hell is Johnny Boy doing out New York City way?"

A disgusted sound came up from her chest. "He wound up there because on a visit he got into a high-stakes poker game at the Hotel St. Francis with a famous gambler name of Arnold Roth."

"Arnold Rothstein," Wyatt corrected.

"Rothstein, yes, that's right. Anyway, Johnny won some kind of nightspot out there, close to Broadway I understand, a fancy layout that would make the Longbranch look sick. My only son is riding high on the hog, Wyatt, turning that joint into what they call a 'speakeasy.'"

The Volstead Act, the Eighteenth Amendment, had passed last July, but hadn't really gone into effect till just a few months ago—January 16, to be exact.

Wyatt nodded. "This Prohibition is making a lot of men wealthy."

"It's also making a lot of men dead," she snapped. "The competition is fierce. New York is full of gangsters, and Johnny has that same death-be-damned attitude as his father—he's laughing off the murder threats from these Italian brutes who are trying to . . . to . . ."

"Muscle in?"

"Muscle in. Indeed." She shifted in the rocker. "I've spoken to Bat about it, on the long distance telephone."

Bat Masterson, Wyatt's best friend alive, had years ago traded the West for the East, and was successfully writing a sports column for some bigtime New York rag.

"Bat? Where does he figure in?"

"He's kept me filled in—you don't think Johnny's talking to his *mother* about all this, do you?"

"Was it Bat's idea, you coming here?"

". . . Let's just say he wasn't against it. He says Johnny has been threatened by one of the most dangerous of a dangerous lot. Bat says . . . how did he couch it? Says this tub of guts Black Hand bastard has put Johnny 'on the spot.'"

Wyatt's eyes narrowed. He knew the term: it meant marked for death.

"Will you do it, Wyatt? Will you go?"

Wyatt Earp—who once upon a time had gone on a months'-long drinking binge after losing his own wife and son, and who in those dark days had stolen a horse and almost got hanged for it—said, "Yes, I will go. . . . By the way, Kate—what's this Black Hand bastard's name?"

"Alphonse Capone," she said.

Wyatt shrugged. "Never heard of him."

# Three

EXCEPT FOR THE TELEPHONE POLES ALTERNATING with palms, this might be Baghdad; or maybe a twister had plopped a Moorish palace down in Los Angeles, between First and Second Streets. Either way, the garish reddish rambling rococo structure on Sante Fe Avenue, with its towers and spires and golden central dome would be Wyatt Earp's portal to the East; but not by camel, or magic carpet: beyond the archway labeled LA GRANDE STATION, the Atchison, Topeka and Sante Fe's *California Limited* would pull that trick off.

Wyatt, in a black suit with four-in-hand tie and a black homburg, could have been a preacher or perhaps undertaker, as he and his alligator valise threaded through the diverse bustle in the station—from overdressed wealthy wives attended by sleepwalking husbands in impeccably tailored suits to the poorest Mexicans and Indians in ponchos and flimsy cottons. The station interior wasn't so fancy, not a harem dancer in sight, though the pretty, white-aproned waitresses of the lobby's Harvey House restaurant did their best to tempt travelers, abetted by the aromas of dishes almost as attractive as they were.

With a 1:10 p.m. train to catch, Wyatt would hold out till dinner on the dining car, also the domain of famed restaurateur Fred Harvey (though onboard Harvey's equally famous "girls" were replaced by colored stewards); and anyway, Sadie had fixed him an early lunch—weenies and sauerkraut, which you might call her specialty if any of the four or five meals she knew how to cook could be considered any way special.

He hadn't married the woman for her culinary talents. When he'd first seen Sadie—Josephine Sarah Marcus, Josie to some, Sadie to most—she'd been in Tombstone performing *Pinafore* on stage at Schieffelin Hall, a cabin "boy" who did a captivating hornpipe dance. He'd only admired her from an audience member's perspective, as this was not long after he and his brothers and all their wives rolled into town.

And Wyatt did have a "wife" at the time, Mattie, a dance hall wench he'd taken up with in Texas who had soon become a drag on his good nature with her incessant nagging, not to mention penchant for liquor and laudanum. He was not proud of breaking it off with Mattie, but neither was he ashamed. Few men could have resisted dusky Sadie in her day, with her full bosom, slim waist, full hips, and that lovely face, big dark eyes, and dimpled chin.

Furthermore, Sadie had been fun and spirited and adventurous, the only human on God's earth who could make Wyatt Earp laugh, besides Doc Holliday. Older now, with more heft on her, hiding it in loose shapeless dresses, she could still toss a sparkling-eyed smile at Wyatt and make him see the dangerous dusky Jewess he'd gone head over heels for. But Mattie—in his mind's eye—why, he could barely form her picture.

She was gone now, since '88, died of the drugs and drink, and he felt some pity for her; some.

Not that Sadie couldn't be a handful herself, what with her gambling habit and suspicious nature. The latter came from Wyatt's weakness for women, a hankering that had lessened with age. The former, well, Sadie could just not understand why Wyatt, an affirmed gambler himself, could begrudge her the occasional bet.

"You're just not a smart gambler," he'd tell her. "And you have no business risking your money that way."

And some of it *was* her money, at least when Wyatt's fortunes were on the ebb not the flow. When money got tight, Sadie's sister would send a check. In a way Sadie's sibling owed the Earps a little support, since Wyatt helped her establish that oil well claim near Bakersfield. But living off his wife's sister did not sit right with Wyatt.

When he looked back on his life with Sadie, he knew his fortunes had fluctuated, but mostly they'd lived well enough, and even flourished. These last three decades or so, he'd combined prospecting with saloon-keeping as they chased the money dream from one boomtown to another.

Sometimes that meant a mining camp, like Coeur d'Alene in Idaho in '84—he and Sadie ran a saloon there—and other times it might be a city, like San Diego with its land boom in '87, where Wyatt wound up owning four saloons (two with gambling halls) and a string of harness horses. The latter he'd loved, connoisseur of horseflesh that he was, sometimes driving a rubber-tired sulky himself, traveling the racing circuit from Chicago and St. Louis to Escondido and Tijuana.

There'd been horse stables in San Francisco, and two saloons in Nome, Alaska, where during that gold rush he'd hobnobbed with playwright-sportsman Wilson Mizner and famous book writers Jack London and Rex Beach, and palled with Tex Rickard, Jack Dempsey's first fight promoter.

Sometimes he and Sadie lived high, enjoying the best quarters in mining camps as saloon-keeper Wyatt concentrated on digging the gold from miners' pockets via drink and gambling; other times, when the Earps were themselves prospecting, a camping-out style of life ensued, which Sadie didn't mind at all, hearty gal that she was.

Finding both copper and gold at the Happy Days mine had provided good income at first—supplanted by Wyatt going into Needles to fleece the troops on payday—though the cost and toil of all that underground work, dropping shafts and such, was considerable, particularly for Wyatt and Sadie, who were getting a little long in the tooth for that kind of work.

Through all the days of horses and saloons and cards and gold, Wyatt had from time to time taken up his long-barreled .45 for local law work or to rent himself out to Wells Fargo or some mining company or even the Los Angeles coppers. Though he thought of himself as a professional gambler, and entrepreneur, Wyatt knew his reputation as a gun-toting Western lawman always followed him.

Hell, he had capitalized on it—often hanging a big sign on his saloons saying WYATT EARP, PROP.—and ever ready to let card players know they were sitting down with a sagebrush celebrity. His attitude was not one of arrogance or pride, but with fame the bane of his existence as it was, he figured he might as well get something out of it.

And, no denying, he was good at lawing. He'd done police

work of one kind or another since he was a kid back in Lamar, Missouri, and between his skills and reputation, carrying a badge— whether public or private—remained a trade he could always fall back on.

This was why he'd allowed himself to get back into the detective game, of late. A few months every winter at the Happy Days hadn't amounted to much in several years. And the cards hadn't been running much better for him than for Sadie, though he felt confident luck would turn his way. This meant the occasional lie to his darling girl: she thought the Bill Hart job had paid one hundred dollars, when four hundred was the true tally.

He had given her the C-note, while the other three C's were currently residing in his left boot. The Sante Fe's much vaunted speed meant he'd be in Chicago, late morning, third day out— with another twenty hours on the *20th Century Limited* before reaching New York. Three hundred was a good stake for the poker games he hoped to encounter on his four days of train travel.

The five hundred Kate Elder had given him, Sadie knew nothing of—just as she knew nothing of the private bank account Wyatt held certain of his earnings in, out of her reach.

He couldn't keep from Sadie that a female guest had dropped by the bungalow yesterday. He would liked to have, only their nosy neighbors would certainly have told Sadie about the well-dressed, well-preserved matron who'd dropped by. But admitting that it had been Kate Elder, that was another proposition altogether.

Sadie and Kate were oil and water, Kate having been a friend of Mattie Blaylock, them having as soiled doves shared various cages over assorted saloons. Even though Wyatt had thrown Mattie over for her, Sadie remained to this day jealous of that poor dead pitiful soul, resentful as hell that Wyatt had once co-habited with "such a creature."

That hadn't been fair to Mattie. In cowtowns like Wichita and Dodge, and likewise mining camps like Tombstone, red-light gals were the only females within hundreds of miles who weren't Indian or Mexican. Who else was a man in that situation expected to lay with?

Still, there was no reasoning on the subject with Sadie, especially when Wyatt brought up the fact that women in the theatrical profession were looked down upon in a similar way, which only sent her flying.

So Wyatt had simply said that the woman who came by was "Katherine Cummings," which was actually Kate's married name via the drunkard blacksmith in Colorado.

"She's a friend of Bat's," Wyatt had said offhandedly.

Sadie had a mixed opinion of Masterson, the negative deriving from Wyatt and Bat's friendship predating her own tenure, the positive from Bat becoming a successful New York sportswriter.

"And why does that mean she has to come around here?" Sadie asked sharply, sitting in the rocker where earlier that day Kate's behind had rested. By now evening had come, with Wyatt and his wife drinking glasses of warm beer in the cool blue night.

"Bat has a job for me," Wyatt told her.

"What kind of job?"

"A detective job. Young friend of his out there is getting some trouble from these Prohibition gangsters."

Her eyes tightened and she looked at her husband as if he had gone dancing around the little porch jaybird naked.

"Why does Bat Masterson have to send all the way across the country," she asked, "to get that kind of help? Don't they have younger detectives in New York City?"

"Yes," Wyatt said, "but not any Bat trusts. He is paying full expenses and there should be several hundred in it."

Sadie's eyes tightened again, but in a different way; then they untightened and her chin crinkled. "I don't care if it's *five* hundred . . ."

Wyatt managed not to blink at her prescience.

". . . it sounds *dangerous*, and I don't want you doing it."

He grunted a laugh. "Practically no danger in it a'tall."

"You know this for a certainty, Wyatt?"

He patted the air with a dismissive palm. "Hell, I've been in one hundred tighter places."

She frowned and rocked. "I know, but you never can tell—this might be the time."

"What time?"

"The time when one of those bullets catches up with you."

". . . Sadie, it's a chance to see Bat again."

"You saw him, when? Just last year, when you and he worked that prizefight in Ohio!" She stopped rocking and trained those brown eyes on him like the barrel ends of twin revolvers. "Anyway, you don't belong to Bat Masterson. And Doc's long dead, and you belong to me now, and I don't want anything to happen to you."

Managing not to react to her mind-reader's mention of Doc, he got up out of his hard chair and gave her a kiss on the mouth. She was still awfully pretty, especially in this light. And she could still dance a mean hornpipe.

"You think that kiss'll buy me off, Wyatt Earp?"

"It had better. I have no money to try."

She had laughed and swatted him, and he had walked back to his chair with several hundred dollars crinkling in his left boot as he did.

"Expenses paid?" she asked.

"All the way and back again."

And on this Kate Elder had certainly not stinted—Wyatt was

traveling first class and, on the designated Pullman car, he settled into his seat by the window, hat in his lap, knowing that the ride out of Los Angeles would initially be a rough one, the tracks running right down Alameda and playing tag with trolleys and horse-drawn wagons and trucks and automobiles. Before long, though, the bustle of the city had been replaced by orange groves whose pleasant perfume wafted through the car, helped by the battery of high-mounted electric fans.

That afternoon he watched Arizona roll by the window in all its scruffy glory. Wyatt had never thought of this country as a barren expanse, particularly not this time of year, when the tans of sandy desert were broken by blossoms, the golden poppies and vari-colored mariposa mingling with the green of shrubs and cacti. He was at home in Arizona's desert, but knew just as well its mountains and valleys, the green pine forests and the Petrified One, too.

He'd made and lost a fortune out there on that sun-shimmering expanse. He ridden shotgun on stagecoaches, he'd led posses, he'd mined for gold, he'd gambled and won, gambled and lost, upheld the law and been chased by so-called law on murder charges.

As he gazed upon that rugged landscape, Wyatt Earp knew that he would always live in Arizona, though he might not ever set foot there again, except perhaps to get out and stretch when this train made a stop.

How often had he ridden across this land in pursuit of rustlers or stagecoach robbers? He and his brother Virgil had spent seventeen days on one such pursuit, following the bastards who murdered shotgun messenger Bud Philpot into the mountains. . . .

When they first came seeking their fortunes in Arizona, Wyatt and Virgil and younger brother Morgan (and occasionally Warren) did not see themselves as gunfighters, no matter how the rest of the world viewed them. Good-natured James didn't bear that brand—everybody knew that particular Earp was strictly a bartender. The rest were gamblers and, on occasion, policemen, hard but fair, aware that maintaining law and order in cattle and mining towns took guts and the threat of force.

But both Wyatt and Virgil had gone sour on police work— killing in the line of duty could do that to a man—and Tombstone had been about getting rich in a boomtown, not helping marshal it; Wyatt's initial plan had been to start a stagecoach line, but others beat him to the punch. So Wyatt bought into the gambling concession at the Oriental, and—in addition to pursuing mining interests—he and his brothers rode shotgun for Wells Fargo, for whom they also did occasional detective work.

Such activities put them in conflict with a loosely organized bunch of local criminals called the Cowboys, Texans for the most part, who rustled across the Mexican border and fenced the cattle through crooked ranchers like Old Man Clanton, whose spread was near Tombstone. The Cowboys, many of them, were brutal killers, leaving behind a bloody trail of slaughtered *federales* and *vaqueros*.

The area ranchers (whether crooked or legit) were Democrats, Southern sympathizers, while the town businessmen were Union-leaning Republicans from back East. The former stuck a glad-handing, unqualified horse's ass called Johnny Behan into the sheriff's chair, where he could ignore Cowboy crime and get rich collecting taxes.

Behan got on Wyatt's bad side when the two men cut a deal whereby Wyatt would not run for sheriff on the assurance that Behan would run unopposed and then make Wyatt undersheriff.

The son-of-a-bitch Behan reneged, of course, but Virgil was a

U.S. deputy marshal by this time, and after Curly Bill Brocius "accidentally" killed Marshal Fred White, Virgil got the town marshal badge, as well. Morgan became a city policeman, and in time Wyatt was appointed county deputy sheriff. A chilly truce developed between Sheriff Behan and the Earps, who for a comfortable stretch were backed up by Doc Holliday, Bat Masterson and Luke Short . . . and with gunhands like that enforcing the law, few challengers stepped forward, anyway few sober ones.

But after Bat left town to help out his lawman brother in Kansas, and Short lit out in the aftermath of a questionable gunfight, Virgil lost the next marshal's election, and the scales shifted to the Cowboy side.

And the Cowboys were in need of some luck, at that, because the Mexican government had increased its *federale* forces, building forts along the border and confronting the rustlers in bloody battle—Old Man Clanton among the Cowboys who justly fell.

This sent the Cowboys reeling into other crime, not just rustling on the American side, but holding up stagecoaches to plunder Wells Fargo shipments.

Then when the new marshal unexpectedly resigned, Virgil got his badge back; and Wyatt decided to take on Johnny Behan for sheriff in the upcoming election. Behan was already stinging from Wyatt stealing Behan's live-in lady away . . . a beautiful young actress from San Fran called Josephine Marcus, nicknamed "Sadie". . . .

A six-thousand-dollar Wells Fargo reward was available for the capture of the killers of shotgun messenger Bud Philpot, and when his posse came back empty-handed, Wyatt approached the new leader of the Clanton clan, Ike, with a deal. Wyatt knew damned well lowlife loutish Ike was in with the stagecoach killers, and proposed that this prize fool lead him to the fugitives in return for the six grand. The glory of the capture, Wyatt knew, would give him a lock on the sheriff's race.

Ike said yes, but when the fugitives turned up dead (at neither Ike's nor Wyatt's doing), Clanton began to fret that Wyatt would reveal the rancher's treachery to such deadly compadres of Ike's as Curly Bill Brocius, Billy the Kid Clairborne and Johnny Ringo. Drunk one night, Ike accused Doc Holliday of spreading Wyatt's "lies" (though Wyatt had leaked not a word) and Ike damned near got himself killed, saved only by Virgil breaking it up.

Still, Wyatt understood Ike's worry over Doc, who did travel the same gambling circuit as the Cowboys, and who drank heavily and talked freely and might drunkenly let the damning tale slip.

One day, in October of '81, Ike Clanton spread threats against the Earps all over town and waved around guns that city ordinance didn't allow him to carry. The Earps cut him a world of slack—Virgil even played poker with Ike and several Cowboy cronies at the Oriental, shrugging off Ike's bluster.

Outside the Eagle Brewery, where Wyatt ran a faro game, he went out to catch some cool night air only to find himself with a whiskey-talking Ike Clanton in his face.

"Let's go for a walk, Wyatt," the boozy, woozy rancher slurred. He was a round-shouldered character, bordering on stocky, with a scraggly goatee.

"Got a game to mind, Ike."

"You can't run forever—tomorrow morning! We'll go man for man!"

"I don't want to fight you, Ike. There's no money in it."

Ike snorted a laugh and staggered off down Fifth Street, then turned and shouted: "I'll get my boys, you get yours, and we'll fetch this feud to a close! How about it, Mr. Wyatt Earp? What are you *smilin'* about? Maybe you don't think I'll be after you all in the morning!"

"Ike."

"*What?*"

"You talk too much for a fighting man."

And Wyatt went back to his game.

Surely the whiskey would drop Ike before need of any bullet doing it. By morning, all this fight talk would be forgotten and Ike would be working off his hangover over coffee in some cantina.

But when Ike spent the next morning staggering from one saloon to another, running his mouth about killing the Earps, Virgil had to disarm the jackass in the street, kissing him along the side of his head with the barrel of a Colt and dragging him into court for a fine.

And later when Cowboy Tom McLaury approached Wyatt on the street to complain about this outrageous treatment of poor Ike, Wyatt had to give McLaury similar treatment—slapping his face, and whacking his skull with the long barrel of the Colt. Shortly thereafter, the Cowboys gathered at Spangenberg's gun shop and made a big show of buying ammunition while Wyatt watched through the window glass.

Any number of times, Wyatt and Virgil might have arrested the mudsills for carrying firearms; but the lawmen preferred to let the Cowboys run out of steam and ride out of town.

They didn't.

Instead, the Cowboys gathered at the O.K. Corral, made more threats about the Earps to various passing citizens, and—two of them leading horses—walked through the corral onto the vacant lot next to Fly's Photography Studio, which was also a lodging house where a certain Dr. John H. Holliday roomed; so drygulching Wyatt's gambler friend seemed a likely reason for this congregation.

Various townspeople informed the Earps of the threats emanating from the O.K. Corral, as the lawmen stood on the sidewalk outside Hafford's Saloon. Any number offered aid, but Virgil, Wyatt and Morgan were professionals who preferred not to involve civilians in enforcement matters.

The trio was about to make their way toward the vacant lot when Doc Holliday sauntered up to offer his help.

"This is our fight, Doc," Wyatt said. "No call for you to mix in."

Doc reeled as if slapped, but his indignation was touched by his usual dark humor. "That's a hell of a thing for you to say to me, sir!"

Virgil handed Doc a sawed-off shotgun and said, "Keep that under your coat."

Taking it, handing Virgil a spiffy gold-topped cane in return, Doc said, "Well, certainly, Marshal—I would not want to create any undue excitement amongst the citizenry."

Virgil, who was not renowned for his sense of humor, only said, "Raise your right hand, Doc."

Doc did.

"Do you swear to—"

"I do. Shall we get on with the ball?"

Then the three blue-eyed, dark-blond Earp brothers and the hollow-cheeked, haunted-eyed blonder Doc started up Fourth Street. The Earps were indistinguishable from one another, six-footers with handlebar mustaches and black Stetsons and long black coats and black trousers with black string ties adorning soft white collars. Doc's hat was a wide-brimmed black but his long coat (worn cape fashion, over his shoulders) was gray, his shirt pastel, his mustache as sweeping as his companions' but his lips pursed in a whistle. The steps of the Earp brothers had a grave inexorability, but skeletal Doc seemed almost jaunty.

The fall afternoon—it was going on three p.m.—was crisp and cold, the wind making their coats flap and slap at their legs, and the icy sting on Wyatt's cheeks only helped keep him alert. Snow dusted the street, making their footsteps crackle; the wooden side-walks under overhangs were empty, but eyes glittered in store-front windows. Word had spread.

"Wyatt," Morgan said softly, the youngest Earp's eyes moving to and fro, "how do we know how many of these damned Cow-boys we're facing?"

"We don't."

"God knows how many have ridden in to back Ike's play. What if they're on horseback?"

"Shoot the horses first."

Doc eyed Wyatt sidewise, amused. "Horse lover like you, Wyatt? This *must* be a serious game. . . ."

The four men turned onto Fremont, and Wyatt slowly scanned the street every which way to Sunday; but the Cowboys could not be seen.

Then the vacant lot west of Fly's came into view, as did a brace of the rustlers: Ike Clanton and his young brother Billy, Tom and Frank McLaury, Billy the Kid Claiborne . . . and Sheriff Johnny Behan.

Behan, a dapper little daintily mustached man in a derby, was talking animatedly to the Cowboys, decked out in their stan-dard gaudy attire, oversized sombreros, red silk bandanas and gay sashes, fancy-pattern flannel shirts and tightfitting doeskin britches, tucked into forty-dollar half-boots. Ike and Tom wore short cowhide coats, the others vests.

As the Earps and Holliday approached, Behan noticed them and ran toward his brother lawmen, glancing behind him nervously and throwing his hands up, as if in surrender.

But when Behan reached them, Virgil and Wyatt and Morgan and Doc just kept walking, and the little sheriff had to tag along like a kid.

"For God's sake, Virgil," Behan said, "don't go down there—they'll murder you!"

Not missing a step, Virgil said, "They're carrying firearms in town, Johnny. I'm just going down to disarm them."

"You don't have to!" Behan had stopped trying to keep up, and, receding behind them, called, "I've disarmed them all!"

Wyatt exchanged glances with Virgil, who moved the pistol in his waistband around to the holster on his left hip and shifted the walking stick to his right hand. This, as Wyatt took it, was meant to show the Cowboys that the marshal was not there to murder them—after all, his gun hand was filled with a harmless cane.

Not approving of this strategy—why was Behan afraid the Cowboys would murder them, if he'd disarmed the group?—Wyatt withdrew his pistol from its holster and stuck it in his overcoat pocket, and kept his hand clamped on the handle, finger on the outer trigger guard.

As the Earps approached, the Cowboys disappeared deeper into the vacant lot. Clearing the corner of Fly's Photography Shop, Wyatt could only see about half a horse. . . .

But as the lawmen advanced, the Cowboys came into view again—standing in a row but with Ike out front, his baby-faced brother Billy with a hand on his holstered sixgun, Frank McLaury, too, his horse behind him. Tom McLaury stood next to his horse with a hand on the Winchester rifle in its saddle scabbard.

Squared-faced, sad-eyed, modestly mustached men, the McLaury brothers, like the Earps, were all but indistinguishable.

The wind spoke first, blowing dust and snow and howling apparent disapproval; then Virgil addressed the Cowboy contingency in a loud, business-like manner.

"Boys, raise up your hands. I want your guns. You know the ordinance."

Palms still on the butts of their six-shooters, Billy and Frank thumb-cocked the holstered weapons, and even against the wind the *klik! klik!* stood out.

At the same time, Ike's right hand was drifting toward his loose shirt, unbuttoned at the breast.

Tightly, Wyatt said, "You sons of bitches have been looking for a fight. Now you can have it. . . ."

"*Hold on!*" Virgil said, raising the cane, revealing the other hand empty of any weapon. "I don't want that."

Too late: Billy Clanton began to jerk his gun.

Wyatt whipped his long-barreled Colt from the overcoat pocket, but did not take aim at Billy, who was a punk kid and not much of a marksman; the one to get rid of was Frank McLaury, a crack shot and dangerous.

So Wyatt gut-shot Frank, who managed not to fall by holding on to the reins of his nearby horse, while Billy indeed missed, and the gunshots spooked Tom's horse so bad, its owner couldn't get a grip on that Winchester. Scrambling behind the nervous horse, Tom got his pistol out and fired over the horse's back, twice.

One bullet struck Morgan, who yelled, "I'm hit!"

Wyatt said, "Get behind me," and put a few bullets into Billy, as gray-white gunsmoke drifted like fog in the cramped vacant lot and lent the frenzied fight a dream-like haze.

Shotgun in his hands, Doc moved into the lot, upper lip peeled back in a ghastly smile, and closed in on Tom behind the fishtailing horse and let go both barrels, catching the Cowboy under the right armpit, sending him screaming and staggering but, somehow, Tom had enough left to sway out into the street.

Doc pitched the shotgun and switched to his more familiar nickel-plated revolver, and threw shots at Billy Clanton, who seemed to be everywhere, shooting at everyone, hitting nobody.

Meantime Virgil had shifted the cane to his left hand and yanked his Colt and started shooting, once at Frank, three times at Billy, one catching the kid in the belly, though the boy kept moving, kept shooting. Gut-shot Frank, leading his horse by the reins, stumbled toward the street, firing along the way. Tom's horse, ever out of control, provided an inadvertent shield for the other Cowboys, and in this moment Ike ran up to Wyatt and clutched his arm, the booze on his breath, the red in his eyes, matched by the terror in his face.

"Don't kill me!" he sputtered; spittle had frozen on his goatee like little icicles. "Please don't kill me. . . ."

Wyatt pushed him away, seeing the man held no weapon, and said, "This fight has commenced, Ike—get a gun, or get away."

Ike scrambled out of the lot and into Fly's, leaving behind him the continuing carnage that he'd so recklessly instigated. Claiborne was gone, too, and now so were the horses, taking off down the street, leaving their owners exposed in the lot.

Belly bleeding, Frank followed his horse, or tried to, staggered past Doc, stopping behind him and, on unsteady feet, his smile grotesque, aimed his sixgun across the brace of his arm at Holliday, saying, "I've got you now, you bastard. . . ."

"Blaze away," Doc said, turning sideways, making a narrow

target of himself and taunting in his drawl, "You're a *daisy* if you do. . . ."

Frank got off a shot that creased Doc's hip but that was all: Morgan, whose wound had sent him to his knees, fired at Frank and caught him under the ear. With that head shot, Frank should have been instantly dead, but he danced around mumbling to himself, although no longer shooting at anybody.

As this happened, Wyatt had whirled to trade shots with somebody in a window at Fly's, probably that goddamned coward Ike. . . .

At the same time Virgil, who'd also been hit in the left calf, staggered over to Morgan, and then Wyatt helped them both out into the street, while Doc was screaming at the finally fallen Frank McLaury, "The son of a bitch shot me! I mean to kill him."

Wyatt went to Doc and said, "Morgan beat you to it, Doc. Let it go."

Tom McLaury lay dying at the foot of a telegraph pole at Third and Fremont. Billy Clanton, shot to hell, was still alive, after a fashion—slumped against a wall, lamely, gamely trying to reload when Wyatt removed the weapon from his dying fingers, and tossed it to one side, not having the heart to take the kid's last few minutes from him.

Anyway, the Earps and Holliday were all out of ammunition, too.

The firing had ceased, and a crowd was gathering. The gunfight was over.

But much else had only begun. Behan wanting to arrest Wyatt ("Not today, Johnny"). The inquest, jail time, the hearing, cleared, charged again, the assassination attempt on Virgil, maiming Virge's arm . . .

. . . and one terrible night, several months later, when Clanton's Cowboy assassins shot Morgan in the back, killed that sweet boy while he and Wyatt played pool.

So many bullets. So much blood.

And yet the Arizona landscape rolled by his window in all its rugged glory, looking like hell and heaven to Wyatt, as if to say, *You've grown older, I'm unchanged.*

When evening came, Wyatt was seated in the steel diner, alone at a table for two, the car a modern marvel of indirect lighting and reflective surfaces, dark polished wood, gleaming metal, with a high, square-arched ceiling. For one dollar, he was served an eight-course meal: grapefruit, olives, salted almonds and radishes; consommé; filet of bass with cucumbers; lamb chops à la Nelson, with broiled fresh mushrooms; roast turkey with cranberry sauce; mashed potatoes and cauliflower; salad; and plum pudding, with cheese and fruit.

And coffee.

The big meal damned near made Wyatt sleepy, but the prospects of the lounge car woke him right up. A dignified dark-wood chamber filled with overstuffed leather easy chairs filled with over-stuffed well-off males smoking cigars, pipes and the occasional cigarette, the lounge allowed Wyatt to enjoy a cigar himself as he made the acquaintance of a dentist, a banker, a mortician and a fellow who owned a Ford automobile dealership, in whose private compartment they all assembled for rye whiskey and a friendly game of poker.

Wyatt's name had been his calling card with these gents, and occasional remarks amid the smoke and liquor and cards would pertain to that.

"Did you really shoot all those badmen in Arizona?" the banker askcd, early on.

"My share," Wyatt admitted.

"What was bad about them?" the mortician asked.

"We were Republicans," Wyatt said. "They were Democrats."

And that, in this group, had been enough.

Wyatt, who drank only a small polite glass, came away with one hundred and fifty-two dollars, mostly extracted from the dentist, who was no John H. Holliday, at cards at least.

Wyatt had the lower berth, and rather than dress for bed in its constricting confines (he was too tall for that, and maybe too old), he used the dressing room at the end of the car and walked back in robe and slippers. He found the steady rhythm of train travel soothing, and dropped off immediately, sleeping better and sounder than an innocent man.

Nonetheless, deep in the night, the screech of steel on steel and the whine of the train making a stop, perhaps more sudden than intended, woke him with a start; and he sat up and lifted a corner of shade and saw just another depot looming in darkness and drifting steam.

Perhaps his earlier reflecting on his Arizona days caused it, but immediately he was back there, at the depot in Tucson, on the train escorting Morg's body. . . .

Wyatt had no intention of making the whole trip to Colton, California, where his parents and Morg's widow awaited—he'd already put together a posse of Doc, brother Warren, gunfighters Texas Jack Vermillion, Sherm McMasters and Turkey Creek Johnson, armed to the teeth, to go out after Frank Stilwell, Curly Bill Brocius, Ike Clanton, Johnny Ringo and Indian Charlie, the assassins who tried to kill Virgil and succeeded in murdering Morgan.

But then Wyatt had been warned that Ike and Stilwell and

maybe several other Cowboys were watching every train coming through Tucson, going on cars with shotguns and searching for the Earps and any associates. So he and Doc decided to accompany the funeral party on the first leg of the journey.

Dusk draped the station as they pulled in, dark enough already to make the town a shapeless sprawl; blue shadows engulfed the desert as it stretched to mountains that were purple silhouettes against a burning, dying sky.

At the station a crowd awaited, as travelers arrived in welcome and departed in farewell and gawkers neither coming nor going got a gander at the Earp party, which the whole territory seemed to know was heading through Tucson that evening. A damned newsboy was hawking papers, shouting, *"Hell is coming! Read about it here!"*

Wyatt and Doc were guarding the wounded Virgil as he and his wife Allie and brother James and wife Bessie as well as Wyatt's "wife" Mattie departed the train to eat in the station's dining room.

On the platform, Doc tugged Wyatt's sleeve, but Wyatt spoke first: "I see them."

Frank Stilwell—the man witnesses said had back-shot Morg and narrowly missed Wyatt in the poolhall shooting—stood in a long duster with a shotgun barely hidden beneath, his affable oval face shadowed by a tan sombrero and a smile contradicted by the frown of a droopy dark mustache. Next to him lurked Ike Clanton, similarly attired right down to the shotgun, though Ike was as usual scruffier in appearance than the typical gaudy Cowboy.

"And," Doc said, as the pair of assassins fell back into the crowd, "they see *us*. . . ."

Neither Wyatt nor Doc ate, and when they accompanied the family back to the waiting private car, Wyatt spotted a string of flatcars about twenty feet down on the adjacent track, noting something glinting off the station's gas lamps.

Something metal.

On the train Wyatt got his brother settled comfortably into a chair, Virgil's wife next to him with her husband's holster and sixgun around her waist in absurd support of their dire situation. And the Earps did make tempting targets in the well-lighted windows of the private car. . . .

Wyatt put a hand on Virgil's good shoulder. "I'll be seeing you."

Virgil's eyes tightened. "I'll be seeing you, too—if you take care of yourself."

Wyatt nodded, gave Doc—in the aisle behind him—a glance that conveyed the need for him to stay with the party and guard them; then, double-barreled shotgun in one hand, Wyatt moved toward the rear of the car and soon was climbing down onto the side of the yards opposite the platform.

At just after seven, darkness had settled onto the station with the gas lamps and illumination of the train making blurry cameos in a stygian trainyard floating with smoke and steam. A cloud-smeared moon added little illumination, but once again he saw the metallic wink off rifle (or shotgun) barrels down on the flatcar, where two men lay prone waiting in ambush.

Wyatt began to run, his boots crunching on cinders, and this alerted the dry-gulchers, who, seeing him and his gun coming, a dark-flapping-coated apparition hurtling toward them, leapt off the flatcar so fast, they left their shotguns behind.

Ike Clanton was in the lead and he disappeared between flatcars, but Stilwell stumbled, and when Wyatt reached him, the oval-faced Cowboy, his sombrero lost in the chase, gazed up and a terror seized him that had nothing to do with the shotgun barrels.

"Morg?" Stilwell asked. "Morg?"

The bastard thought Wyatt was the ghost of the man he'd murdered!

"No," Wyatt said. "And you won't be seeing him where you're headed."

Stilwell bolted to his feet and his wild-eyed face was inches away when he grabbed Wyatt's shotgun by its barrels—desperately trying to wrest the weapon away instead of jerking the holstered sixgun at his side . . .

. . . and Wyatt let go with both barrels, so close to the Cowboy, the roar was muffled and the man's shirt caught fire.

Stilwell rose off the ground a little, just a little jump, and tumbled backward into a formless pile, flames around the wound crackling and then dying themselves.

Suddenly Doc was at Wyatt's side and the gambler's nickelplated revolver barked four times, downward, hitting the dead man in selected places.

Wyatt gave his friend a curious look and Doc shrugged. His smile was awful.

"Can't let you have all the fun," Doc said. "Much less credit."

They looked for Ike, but the yellow cur had as usual skedaddled, and soon the train was on its way, Wyatt and Doc walking along either side of the car. Before the train pulled from the station, Wyatt looked up at the mournful face of Virgil in his window and raised a forefinger, and mouthed, "One for Morg."

More would follow.

The lookout, Indian Charlie, Wyatt gave a fairer chance than Morgan had received—an *uno dos tres* before sending one two three bullets into the bastard who'd taken twenty-five dollars to make sure Morg's killer, Stilwell, wasn't interrupted.

And of course Curly Bill, at the Iron Springs shoot-out, with assorted other Cowboys also cashing in. Finally Johnny Ringo, whom he and Doc had taken out, though few knew how they'd managed it, the law calling it suicide.

Wyatt shut the curtain on the steam-drifting depot and lay back in the berth. Not by nature a reflective man, he could not at first fathom this rush of memories; finally he guessed it was Kate Elder showing up and springing a Doc Holliday, Jr., on him, and the prospect of seeing Bat Masterson, and a ride through Arizona where, like Frank Stilwell in that Tucson trainyard, a man could expect to see a ghost or two.

Then he was asleep again.

The rest of the trip brought occasional memories—such as when the *Limited* passed Trinidad, New Mexico, where Bat had been sheriff, and Wyatt had to ask him to go fetch Doc in Denver on a phony extradition so the Tombstone murder charges didn't catch up with him. And also Dodge City, Kansas, which had put Wyatt on the map, and maybe vice versa.

But, mostly, he dozed in his seat between big, wonderful meals, and played poker half the night with men of means who were just delighted to lighten their wallets for the chance to sit down at cards with a real American hero like Wyatt Earp.

Who was he to contradict the sons of bitches?

# Four

A SEVERAL-HOUR STOP IN CHICAGO—WHERE HE had come into LaSalle Street Station but had to walk over to Dearborn Station to catch the *20th Century*—meant Wyatt Earp did not reach New York City till late afternoon Friday.

Alligator valise in hand, he made his way from the platform into the elegant cavernous echoing concourse with polished marble everywhere and afternoon sunlight slanting in like swords in a magician's box through windows taller than most buildings. Grand Central Terminal had been built only six or seven years ago, on the site of the old one; but this grandiose gateway to New York already felt like it had been here just a little longer than Egypt's pyramids.

The crowd was considerable, a mix of travelers coming and businesspeople going, with the red hats of colored porters bobbing in the bustle.

How odd to be in a station with no smell of smoke, no carbon fumes, the trains themselves hidden away like poor relations. The vast vaulted ceiling was nighttime blue with the expected stars, though slowing to squint up at these indoor constellations, he thought they weren't quite right. Were they backwards?

Shrugging, he skirted the central circular information booth past ticket booths and up the gentle slope toward the street, past the glass of restaurants, bars, barbershop, drugstores, and more. On his way, he was jostled without apology perhaps half a dozen times, but no one had tried to pick his pocket, which was politeness of a sort.

Frontier reputation aside, Wyatt was no stranger to a big town—he'd lived a good ten years in the City of Angels, and Denver, Kansas City, St. Louis and even Chicago had been his gambler's stamping grounds. But hitting the sidewalk at the corner of Forty-second Street and Vanderbilt Avenue on a cool spring afternoon, he was not fully prepared for *this* big a town.

With its shifting sea of pedestrians and its bedlam of motor and streetcar traffic—horseless carriages outnumbering horse-drawn by a wide margin—Midtown Manhattan stopped Wyatt Earp in his tracks. He stood as motionless as the Greek statues that surrounded the massive clock surmounting the imposing terminal, frozen heroes who towered over him even as the buff skyscrapers towered over them, like tombstones in the graveyard of God's sky . . . not that he could make out much sky.

The taxi driver who took Wyatt to the *Morning Telegraph* at Fiftieth Street and Eighth Avenue provided plenty of local color along the way, including that the newspaper was quartered in what had been an old streetcar stable, back before the cars had been electrified.

"You wouldn't expect to find a paper this far uptown," the

hackie said, a little hook-nosed feller in a blue plaid cap, about two blocks from their destination. "You heard of Park Row?"

"No."

"Well, that's Newspaper Central in this burg. Most of the other dailies are down there. Of course, the *Telegraph* is not your typical rag."

"That so."

"Well, you're going there. You must know."

And he did know: the paper his old friend Bat worked for specialized in theatrical, financial and sports news, with horse racing edging out boxing by a nose.

He did not reward the chatty cabby with anything more than the nickel tip he'd intended, and soon he and his valise were threading through a second-floor city room adrift with blue tobacco haze and alive with typewriter clatter and littered with small cluttered desks at which shirtsleeved scribes toiled and smoked, except for a poker game on the periphery, where copy was being proofed between pots. Passage was made difficult by a variety of humans in the aisles, loud guys with louder clothes sporting derbies or boaters and sucking ciggies or chewing stogies and who belonged either to the gambling or show-business worlds, while bobbed-haired chorus girls sat perched on desks displaying plenty of calf and patiently filing their nails, waiting for reporters banging away at the keys in a hurry to rush through work before coming out to play.

Wyatt didn't ask directions of anybody, since few of these people worked here. Besides, he could see Bat through the glass in one of a quartet of window-and-woodframe offices at the far end of the city-room chaos. Bat's back was to him, but the oval skull was unmistakable, as were the broad shoulders on the medium frame. No typewriter for those gunfighter's hands: Bat was working with pen and ink, scratching away at foolscap.

Wyatt knocked on a sliver of woodframe, rattling the window that said SPORTS EDITOR but lacked Bat's name, and Bat swiveled on his chair and the familiar light-blue eyes widened under the thick slashes of dark eyebrow.

From the start they'd been dissimilar in appearance—Wyatt tall and slim, Bat a good four or five inches shorter with a broad chest and compactly muscular. When they'd met in the buffalo camps in '72, Wyatt was at twenty-four an old hand at frontier life, Bat at seventeen a greenhorn.

But not enough years could pass to prevent Wyatt recognizing those blue-gray eyes—intelligent, perceptive, sharp and, when called for, cold. He recognized them because he had them, too. Doc had once commented on the effect the two "spooky-eyed lawmen" could have, side by side, upon some "poor pitiful miscreant."

In his shirtsleeves, a dark brown Windsor-knot tie loose around his collar, and crisp-creased light brown trousers (a matching coat hung with a black flat-topped derby on a coat tree), Bat was out of his chair like a man shot out of a cannon. He ushered Wyatt in, shaking his hand pump-handle-style and guiding him to a leather-cushioned couch under the row of windows, putting the city room to his guest's back. Hands on his hips, Bat grinned and shook his head and chuckled, as he appraised his old friend.

"Wyatt," Bat said, "you just don't change—your hair goes white, and that's about the sum total. I know it sure as hell isn't clean living!"

Bat, considering he was in his late sixties, hadn't changed much, either—a slight paunch and his hair was more salt than pepper, and the trim mustache was gone. But even now Bat had a snub-nosed, dimple-chinned boyish quality.

"Bartholomew," Wyatt said, "you look well-fed."

Half a smile dimpled a cheek as plump and rosy as a baby's. The wordsmith seemed to appreciate the layered insult expressed so succinctly, starting with Bat despising his given name "Bartholomew" and having long ago affected "William Barclay" Masterson.

Bat drew his swivel chair up and sat facing Wyatt with hands on knees and both sides of the smile going, now. "If you're implying I've gone to seed, I'll have you know I cleaned the clock of a younger man just last week, in the lobby of the Waldorf-Astoria."

"I was thinking more along the lines you'd got fat. Who was this crippled youth?"

Bat drew a package of Lucky Strikes from his breast pocket, did not bother offering a cigarette to Wyatt, knowing his friend smoked only cigars, and lighted up. "Remember Colonel Dick Plunkett? Arrested Ed O'Kelly in Crede for killing Bob Ford?"

"I remember him. I don't remember him being a colonel."

Bat let out a smoke-exhale laugh. "He was just another deputy. Deputies were a dime a dozen in those days."

"Yeah, and we were two of 'em. Only this Plunkett's surely no youngster."

"No, but he was in the company of a cocky young editor from some Texas paper or other, feller setting up interviews. The two were telling every reporter in town except yours truly, of course, that Bat Masterson was a fraud and a fake and a phony and held in low opinion by *real* Westerners."

"A shame," Wyatt said.

Bat shifted in the swivel chair. "I believe the point was to get Plunkett enough publicity to land himself a spot in a Wild West Show. Which is a fine place for a broken-down nobody like Plunkett and I would not begrudge him—but making a goat out of me to get himself some glory? Would I put up with that?"

"Likely not."

"Anyway, Plunkett was carrying this old six-shooter with him, and you know, I still carry a marshal's badge in the state of New York, Teddy Roosevelt arranged it some years ago . . . it's mostly honorary now, but as I say, I showed the 'Colonel' the badge and shoved him, just a tad. . . . Are you listening?"

"I can listen with my eyes closed."

"Oh. I thought maybe you dropped off for a nap there, elderly gentleman that you are."

Wyatt opened his eyes. "No, I was just trying to picture this fascinating tale. Maybe with Bill Hart in the lead."

Bat grinned and the cigarette almost fell from his mouth as he said, "You know, he'd be good as me. That would make a hell of a movie, Bill Hart playing me. Where was I?"

"Shoving some codger around in the Waldorf lobby."

"Right. Well, the young pipsqueak from Texas, the editor, name of Dinklesheets . . . Dinklesheets! What the hell kind of name is Dinklesheets, anyway?"

"A stupid one."

"This Dinklesheets hauls off and pastes me one."

"Do tell."

"So I pasted him back, knocked him down. Promptly, he was hearing birdies tweet and bleeding out his mouth. But old Plunkett still had that gun on him, so I shoved my hand in my jacket pocket and indicated I had the drop on him, and the old boy just put up his hands and didn't even bend to dab the blood off from the corners of his companion's damaged mouth."

Wyatt said, "You still carry a gun?"

"Time to time," Bat said, then lifted the deck of cigarettes from his breast pocket again, "but I was just pointing a pack of these at 'im. That's about the whole story. Hotel detective came up and requested I leave."

"And of course you're not one to stay where you're not wanted."

"Not me!" He tapped cigarette ash onto the filthy wooden floor. "Listen, your timing is good as ever. I just put the finishing touches on my Sunday column. The evening stretches out ahead of us in possibility like an endless prairie."

"I don't mind you being a writer," Wyatt said with a frown. "But please God don't talk like one."

Bat ignored that, slapping his thighs, getting to his feet. "You'll stay with Emma and me at our apartment, of course."

"I'm not one to impose . . ."

"Of course you are, but you won't be. Emma has a fondness for you resulting from never ever having spent much time with you. And I've misled her, because I speak so highly of you since, of course, it only enhances my standing."

"Of course."

"Let me just arrange for an office boy to walk your bag over to the apartment—just a few blocks from here, but we're not headed that way."

"Where are we headed?"

But Bat didn't answer, stepping out of the glassed-in office with Wyatt's alligator bag and returning in two minutes empty-handed, having sent a harried-looking lad off with it.

"Hope you didn't eat on the train," Bat said.

"Not since lunch. After four days, even Fred Harvey's cooking gets tiresome."

"Well, we'll have a wonderful meal, take in a fight, and along the way I'll fill you in about this kid of Doc's. Chip off the old block."

"A mean drunken lunger with a nasty sense of humor?"

Bat shook his head. "Not a chunk, a chip—grab your hat. . . . Couldn't you have worn a Stetson?"

"This is a Stetson."

"No, I mean a *Stetson*, with a nice wide brim. I'm going to be introducing you around as Wyatt Earp and in that goddamned homburg, you just don't look the part."

With this, Bat snugged his tie and donned his trademark derby; he seemed to have abandoned the other trademark, his gold-topped cane, but Wyatt noted the limp from the King gunfight was still present.

"When did *you* ever wear a Stetson?" Wyatt asked his friend, who was holding the office door open for him.

"Never. I always had more dash than you, Wyatt—but you have to give people what they expect. Reality isn't the point—it's the perception of reality." He shrugged. "That's show business."

They took a taxi and the noise of traffic—the blat of automobile horns, the clang of trolley cars, the wheeze of double-decker buses, the harness rattle and wheel-clank of horse-drawn wagons—made conversation too much trouble. Wyatt watched the bustling burg go by and understood, suddenly, Bat's Stetson talk—hard to stand out in a city of six million.

Though Wyatt had wound up on the West Coast and Bat here on the East, their paths had been much the same. Both had ridden every trail the frontier had to offer, bucking the odds in high-stakes games, going to the aid of friends and family, trouble-shooting with and without a badge in cow towns and boomtowns and assorted hellholes of every stripe.

Bat's luck, like Wyatt's, had run hot and cold and back again, again and again . . . but by the time adventuring and drifting had lost its appeal, each man had enough of a stake built up to settle in one spot.

Times Square, just after six o'clock, was in all its electric glory, the sun having set to turn the illumination job over to Edison. Already Manhattan was taking a blazing bath—lights of blue, green, yellow, red, even white, letters whirling and tumbling and encouraging this soda pop and that candy bar, painting flashy, flashing tributes to Wrigley's Chewing Gum and White Rock Water and assorted cigarettes and tires and toothbrushes and automobiles and even a laxative or two, electric placards extending from buildings, sometimes at angles, in a modern geometry at once exciting and garish.

Bat saw Wyatt taking it all in and the New Yorker's smile had smug pride in it. "Twenty-thousand electric signs in this space," Bat noted. "Twenty-five million candle power. . . ." Then Bat's expression turned a shade melancholy, as he added, "Still, it's not as bright as it used to be."

Between the blinking billboards were the marquees of movie palaces and theaters, sometimes sharing the same names, as film stars like Douglas Fairbanks and Fatty Arbuckle were currently trodding the Broadway boards.

"Seems bright enough to me," Wyatt said.

"In any case, you should be comfortable here."

"Yeah?"

"Broadway started as a cowpath."

They were let out on the east side of the Square between Forty-third and Forty-fourth Streets in front of a long low-slung yellow structure whose electrical sign, oddly, bore no name, just some hybrid creature, half lion, half eagle, flapping its lighted-up wings over the pavement.

"What the hell's this?" Wyatt asked, glancing up.

"That's a griffin. Mythological beast—you know, like the Western gunfighter. The restaurant is Rector's, which I imagine even an uncouth dweller from the hinterlands like yourself has heard of."

A grandly uniformed doorman holding back a nonexistent crowd undid the velvet rope for them and allowed them to pass.

As Bat led him into a revolving door, Wyatt said, "Thought for a minute there you joined a lodge."

But the interior was no Moose or Elks hall, rather a spacious expanse made to seem more so by floor-to-ceiling mirrored walls; the walls were gold and green brocade, the Louis XIV decor elegant under the sparkle of endless crystal chandeliers.

Wyatt had of course heard of the famous restaurant, and was surprised to see it barely half-filled, supper hour, Friday night. Further, the crowd did not seem terribly distinguished, running largely to older businessmen with young well-rouged women who could have carried their skimpy clothes in their handbags, except for the bulk of an occasional silver fox or mink jacket.

At their table with its linen cloth and fine china and sparkling silverware (all bearing that "griffin" symbol), Bat was in the midst of polishing off a dozen oysters, indulging in a side serving of nostalgia.

"Not long ago," Bat was saying, between oyster slurps, "you'd see Lillian Russell gliding down that aisle with a long train behind her, layers of whispering silk. Gypsy band would be playing. Unforgettable."

"Hmm," Wyatt said, in the process of putting away half a dozen soft-shell crabs.

"Right over there, you could see Diamond Jim Brady, an oversize napkin stuffed in his collar, polishing off six or seven lobsters.

Your pal Mizner, from Nome, used to say Brady liked his oysters sprinkled with clams and his steaks smothered in veal cutlets."

"Umm," Wyatt said, working on another crab.

"I just squint and I can see them all. . . . Ziegfeld and Anna Held. Charles Frohman. Victor Herbert. Another Alaska pard of yours, Rex Beach, he liked to hang out here, and O. Henry, the short story writer. What a grand place."

"What happened?"

Bat shook his head. "What happened to every decent lobster palace in this town? Prohibition! The men go off to war and the women stay home and push these damned abolitionist laws through, and restaurants like Rector's and Delmonico's can't cook with *wine* anymore! And a man can't have a decent meal with a bucket of champagne at his elbow!"

As if to underscore this travesty, Bat took a swallow of iced water.

Then he began to rant again: "And now Delmonico's is *closing*! And this joint may change its name to some French nonsense. Can you imagine?"

"How are the steaks?"

The steaks were excellent, huge and bloody, the way both men liked them; but Bat wasn't through.

"All the great old bars, the fine restaurants, the wonderful cabarets, shutting their doors while these goddamned speakeasies and blind pigs take over."

"Speakeasies," Wyatt said thoughtfully. "Doc's son—Johnny. That's what *he's* gone into?"

They were on to coffee now.

Bat nodded, stirring in sugar. "He used to have an honest trade, like his father."

"Denistry, you mean."

"Hell, no! Gambling!" Bat leaned forward conspiratorially, though the tables fore and aft were empty. "He's damned good at it, Wyatt. He can read the cards and he can read the people."

"Does sound like Doc's son."

"While back, Johnny got in a high stakes game with a feller at the St. Francis Hotel. Running with a real roller crowd, Wyatt— Rothstein himself was in that game."

"Arnold Rothstein?"

Bat nodded.

Rothstein, the so-called brain of the New York underworld, was the famed fixer who rigged last year's World Series. Which struck Wyatt as both un-American and a hell of a feat.

"Anyway," Bat continued, "it was a few weeks before this goddamned Volstead Act went into effect. A guy who owned six saloons around town bet all six and his whole stockpile of liquor on aces full over jacks."

"Who could blame him?"

"Guy himself could." Bat raised an eyebrow. "Johnny had four deuces."

Wyatt sipped; his was black. "Saloon guy must've been in a reckless frame of mind, with the Prohibition coming."

"Drunk, reckless and despondent about his whole general state of affairs. That, and four deuces, was all it took."

"What happened?"

"Paid up. Killed himself, week later."

Wyatt shook his head impatiently. "Not the saloon guy—what did Johnny do with six saloons on the eve of Prohibition?"

"Oh. He held on to the liquor supply and sold the saloons to Rothstein, for a pile . . . and used the pile to buy an old brownstone on West Forty-fifth."

"And that's the speak?"

"That's the speak. Holliday's. I'll take you there."

"Now?"

"Hell no!" Bat threw his napkin down and grabbed the check. "We have the fights, first."

Madison Square Garden was a palace of yellow brick and white terra cotta with a nude statue of Diana the Huntress on top of its central tower—and to Wyatt, one unlikely venue for a boxing match.

The block-long affair, bounded by Madison and Fourth Avenues and Twenty-sixth and Twenty-seventh Streets, housed (among other things) a theater, restaurant, concert hall, and a roof garden where ten or fifteen years ago its esteemed architect, Stanford White, was shot by his former mistress's husband, Harry Thaw, a loony Pittsburgh millionaire. You didn't have to be a New York native to know about pretty showgirl Evelyn Nesbit and the ruckus she'd caused—just needed to have read the *Police Gazette*.

Wyatt had.

Even with the Garden's history of carnage, the boxing match seemed at odds with the structure's fussy pink rococo interior. But once inside the vast arena itself (first erected, Bat said, for horse shows), clouds of cigarette and cigar smoke compensated, as did loud enthusiastic fight fans, peddlers of roasted peanuts and hot dogs, and ringside seats. Tiers of balconies on all four sides were draped red-white-and-blue, while high over the ring, under skylights, black bell-shaped speakers emitted occasional, largely unintelligible announcements.

Wyatt sat between Bat and a thin, thin-lipped, grave-featured chain-smoker whose brown hair was shellacked back and who wore wirerim glasses behind which yet another pair of pale blue eyes lurked.

"Wyatt, this is my friend Al Runyon," Bat said, over the arena din. "Al, this is Wyatt Earp who I've told you about."

Cigarette clenched tight in the slash of his mouth, Runyon nodded and Wyatt shook hands with him, a quick, solid shake.

Bat leaned in and whispered: "Kid's a big booster of yours. A real fan. He writes under his middle name—'Damon.' Maybe you've seen his work."

Wyatt had indeed read Runyon's sports columns. The dude was well known nationally as a real expert on baseball, boxing and the ponies. And Runyon *was* a dude: the columnist's suit, a natty light brown plaid, was without a wrinkle and his floral tie bore a diamond stickpin. He was poised to take notes with a hand that bore a huge pinky ring.

Wyatt said to the "kid" (who was around forty), "Read your stuff. It's good."

Runyon, deadpan, flicked Wyatt a look, and the cigarette bobbled as he said, "Thanks," then returned his attention to the ring, where the fighters were already in their respective corners and an announcer with a megaphone was wandering between them.

That was the extent of the conversation between Wyatt and his "big fan."

The fight was a good one, two heavyweights, Billy Miske— who had given champ Jack Dempsey a run at it in two hard battles—and another real contender, Bill Brennan.

Bat, however, wasn't impressed with either man, and between rounds said to Wyatt, "Your prime, you could've taken out either one of these bums."

Then Bat leaned across Wyatt to say to Runyon, "Al, you're sitting next to the best natural boxer I ever saw. Known him since the early '70s, and nobody could scrap with his fists like this feller."

Wyatt said slowly, "Bartholomew. . . ."

Bat ignored that, still leaning. "Few men in the West could whip Wyatt in a rough-and-tumble, forty years ago, and I think he could give these youngsters a hard tussle even today."

Runyon's eyes tightened behind the wireframes, he nodded a little, and he returned his attention to the bout as the bell clanged.

"These guys are genuine tango experts," Bat said bitterly.

But Wyatt thought it was a pretty good scrap, a view highlighted by them sitting close enough to feel the flying flecks of sweat and blood.

Between the next rounds, Wyatt asked Bat, "What do you know about this kid Caponi who's giving Doc's boy a bad time?"

Bat nodded toward Runyon. "Ask Al—he's an expert on these hoodlum types."

Without looking at them, Runyon said, "It's Capone, not Caponi. One of Yale's crew. He's a comer."

Wyatt asked, "Tough?"

Runyon, lighting up his latest cigarette, nodded.

Brennan knocked Miske down in the seventh round, and while the ref stood over the fallen fighter counting him loudly out, Bat admitted, "That gets him closer to a match with the Mauler, who will murder him."

This was a reference to Dempsey's nickname, the Manassa Mauler. Wyatt was pretty sure Runyon had coined that moniker, but didn't ask for confirmation.

Bat hadn't taken a single note during the fight, maybe because he'd already written his next column; but Runyon had filled half a notebook, writing without looking at the pages, just the match.

The solemn dapper plaid-clad reporter rose with Wyatt and Bat, asking the latter, "Doyle's?"

Bat said, "Not tonight."

Runyon nodded, then nodded to Wyatt, and cut like a blade through the packed aisle, in a hell of a hurry. Maybe he was going off to file his story.

As the two old friends took their time moving up the aisle in the smoky, echo-ringing arena, Bat said, "Al got a real charge out of meeting you."

"Yeah. Pissed himself, he was so excited."

Bat laughed, once. "No, Wyatt, really. He's just a listener, is all. But he's from out West himself; his daddy was with Custer."

"If so, daddy got scalped."

Bat shrugged. "That's a point I never pursued. . . . But Runyon's a good man, thinks of himself as a Westerner at heart, idolizes fellers like me and you."

Wyatt gave Bat a sideways look.

"On my oath! I know him from way back in Colorado days—he was on papers in Trinidad and Denver, both. And now he's a big shot, just signed a contract with Hearst."

"Well. Liked to talk my ear off."

Bat grinned. "Yeah, makes you look long-winded. Kind of nice seeing you put in that position. Anyway, if we need any help, he has connections, including underworld."

"What is 'Doyle's'?"

Bat's grin faded. He shrugged. "Just a joint."

"What kind of joint?"

". . . Billiards."

So that was it. Wyatt had never set foot in a pool hall since the night Morgan was shot in the back and sent sprawling onto the green felt.

"Don't let me stop you," Wyatt said.

"Naw. Not in the mood. Let's get a bite."

Wyatt blinked. "After Rector's?"

"That was forever ago! Anyway, watching those bums do the Castle Walk famished me! Come on!"

The next stop was on Sixth Avenue, opposite the Hippodrome—Jack Dunstan's, where the decor was as plain as Rector's had been opulent, and the aproned waiters looked more like fighters than either heavyweight had.

Bat held court in a corner booth over seltzer lemonades and tongue sandwiches on rye; Wyatt had two Coca-Colas and a single sandwich, corned beef on rye. A parade of people came over to say hello, coming and going, and Bat introduced Wyatt to a score of Broadway characters, fight managers, press agents, actors, playwrights, and Wyatt shook enough hands to damned near work up the appetite for his sandwich. He recognized not one name and committed none to memory.

A sort of impromptu floor show was provided by the waiters, who formed a flying wedge to escort a rowdy gaggle of disorderly collegiate types out onto Sixth Avenue.

Finally the social hour passed, and Wyatt and Bat were left to themselves. This meant a round of steaming coffee, richer and hotter and frankly better than Rector's, and Wyatt asked, "What is this Capone after? And who is Yale?"

"Frankie Yale," Bat said, lighting a Lucky, "Brooklyn gangster, looking to expand his territory. These are new days, Wyatt, nasty days—like Dodge or Tombstone, only it's tommyguns not sixguns."

Over the rim of his coffee cup, Wyatt asked, "What's a tommygun?"

"Thompson submachine gun. Spits bullets."

"How fast?"

"Fifteen-hundred rounds per minute, fast."

Wyatt offered up a small, slow whistle.

"Trench gun, built for use in the Great War," Bat continued cheerfully, "a little too late to get into the action . . . but right in time for Prohibition."

Wyatt frowned. "What do these gangsters want from Doc's kid? Move in on him and take over? Put him out of business? Or just get their piece?"

The protection racket had been around a long time. Wyatt and his brothers had been accused of it in Tombstone, though that was bunkum. A lawman deserved a taste.

"Yale isn't in the speakeasy business," Bat said, "though he does have a dance hall on Coney Island that isn't afraid to serve up a beer."

"What do they want from Johnny, then?"

"To sell *him* booze. Only Johnny doesn't need their booze, having plenty of his own."

Wyatt glanced at a round clock on an off-white plaster wall broken by a black electric cord. "Gettin' on to midnight. So we'll save dropping by Johnny's speak for tomorrow?"

Bat's eyes narrowed and his grin widened. "You *are* an old man, Wyatt. Hell, we're just getting going. The Forties don't start roaring till midnight."

Wyatt's eyes tightened. "Don't you mean 'Twenties?' "

Bat laughed. "Wyatt, Wyatt. . . . Still a farm boy at heart."

Wyatt smiled just a little as he eased out of the booth. "Well, then, Bartholomew, being as you're a city boy . . . I'll just let you pick up the check again."

# Five

T HE ROARING FORTIES—AS BAT EXPLAINED TO
Wyatt on their next taxi ride—was the Times
Square/Broadway area itself, Forty-second Street
and the other "forties." This seemed to be a loose
definition, as the "speaks" in question were set
up between Fortieth and Sixtieth Streets, chiefly
in old brownstone residences.

"Springing up like mushrooms," Bat said.
"Sometimes the poisonous kind."

The better-class brownstone speakeasies operated as clubs with private memberships and
high-tone names like the Town and Country or
the Bombay Bicycle Club or Louis's or Anthony's
or, for that matter, Holliday's.

"But now that we're a couple months into
this grand new experiment called Prohibition,"
Bat said, "the gangsters have really been moving

in—sometimes taking over, other times just peddling their liquor."

The two men were in the backseat of a Ford taxicab.

Wyatt asked, "Why don't they open their own joints?"

"Oh, they're starting to—delightful upholstered sewers like the Hotsy Totsy, the Silver Slipper, the Fifty Fifty—you can get shots of both varieties there: alcoholic *and* ballistic."

Wyatt chewed on that for a few moments. Then he asked, "How many hoodlum factions?"

"How many fingers you got? And maybe you should break out your toes."

". . . Before long, you could have the Manhattan version of a range war."

Bat laughed without humor. "You're tellin' me. So far, though, the only turf invaded belongs to independents like Johnny. Now, across the river, the micks and the guineas are squabbling to beat the band . . . which is why Frankie Yale is sending his young emissary Capone around, looking for new territory, this side of the Brooklyn Bridge."

Traffic on West Fifty-second, between Fifth and Sixth Avenues, was as congested as Times Square itself. They weren't close to their address when Bat paid off the hackie and the two men walked the rest of the way in the brisk April air.

"Damn near without exception," Bat said, gesturing, "every house on both sides of this 'residential' cross-street is a speak."

The houses were unfailingly dark, shades drawn and windows sometimes painted out, black. You'd have thought funeral wreaths should be hanging on every door; yet the curbs were bumper-to-bumper with parked autos, and the sidewalks were busy with laughing couples, on their way somewhere, and not a funeral.

"Of course," Bat was saying, "Johnny never refers to *his* joint as a speak—it's strictly a *night*club. . . ."

"There's a difference?"

Bat chuckled, shrugged. Derby at a raffish angle, he moved along jauntily but not quickly, that old gun-battle leg wound still slowing him some. "In Johnny's view, there's a world of difference. At a speak customers drink, at a theater they see a show, at a dance hall they dance—at a nightclub, they get the whole shebang, and more."

The three-story brownstone where Bat stopped also looked asleep, windows dark; hell, it was well after midnight, why wouldn't they be?

Still, Wyatt started up the seven or eight steps to the raised entrance . . . only to have Bat tug at his friend's coat sleeve and shake his head, as if scolding a backward child.

"No one gets in that way," Bat said, and led Wyatt down the half-dozen steps to basement level.

Dreary and unlighted, the basement entry sported a forbidding black metal door. Bat rang the unmarked bell and a peephole panel shuttered open, exposing a single hard appraising eye.

No password or display of any membership card was necessary in this instance. The peephole slid shut, the heavy door swung open, a simian in a tuxedo said, "Good to see youse, Mr. Masterson," and led the two guests through a series of interlocking doors on to adjacent vestibules and finally into Holliday's itself.

"Have a good evening," said the slope-foreheaded guardian of the gate, and disappeared back inside his world of locks and doors and entryways.

The interior of the nightclub (and "speakeasy" truly did not do it justice) damned near tempted Wyatt to smile.

In tribute to his late daddy, Johnny had provided an under-stated but distinct Wild West decor—the spirit of Dodge's Long Branch and Tombstone's Oriental lived in this forty-by-eighty-foot tin-ceilinged cellar.

About as authentic as a Tom Mix picture, Holliday's was none-theless a nice blend of cantina and saloon. The walls were pale yellow stucco, decorated with a sprinkling of rustic-framed West-ern and Mexican paintings, with arched recessions in walls home to little statues of cowhands on bucking broncos and slouchy In-dians on sleepy ponies. The many tables were small, square and covered with brown-and-white checkered cloths, their chairs simple, rounded wooden straightbacks.

Even the Chinese lanterns, providing much of the low-slung chamber's scant illumination, weren't out of place: Wyatt had seen them used in many a watering hole out West.

Entering, you looked across the seated patrons through the blue haze of cigarette smoke to the bar—no stools, strictly a serv-ing station—a roughhewn pine affair that resonated within Wyatt's memory. Of course, this was more Pony Express way-station-style than, say, Tombstone's Crystal Palace, where the bar had been an endless expanse of mahogany. But in a business wherein occa-sional raids, for real or for show, might include ax-wielding intrud-ers, pine seemed the prudent choice.

Two bartenders, both with handlebar mustaches and black hair slicked back and aprons over white shirts with black bow ties, selected bottles from the pair of pine-shelf bookcase-like displays that left room between for a gilt-framed oil of a reclining Spanish lady wearing a shawl and a rose and a smile. Above the entire affair, all that remained of a longhorn steer was on impres-sive display, horns looking sharp enough to give a visiting bull-fighter a shiver.

Wyatt had set foot in a speak or two in L.A., and knew the rows of liquor bottles behind the bar were an exception, not the rule—real labels with such familiar names as Johnny Walker and Jim Beam beamed at patrons not used to actually seeing what they were drinking.

Wyatt knew the rules in an establishment like this—some gents might bring their own flasks, and the club would charge for set-ups, maybe two bucks for a pitcher of water and/or ice, or a buck and a half for ginger ale and/or a buck a bottle for White Rock. Most patrons bought liquor at the clubs, however, particularly one with Johnny Holliday's impressive supply of the genuine article.

Pretty things in peasant blouses and short red flared satin skirts with mesh hose were weaving in and around the tables selling various wares from trays shoulder-slung like feedsacks: cigarettes ran a buck a deck; rag baby dolls (for your baby doll) a fin; and red-rose corsages also a fin—artificial flowers a buck. Purchases were not encouraged, they were expected, as were generous tips—guys did not want to look like tightwads to dolls, either the one they'd come in with, *or* the one pushing cigarettes or rag dolls or flowers, real or false. . . .

Behind and right, as Wyatt and Bat stood just inside the place, was a hatcheck stand, where Wyatt and Bat left theirs with a redhead in a fringed buckskin vest over a yellow blouse with a gaily colorful bandana knotted at her neck. To the left a hostess station was "manned" by a similarly garbed brunette. This was the standard waitress attire, as well, and four such cuties in short buckskin skirts were conveying drinks of trays to the clientele—cowgirls out of Ziegfeld.

At the far left was a little stage, the fairly low ceiling allowing room for only a baby grand piano and two tiers of musicians, saxophone, trombone, drum set, violin, trumpet and clarinet, who happened to be filing onto the platform right now, like a little tuxedo army. A parquet dance floor out front would accommodate maybe a dozen couples, if they didn't mind rubbing shoulders and other surfaces.

The brunette hostess knew Bat from way back and led the two men to a reserved table ringside. One of the bandana-sporting waitresses got there right away, and Bat ordered bourbon straight up and Wyatt asked for a beer.

Wyatt surveyed the scene. The well-dressed crowd was largely young—bored with well-paying jobs, hell-bent for fun, ready to pay sky-high prices for the privilege. A certain number of sugar daddies with dollies were sprinkled around at the postage-stamp tables, too. Still, this was mostly kids—some exercising their silver-spoon heritage, others making a decent living and out to blow some of it . . . but kids. Who else could hang out at joints that didn't open till midnight, and carouse club-to-club till five in the morning?

The answer to that question could be found among assorted famous faces sprinkled around the room—famous at least in Manhattan terms.

"Those two boys," Bat said, leaning in confidence, "are Yankees stars—hour and a half ago, their dates were on stage with the *Follies*. . . . That dame is a Park Avenue hostess with more dollars than sense, and the pansy with her is her favorite art dealer, who specializes in 'modern' stuff, you know, squiggles and squares? . . . *That* dame is married to the biggest banker in town, only the smoothie she's with isn't him. . . . And that distinguished dub? An editor at the *Times*, whose wife no doubt thinks he's burning the midnight oils pounding out an editorial on world affairs."

Instead, said editor seemed to be pounding out a domestic affair with a blonde.

"No food served down here, by the way," Bat said, as if Wyatt had asked him.

"After Rector's and Jack Dunstan's," Wyatt said, "I may not eat till next Tuesday."

Bat lifted a forefinger. "Well, when you get around to it, you can get sandwiches and steaks upstairs."

"Where's our host?"

"Johnny'll make an appearance. After Tex."

"Tex?"

The answer came not from Bat—because the band chose that moment to start playing a jazzed-up version of "Pony Boy"—but from the glittering, leggy apparition that appeared from the wings, "riding" onto the stage slapping her hip and waving a bejeweled white Stetson.

"I told you, Wyatt," Bat whispered. "A Stetson makes a statement. . . ."

Everything about the woman onstage made a statement. Attractive in a sleepy-eyed, cartoonish way, her full figure ensconced in a sequined form-fitting gown, several loops of pearls around her neck and riding her generous bosom, her wrists heavy with glittering bracelets, her marcelled hair almost touching her shoulders, she snugged the jewel-sparkling Stetson onto the peroxide 'do at a rakish slant and a wide red-rouged mouth that somehow opened wider to say: "Hello, suckers!"

The audience exploded in laughter and applause.

From the bandstand, a trumpet player brought down a spare stool for her to perch on and, as she got settled, she made a lewd throaty throwaway remark—"Horny little devil, aren't you?"— that killed the crowd.

Wyatt shook his head, thinking, *Big city, small world.* . . .

"For you newcomers," the brassy blonde was saying, in a deep but full-bodied drawl, "my name is 'Texas' Guinan. I was raised in Texas, schooled in a convent, and ruined right here in Manhattan!"

That got a big laugh, but she topped herself: "Most recently, at two o'clock this afternoon!"

More howls.

Newcomer though he was, Wyatt needed no introduction to Tex Guinan. She had been a discovery of his friend William S. Hart's, an actress with both rodeo and vaudeville experience who had briefly become a sensation as the silver screen's first cowgirl in such epics as *Wild Flower of the Mountain Range* and *South of Santa Fe.*

She was talking about that right now, telling the audience she had a new picture out.

"It's called *The White Squaw*," she said, "and, as you might expect, I have the title role. My last few horse operas have been flopperoos, so I need you good people to crawl out of bed at noon tomorrow, and take in a damn matinee! Why, I risked my . . ." She shifted on the stool. ". . . *life* makin' that picture for my public. I did. Truly did—we shot this one in the wilds of Long Island."

Her material was fair but her delivery was slaying them. Even if the audience was mostly at least a little high, she was good, Wyatt thought. Even better than in the movies, though she sat a horse every bit as well as she did that stool.

"You know, when I started out in pictures, four or five years ago," she said, "they called me the female William S. Hart. Picture ol' Bill in a dress and lipstick, and you'll see that wasn't any *compliment!*"

This went on for a while and Wyatt noticed her, almost imperceptibly, spot him at the ringside table. A small real smile flickered in the midst of the big fake one, but she did not miss a beat of her comedy routine, nor did she embarrass him by introducing him from the audience.

Which she could easily have done.

Right now she was pointing to audience members, saying, "Hello, Corrie! . . . Hello, Jimmy. . . . Is that you, Charlie? Why, Charlie, I spotted an old flame of yours on the other side of the room. . . . Well, Diana! I thought Rafael was *my* hunk of manhood! . . . Say, Harry, where's your wife? You *do* still love her? . . . I'm *so* glad to hear it. . . ."

Perched on the stool, she sang a couple of songs to piano accompaniment, needing no megaphone to be heard, delivering numbers with more gusto than skill, jazzy tunes like "Won't You Come Home, Bill Bailey" and "When My Baby Smiles at Me."

Finally she stepped off the seat and the band came in as she sang a loud, brassy "Swanee," doing a broad, funny imitation of Al Jolson, after which the boys went into "Pony Boy" again and she flounced offstage, waving her jeweled Stetson. When she returned to much applause, three girls came from either wing to "ride" onstage and join her and add words to the song, and at least one of the half dozen was off-pitch, not that it mattered.

They were beauties in white and black-spotted cowhide-pattern bra and panties and high heels, kicking lovely showgirl legs and doing little dances, sometimes with their perky backsides to the audience. One of the girls, a petite Kewpie-doll brunette, was half a step behind, but that didn't seem to matter, either.

"*Po-ny Boy, Po-ny Boy,*" they sang, "*won't you be my To-ny Boy? Don't say no, Here we go, Off a-cross the plains. . . .*"

It wasn't exactly good, but it was fun, and certainly gave the old pecker something to work on, and Wyatt found himself clapping in rhythm with the rest of the audience and, finally, even singing along.

*"Gid-dy up, gidy-up, gid-dy up, whoa! My Pony Boy!"*

Then Texas Guinan strutted back onto the stage and gestured to the little chorus line, saying, "Let's give the little girls a great big hand! What do you say? Come *on* now! Ladies, take a bow!"

One big hand after another was willingly delivered by the audience, as the revue went on for another good half hour, growing increasingly silly but making the audience a part of the show in a manner that was irresistible, particularly to those drinking heavily . . . which was just about everybody but Wyatt and Bat.

About midway, Texas went out among the crowd and passed out noisemakers, as if tonight were New Year's Eve (Wyatt had a hunch every night was New Year's Eve at Holliday's). She sang a few more numbers, with the dancers backing her up (no harmony, unison seeming challenge enough), then circulated around, talking, talking to customers, particularly ringside— though she had the sense to steer clear of Wyatt—and made cheerful fun of them.

Bald men ringside were practically guaranteed a kiss on the blushing noggin, with a Tex lipstick print left behind, and when they weren't bald, they got their hair ruffled. When a self-professed dairy farmer from Des Moines handed out fifty-dollar bills to each of the six chorines, Texas cheered him with, "Well, what do you say, folks? Give the big butter-and-egg man some love and affection!"

They did, mostly by working those noisemakers.

Wyatt found it interesting, even impressive, that Texas maintained control even as the show appeared to be careening into chaos, in particular an invitation for audience talent to perform that resulted in a birdcall specialist, an Eddie Cantor imitation ("Margie," to balance out her Jolson) and a song from an amateur composer who was no competition to Irving Berlin.

After the "Pony Boy" finale reprise, the chorines came out to wild applause and sang as an encore a song about cherries that Wyatt wasn't familiar with, though the audience clearly was, chiming in the chorus—"*Cherries! Cherries! Cherries!*" Then one of the girls produced a basket of cherries and went out into the crowd and fed them to damned near every male in the audience. Wyatt included.

Bat sucked on a stem and commented, "I'm a mite surprised these girls have any cherries left to give away. . . ."

After Texas flounced off in a flash of pearls and jewelry, and the girls trotted off to the wings waving and blowing kisses, Wyatt turned to Bat and said, "If they'd tried that at the Bird Cage back at Tombstone, what would have happened?"

Bat chuckled. "An impromptu dramatization of 'Rape of the Sabine Women,' maybe?"

"At least," Wyatt agreed.

"Times change."

"They do. But people don't."

Texas Guinan, however, did change—her clothes, anyway, trading in her spangly gown for a tasteful rose-colored dress with cream lace collar and only a single string of pearls to suggest her former persona. She slipped from the wings to the ringside table, and though some audience members spotted her, they were not rude or drunk enough to bother her, since she was clearly joining friends for a chat.

Tex seated herself next to Wyatt—he and Bat were using half of the four chairs provided with a table barely big enough for two—and clasped his right hand with both of hers. She squeezed. The warmth gave him a tingle.

"It's been a while," she said.

"Good five years," Wyatt said.

"Nice to see you, too, Tex," Bat said.

"Why should I talk to you?" she said to Bat without looking at him. "You almost never mention me in your column."

"Tex, I mostly write about the fights."

"Shoulda seen the one we had in here last night." Her eyes, big and brown, remained on Wyatt. "I shoulda known you'd show, one of these days. Even if Manhattan isn't exactly your territory."

"Well, Tex . . ."

She waved a hand with a pearl ring on a finger. "I didn't mean you'd come looking for me." Her eyes narrowed shrewdly. "You musta heard about *Johnny*. You musta wanted to find out if this young apple really did fall off your old doctor pal's tree."

Bat smiled as he lighted up a Lucky.

"Tex," Wyatt said, withdrawing his hand but patting hers, "you have a real way with a crowd."

Her eyebrows went up and her eyes widened. "Yeah, well my days on the silver screen are pretty much over. Times and tastes have shifted, and I don't seem to be getting any younger . . . so, what the hell, I shifted, too. . . . You know, Johnny himself found me."

"Didn't know you were lost."

Her laugh was even lower and throatier than her speaking voice.

"Well, I was taking in this new restaurant . . ." She flicked a glance at Bat. "The Gold Room. You know it, don't you, W.B.?"

Bat nodded. "I was there that night, Tex. Remember?"

"Vaguely. . . . Anyway, it was opening night and Sig Romberg got up out of the audience to play the piano, and I was about two sheets to the wind, and got up and got to singing, and then I started dragging celebrities up outa their seats . . . to sing a tune or two? Gold Room was supposed to close at one a.m. but we were still going strong at five-thirty."

Bat said to Wyatt, "Johnny was in the audience, impressed by what he saw, and the rest is history, or soon will be."

With a gesture toward the stage, Tex said, "I've been up to this nonsense for over a month now. And the word has spread . . . kinda like the prickly heat."

Wyatt laughed a little; she seemed to want him to.

Her eyes narrowed. "And how's Sadie?"

"Good. Fine. Wonderful."

Texas smiled, upper lip curling, and turned to Bat. "Whenever he says three words, when one's sufficient? Gives me pause."

With a little too much edge, Wyatt said, "Things are fine."

Texas seemed mildly hurt, but she still managed another smile. "I'm not lookin' to cause trouble, Marshal. I always say, a man who will cheat on his wife will cheat at cards. And you never cheat, right, Wyatt? At cards?"

Wyatt had been known to rig a game for a fool, so he knew damned well she was needling him. But Texas knew damned well their fling out in Hollywood had been during one of those occasional times when he and Sadie had been on the outs. During such rocky patches, he had been known to seek solace.

Calling it "cheating" was ungracious.

Seeing him bristle, she patted his hand. "Anyway, it's good to see you, you goddamned rascal. . . . If Johnny was coming down tonight, he'd have done it by now. Why don't you let me take you upstairs to meet the boss?"

"Why don't you?" Wyatt said.

And the three went upstairs.

# Six

THE STAIRWAY ONTO THE MAIN FLOOR EMPTIED out from under another stairway into a fairly generous hallway. To the right was the cage of a small elevator (marked EMPLOYEES ONLY) next to a recessed rear doorway similarly marked, from which came the clatter and clamor of a kitchen.

Texas and Bat led Wyatt left, past several closed doors at right labeled PRIVATE and past the wide, velvet-roped-off staircase at left. Just beyond that, a double-doorless doorway opened onto a dining room about a third the space of the nightclub floor below.

The dining room was a simple affair, a dozen brown-and-white-checkered cloth-covered tables (though larger than the nightclub's) in what had obviously been the dining room of the brownstone in its years as a residence. Tellingly, the walls bore a faded floral wallpaper that had nothing to do with the occasional framed Western-landscape prints, and the atmosphere was limited to waiters whose mustaches, slicked-back hair, aprons, white shirts with string ties and black trousers matched the uniform of the bartenders below.

Well-dressed patrons (strictly couples) filled only half of the tables, though the pleasing aroma of the steaks and stews and hamburger sandwiches floated invitingly into the hall. Someday, when Wyatt felt the need to eat again, this would be a possibility.

Bat, at Wyatt's elbow, said, "Restaurant's really just a courtesy to the club patrons. But decent grub."

Wyatt eyed his friend. "If you'd like to inhale a T-bone or two, be my guest."

Bat twitched a smile. "Let's get you and Johnny together. That's a meeting long overdue."

"Is he expecting me?"

"No." Bat pointed a finger. "Though . . . I expect Tex is announcing you about now. . . ."

Wyatt wheeled toward where Bat was indicating. At the middle of the three doors that interrupted the wall of woodwork and pale-blue brocade wallpaper with faded patches where pictures once hung (more ghosts of the residence), Texas was leaning in.

Momentarily a figure brushed past Tex so quickly that the formidable woman got damned near bowled over—not that she seemed to mind, her wide mouth turning up in a one-sided smile that threatened to drive her cheek into her ear.

The figure was male, hurriedly putting on and straightening a gray suitcoat over a pastel yellow shirt and snugging a darker yellow necktie that bore a jeweled stickpin, a diamond possibly. His trousers were black and perfectly creased, and the combination of gray coat and black trousers gave Wyatt his first jolt.

When the young man—not that young, early thirties, but young enough—planted himself before Wyatt and smiled shyly, in an almost childlike manner, and extended a hand . . .

. . . Wyatt felt as woozy as a cowpoke at the Long Branch who'd had much too good a time.

"I don't mean to embarrass you," the young man said, "but I have so looked forward to this moment."

The boy (and Wyatt could only think of him that way) stood near Earp's own six-foot-something. His hair was sandy, his eyes large and dark blue and as piercing as a blade. His cheekbones were as high and sharp as an Apache's, his jaw line broad and strong. Clean-shaven, he even had that familiar paleness of flesh given to a father afflicted with tuberculosis; but his was the indoor pallor of the gambler, not the lunger.

And, my God, but his clothes were immaculate—finely tailored, worthy of Savile Row. Hell, maybe he'd gone over to London for these threads, and that crisp yellow shirt. Had the boy researched his father, or had that penchant for pastel been born into him?

Dr. John Holliday, Doctor of Dental Surgery, stood before him, as if Christ had come while Wyatt wasn't looking and resurrected the reprobate's sorry ass.

Only Doc had never looked this healthy. At this age, Doc had had but a few years to live, and would have weighed in at maybe one-hundred-and-twenty pounds. This lad was a sturdy one-seventy, and the weight and general air of good health was the only indication that this apparition was real, and the son, not the father.

That, and the lack of a handlebar mustache; Wyatt had never seen Doc sans 'stache.

Johnny Holliday's hand lingered in the air and his smile had just begun to fade when Wyatt finally grasped the hand in a firm, warm shake.

"My apologies," Wyatt said. "I thought I'd seen a ghost."

This seemed to please Johnny, who grinned at Tex (at his side) and then Bat (at Wyatt's).

"Mr. Masterson told me I was a ringer for my pop," Johnny said. His voice was Doc's, too, a mellow second tenor, but minus the Southern drawl. "And I've seen a few pictures of him, thanks to my mother. But this is the first time I've garnered this reaction."

Wyatt sighed, smiled just a little. "I've had two good friends in my life, Mr. Holliday. This so-called reporter standing next to me, and your late father. Seeing the image of him, standing before me, well, it gives an old man pause."

The boy beamed. "I'd be honored if you called me 'Johnny,' which my friends do."

"The honor's mine, Johnny. And my name's Wyatt."

"Yes, I, uh . . . am familiar with you and your name, sir. And I hope, at some point in the not-too-distant future, you might sit down with me, and tell me about my father."

"He was the bravest man I ever knew," Wyatt said. "Or perhaps the most reckless. That's really the whole storehouse."

Johnny, whose eyes shone, said, "We'll see . . . Wyatt."

"And," Wyatt said, with a thumb at Bat, "don't honor this journalist by calling him 'Mister.' His name is Bartholomew, if you're wondering."

"Reeeeally," Johnny said, amused and surprised. "Here I thought it was 'William'—"

" 'Bat' is fine, son," Bat said, his smile touched with irritation.

Tex took Johnny by the arm, affectionately. "I think this is about to become a clubhouse where no girls are allowed . . . and, anyway, I have to go upstairs and start getting ready for the next show."

Johnny nodded and patted the hand on his arm. "How's the house?"

"Packed."

"Problems?"

"No. No sign of your . . . new friends."

He nodded. "Louie's supposed to keep them out, but those fellas have their ways."

Wyatt and Bat exchanged glances, but said nothing.

With a little-girl wave, Tex hip-swayed back toward the elevator. The view was nice enough, but Wyatt thought she was trying a little too hard.

Johnny's eyes went to Wyatt's. He gestured toward the dining room. "Care for anything, gentlemen? We keep the kitchen open all night."

"Bartholomew might want to eat a rump roast or maybe a kettle of stew. But I'm not inclined, thank you."

Bat waved that off. "Son, I took him to Rector's, top of the evening, then later to Jack Dunstan's. He's still in shock from seeing how people of means satisfy the need for sustenance."

Wyatt jerked a thumb at his friend. "Does he talk to you like that, Johnny, all the time? This writerly nonsense?"

Johnny held up his hands, as if in surrender to a stagecoach robber. "I abstain."

Bat said to Wyatt, "You weren't complaining when I wrote that piece on you."

A magazine article on Wyatt's lawman days, written by Bat and somewhat true, had indeed sparked the Hollywood interest of Bill Hart, Tom Mix and others. But Bat didn't need to know that.

"After all of the lies the newshounds told about us," Wyatt said to Bat, good-naturedly riding him, "the very thought that you could join the enemy camp—"

"Why don't you join the twentieth century, Wyatt," Bat said with snap in his words. "I traded in my sixgun for a typewriter . . . and words are weapons, too."

"They surely are," Wyatt admitted. "They've killed my reputation often enough."

Johnny stepped forward and put one hand on Wyatt's shoulder and the other on Bat's. "Why don't we repair to my office, have some brandy, and if you fellas want to wrestle, why, I'll just referee."

They laughed and followed him.

The office was the library of the former residence, a spacious chamber of dark wood and walls that were mostly bookshelves with volumes that included medical tomes as well as the complete leather-bound works of Shakespeare and Dickens, and well-read popular editions of Bret Harte, Jack London, Rex Beach and Mark Twain.

Several framed maps, old ones of Arizona and Texas and regional Western maps, took up much of the available wall space, as did an oil painting that Wyatt at first thought was of Johnny himself, but on closer examination proved to be of the boy's father, a romanticized version of a widely published photograph.

Soon Wyatt was sitting in a most comfortable red leather chair across from his host, and Bat next to him in a yellow leather version (matching a three-cushioned couch against the right wall), both men having been provided generous snifters of brandy. The flavor of the dark liquid was matched by the pleasant warmth it brought to the belly.

Johnny's desk was a massive cherrywood affair piled with ledgers and paperwork. He had got himself a snifter, too, but it sat on the desk while its owner leaned forward with elbows resting on a blotter and fingertips tented.

"I am so pleased and privileged to meet you, Wyatt," Johnny said, "that I am willing to overlook why you came."

Wyatt shrugged. Sipped. Said, "Why did I come?"

"Because my mother asked you to. Because my mother thinks

I've gotten myself into . . . as she so quaintly puts it . . . 'dangerous straits.' "

"Most dangerous straight I know of," Bat said lightly, "is trying to fill one, inside."

Wyatt cocked his head and said, "Did your mother tell you she'd talked to me?"

"No." Johnny's childlike smile flickered with deviltry, so like his papa's. "*You* just did."

Bat chuckled. "Kid's a card player, Wyatt. Told you as much."

Wyatt gestured behind him. "What's in the adjacent room?"

Johnny's eyes narrowed, the question seeming to him a non sequitur. "Nothing. It's a music room. Or it was till I had the piano moved to the bandstand, downstairs. Fireplace, not much space. I'm not utilizing it, presently."

Wyatt nodded. "This is a three-story building?"

"Yes." Mildly confused, Johnny sat forward. "Why, do you want a tour?"

"Right now? Just in words. So it's three floors, four counting the basement."

"Yes. The kitchen's on this floor, in back. Floor above I turned into a dressing room for the girls, star dressing room for Miss Guinan, and I have a couple of guest rooms. Top floor is my apartment. . . . Why? What's on your mind, Wyatt?"

"Nothing. Just getting the lay of the land."

Bat was looking at Wyatt curiously.

So was Johnny, who said, "If you have a message from my mother, Wyatt, I'm willing to listen."

Wyatt shook his head. "No you aren't. You've already listened to her, haven't you? Or heard her, anyway."

"Yes. Of course. . . ."

"And Bartholomew here's tried to talk sense to you?"

Johnny grunted a laugh, sat back in his chair. "On a weekly basis!"

Bat gave Wyatt an earnest look and said, "I've done my best, Wyatt. Truly I have."

Johnny laughed some more—a dry, familiar laugh; Doc's laugh. Gave Wyatt a shiver as the young man said, "And with all due respect, Mr. Masterson . . . Bat . . . you have made less than a convincing case."

Bat frowned, offended. "I object! I've stated the case against this enterprise with passion and precision!"

"All the while," Johnny said, "you were tossing back bourbon and filling your eyeballs with my chorus girls and enjoying the speakeasy life like you were born to it."

Had Bat moved any farther forward in the leather chair, he'd have been on the floor. "Now, I never said this life didn't have its appeal. Who doesn't like a drink? Who doesn't like a damsel? You've got Tex Guinan in your hip pocket, and she's the toast of the town! That whelp Winchell's calling her the Queen of Broadway!"

"Then what," Johnny said, crisply polite, "is your problem?"

Bat flopped back in the chair and waved his hands. "I don't have any problem! I'm just a paying customer . . ."

Johnny raised an eyebrow. "Paying? When did this new policy begin?"

Bat swallowed thickly, then said, "I simply mean, that this life, this night life, has great appeal. And it has enormous possibilities for making money. I don't deny that. In fact, that is the very *point* . . ."

Wyatt said, "With liquor illegal, the gangsters are bound to move in."

Bat's eyes whipped to Wyatt's. "Exactly! This town is brimming with bastards in Borsalinos just waiting to take over, and kill you for the privilege. Wyatt, it's Tombstone redux—only these characters from Brooklyn make the Clantons look like kindergartners!"

Wyatt swiveled to Johnny. "Well, son?"

Johnny shrugged, rocking gently in his chair. "Mr. Masterson . . . Bat . . . is right. The rewards are considerable, and so are the dangers. When you were my age, Wyatt . . . Mr. Earp . . . weren't the conditions the same?"

Bat said, "No comparison!"

Wyatt said to Bat, "*You* just made one."

Johnny continued: "Manhattan's a boomtown, Wyatt! Do I even have to tell you? These speakeasy days are the new Gold Rush!"

Wyatt, feeling the old tingle, quietly said, "Johnny . . . let's put these hoodlums aside. Where do the police stand in this?"

He flipped a hand. "We pay them off weekly. They're no help to us, but no hindrance, either. I'm told we'll eventually have to help them stage some raids, for the papers . . . but we'll have plenty of notice. Just in case, I only keep what I need on hand . . . by way of liquor, I mean."

"What about the federals?"

"Some of them are honest, most aren't. Right now, we have them on the pad, too."

Wyatt nodded, sat with his hands folded over his belly. "So you do have considerable overhead."

"No denying it," Johnny said. "But I own this building outright, and my supply of liquor? I calculate it will last me at least five years."

Bat said, "If *you* last five years."

"Life is like business," Johnny said with a shrug. "A risk."

Bat was shaking his head as Wyatt asked, "What do you intend to do, once you run out of product?"

Johnny slapped the air. "Hell—retire. In five years, I'll be independently wealthy. The hoodlums can have it."

Wyatt said, "Hmmm," and mulled that.

Bat said, "Johnny, quit painting this rosy picture and tell Wyatt about this character Capone, and his boss, Yale."

Johnny rocked some more. "Nothing much to tell. They all work for a smart slick guinea named Torrio, who operates mostly out of Chicago. They're not trying to take over."

Wyatt frowned. "They aren't?"

"No. They're just using their old Black Hand extortion techniques to force me into using them as my distributor. But I don't *need* a distributor!"

"Because of the supply you won."

Johnny chuckled. "Oh, you heard about that, did you?"

"Yeah. You got this brownstone, you won half the liquor left in New York, playing poker. . . . This Brooklyn bunch—they don't run speaks?"

Tiny shrug. "They own a few—but on *their* side of the river. Biggest joint's in Coney Island—one of Yale's two or three headquarters."

"Is he dangerous?"

"Yale? I can't really say. He's feared, all right. But it's this plump kid, who does his enforcing, that has everybody's underwear riding high."

"Capone."

"Capone. He's maybe . . . twenty-one, twenty-two? You see, they're having trouble in their own backyard, with the Irish hoodlums moving in on them. That's why they're trying to expand over here . . . but it's not going to work out."

"Why?"

Johnny threw his hands in the air. "There's too much competition over here already! And Arnold Rothstein, who is a personal pal of mine, has connections with every faction in Manhattan. He's the peacekeeper. Plenty for everybody, he says."

"Good philosophy."

Johnny folded his arms and an eyebrow rose slyly. "Now, I might be able to throw Yale and Capone a *bone* . . ."

But before Johnny could finish that, Tex stuck her head in the door, string of pearls dangling like a noose. Her expression was grave.

"Trouble," she said.

Johnny's chin lifted; the dark blue eyes were hard and glittering. "Not our Brooklyn friends?"

"*Your* Brooklyn friends."

"Capone?"

"Himself . . . and two bully boys."

Wyatt glanced at Bat, whose expression was as grave as Tex's. Wyatt, however, was smiling, just a little. This was a nice piece of gambler's luck, being here when the hoodlums came to call.

Johnny was up and coming around the desk. "How'd the bastards get in?"

Tex met him half-way, stopping him with her hands on his chest, while Wyatt and Bat remained in their well-padded leather chairs.

She said, "They tagged in after two toney couples who Louie recognized as regulars. Louie's tough, but with three Brooklyn boys packing heat? Forget it."

Moving past her, Johnny said, "I'll handle these sons of bitches. Louie and the other boys can back my play, and—"

Wyatt said, "Johnny. A moment."

Johnny froze and said, "Oh, Wyatt, that's generous as hell, but I can't ask you to—"

"I'm not offering anything." His eyes went to Tex. "Are they causing trouble? Bothering the clientele?"

"No! Not yet, anyway. They're just sitting at one of the tables, listening to the band and watching couples rub against each other."

"Maybe they're here for your show."

Tex's eyebrows hiked. "Yeah, to bust *up* my show!"

"Have they ever gone that far before?"

"No, but they've threatened—"

"Tex, what do they say they want?"

"I didn't talk to them."

"Did your friend, uh, Louie? Did he talk to them?"

"Yeah. Of course."

"And?"

"And Capone and his cronies, they say they wanna talk to Johnny in private." Her eyes found Johnny's and she gripped his nearest arm. "You can't do that. They get Johnny alone, and God knows what they'll pull. It's an invitation to dine, and I don't mean on steak or stew."

Wyatt, still seated, said, "Send them up."

Wyatt was addressing Tex, but Johnny answered, "Receive them in my own office?"

"Sure. It's business, isn't it?"

Johnny, who already had a good head of steam worked up, paused and thought. "I suppose . . . I suppose it is."

"Keep it cool." Wyatt raised a forefinger. "Plenty of time later, to get hot."

Tex turned to Wyatt, eyes flashing, nostrils flaring. "Are you completely out of your mind, Wyatt Earp?"

"That has been suggested," Wyatt said. Then to Johnny: "Have her send them up. Bat and me'll back your play."

Bat said, "We will?"

Tex, hands on her hips, said, "Pardon me, but a couple of duffers like you are gonna take care of young turks like this?"

"I rode a young filly once," Wyatt said, "and she didn't complain."

Tex's mouth fell like a trapdoor, and then she roared with laughter and waved a dismissive hand in Wyatt's direction. "Sweetie, whatever you get, you deserve! . . . I'll go get our 'guests.'"

And she was gone.

Johnny was just standing there frozen, like Lot's wife getting a gander at Gomorrah.

Wyatt gestured with a finger. "Got a rod in that desk, son?"

Johnny swallowed. Nodded. "Top drawer, right."

"Then get behind it, and open it an inch." Wyatt rose, and looked down at the still seated Bat, who seemed a mite bewildered. "Come on, Bartholomew. Cheap seats should be sufficient, for a show like this."

Bat's eyes narrowed, but he got to his feet, and followed Wyatt over to the yellow couch, where both men sat.

In about two minutes, a character bounded in, a big heavyset kid with an immediately commanding presence.

"Johnny," he said. "Good to see you again. You look like a million fucking dollars."

A pudgy hand bearing a pink-jeweled pinkie ring was thrust forward and Johnny, not rising, took it briefly.

From Wyatt's vantage point on the couch, all he'd seen so far was a blur of purple—Johnny's guest was six feet tall and four feet wide, a small building of a man wearing a purple suit, beautifully tailored.

As the newcomer swung around to take in the rest of the office— including the two men seated on the sofa—he presented Wyatt with a good detailed look. The rest of the wardrobe was equally as nattily tasteless: a lighter purple shirt, a deep purple necktie (like Johnny's tie, this one had a diamond stickpin) and a pearl-gray Borsalino at an angle so sharp it cut across his left eye. The shoes were white and pointed and perforated.

"Mr. Capone," Johnny said with half a nod.

Mr. Capone had a wide round face with full, reddish lips, a broad flat nose and light-gray eyes under dark shaggy slashes of eyebrow, and no neck to speak of; his complexion had an olive tinge though the plump cheeks were boyishly rosy.

He waved toward the doorway and two men in dark suits and black fedoras stepped into view. They stood as if they were smuggling bricks under their arms, which told Wyatt they had guns in holsters under every armpit. But two-gun kids had never impressed Wyatt Earp.

Capone himself, if he was armed, either had a better-cut suit (no doubt of that) or a physique that obscured shoulder-stowed weaponry.

Oddly, the corpulent gangster said to his flunkies, a pair of interchangeable dead-eyed pasty faces, "Be polite," and both men took off their fedoras, which they held in their left hands. This served to make them look less alike, as one was mostly bald and the other had a full head of greasy, curly hair.

What was odd, however, was Capone requesting this respect while leaving his own Borsalino in place.

Capone turned to Wyatt and Bat and said, "Don't get up."

Wyatt said, "Don't worry."

Capone's eyes, which had a bulginess to them, managed to turn tiny as they studied Wyatt, and then Bat. The hoodlum was smiling but the smile had a faint quiver in it, now.

Something in the faces of these old men—perhaps the spooky light-blue unblinking eyes—had stopped him for a moment.

To Johnny, Capone said, "Am I interrupting some kind of family reunion?"

Johnny's eyes narrowed. "Why?"

"I thought maybe these was your grandpas or some such."

"They're friends."

Capone grinned at Johnny and then grinned at Wyatt and Bat. "You run with a kinda old crowd, Johnny. . . . Who are you, Granddad?"

The question had been addressed to Wyatt Earp, who said, "Wyatt Earp."

Capone took that like the small punch it was and, thick spittle-flecked lips still smiling, chuckled and said, "Like in the dime novels?"

"Like," Wyatt said, "in the dime novels. And this is Bat Masterson."

Finally Capone swept off his hat, bowing, revealing thinning black hair. "Well, what an honor. Regular Wild West show in here. Where's Wild Bill Hickok?"

"Dead," Wyatt said. "So is Buffalo Bill, but I believe his troupe is in Philadelphia, should you want to catch a train and a show."

Capone's smile curdled and his eyes seemed to be wondering if he'd been insulted or not.

Then, gesturing with the fancy hat at Johnny, he said, "That's right! That's right. . . . You're supposed to be Doc Holliday's kid, aren't you?"

Johnny said nothing. Didn't even nod.

Capone tromped closer to Johnny's desk. "I always figured that was just talk. Just a gimmick, 'cause of you hiring Texas Guinan and dressing your speak up, Wild West–style. So you really are Doc Holliday's kid? He was sick or something, wasn't he?"

"What do you want, Mr. Capone?"

"Mind if I sit?"

"Do I have a choice?"

Capone sat. He crossed his leg and rested an ankle on a knee. Wyatt got a glimpse of purple sock.

"Of course I've seen you around, Masterson," Capone said without looking back at him. "You were one of them cowboys, too, right? And now you hang around racetracks or something."

Bat said nothing. But Wyatt noted his friend's eyes had turned very hard and very cold.

"Anyway," a genial Capone was saying to Johnny, "you've had plenty of time to think over our offer. Mr. Yale has been generous in giving you lots of rope." Capone glanced back, grinning. "You old cowboys know about rope, don't you?"

"Thrown one over a tree or two," Wyatt said.

Capone's eyes got tiny again, but then he turned back to Johnny. "We're not a bunch of goddamn bootleggers. We're not making our own stuff. We're importing the genuine article from Canada. Real label product."

Johnny sighed. "Mr. Capone, I've explained to you at length— I have my own supply of 'real label' product."

Capone's nodding was exaggerated and protracted. Then he said, "Mr. Yale is aware of that. He understands you have years and years worth of product, stored away someplace."

"I have no control over what Mr. Yale 'understands.'"

"That's right, you don't. And don't forget that." Capone's hand slipped under his purple suitcoat and Wyatt was just starting to rise when he saw that the fat fingers were withdrawing a thick cigar.

Wyatt settled back as one of the flunkies lighted the cigar for Capone, who bestowed a nod, and got the oversize stogie going, taking his time about it, and then said to Johnny, "Mr. Yale is willing to offer you a good sum of money for that stored-away product. A generous sum. A Christian sum. He will even give you a sizeable discount, when he sells it back to you."

"Why would I want to do that?"

"Good business. Good business. With years' worth of product, well, there are considerations."

"Considerations."

"Such as, could that product go bad, over time? You serve bottled beer, right? Your whiskey and such, well, it will stand the test of time. But beer is like milk. It don't have to get spilt to go bad."

Johnny was nodding now, and his voice was fairly amiable as he said, "You're right. My supply of beer will be gone, in six months. I'll need a new supplier. And I'm willing to talk to you and Mr. Yale about that."

Wyatt glanced at Bat; both men realized that this had been the "bone" Johnny had mentioned.

But Capone was shaking his head and waving a pudgy hand which had the pool cue of a cigar between thick fingers, smearing the air with blue smoke.

"Beer won't do it, Johnny. No, sir. You see, we could be real pricks and come over the bridge and start taking over speaks—"

"Maybe Arnold Rothstein," Johnny interrupted with an edge, "and his various good friends would frown on that."

"Fuck Arnold Rothstein. Rothstein is a gambler and he should stick to his goddamn cards." Capone sat forward and the leather chair, where Wyatt had sat, groaned like a cavalry officer taking Indian torture. "We got no interest in the retail side. We are strictly wholesale. And there's gonna be wholesale fucking *trouble* if you don't sell out to us and then start buying. *Capeesh?* That means 'understand'—understand?"

Capone crushed the big fresh cigar in a glass tray on the desk;

the waste of what must have been an expensive smoke made a certain wanton violent point.

Johnny raised a hand, gently. "Mr. Capone, I'll consider your offer. For now, I have a club to run. You're welcome to go downstairs and take a table and watch the show. As long as you behave yourself."

Capone was out of the chair like a cannonball. His hands were on the desk and he was leaning his fat florid face right into Johnny's pale skinny one and shouting, "Are you saying we ain't civilized, Mr. Yale and me?"

Wyatt was astounded by how fast Bat moved.

And the bum leg wasn't a factor, at all, the bulldog Bartholomew suddenly past the chair and was behind Capone and sticking the small snout of a revolver between the fat folds of the hoodlum's neck.

"Time for you and your boys to go," Bat said.

The two flunkies were moving forward.

Wyatt took the closer one, and wasn't even fully off the couch when he kicked the hood behind the left knee. The world went out from under the guy—this was the bald one—and Wyatt knelt and withdrew the two revolvers from under the fallen flunky's shoulders to point up at the astounded curly-headed one, who hadn't even gone for his own guns, yet.

Rising slowly, Wyatt said, "I have to agree—you fellers need to move on."

Johnny's gun was out of the drawer, in hand, and the three of them—Doc Holliday's boy and Bat Masterson and Wyatt Earp—ushered their three Brooklynite guests out via the seldom used front door. Wyatt brandished only one of the two guns he'd commandeered, sticking the other one in his waistband, thinking a pair of guns was redundant and a trifle showy.

Considerable restraint was displayed, when none of the guests got kicked in the ass as they started down the eight steps to the sidewalk.

Capone looked back to glower, "You fucked up bad."

This seemed generally directed, but Wyatt responded.

"Maybe so," he said, pointing a gun at Capone's jack-o'-lantern head. "Not too late to kill you."

At this, the three hoodlums scurried into the night, almost bumping into several well-dressed couples on the sidewalk who were making the speakeasy rounds.

Inside, the handful of diners—who had witnessed the conveying-by-gun of these guests out the door—were on their feet and milling around wide-eyed, whispering. The pair of waiters looked startled, too.

"Nothing to worry about, folks," Johnny assured them, tucking his revolver (a little pearl-handled nickel-plated number) in his suitcoat pocket. "Your meals are on the house tonight."

Then their host led Wyatt and Bat back into his private office.

"Now do you see what I mean," Bat whispered to Wyatt, as they settled into the leather chairs and Johnny got back behind his desk. "Do you see why this boy's mother wants you to talk sense to him?"

"I intend to talk sense to him," Wyatt assured Bat. Then he turned back to Doc's son and asked, "Johnny, have you considered putting some gambling in?"

Bat covered his face with a hand.

"You've got plenty of wasted space for it," Wyatt was saying. "That front music room, we could start with a table in there—faro or poker. Lots of folks in this town might get a kick out of playing a hand or two with the likes of old Wyatt Earp . . . if I don't sound too immodest."

Johnny was rocking back in his chair, smiling, laughing softly. "No . . . No, Wyatt. You don't sound immodest at all."

# TWO

# BUCK THE TIGER*

*gambler lingo for: defy the odds

# Seven

AL CAPONE WAS NO FUCKING THIEF.

In this, the twenty-one-year-old business-man from Brooklyn took great pride. Sure, back when he ran with kid gangs, he was involved in the typical petty pilferage of such good-natured childhood pastimes as lunch money extortion, and knocking over pushcarts and scattering bread bins, taking free samples in the wake. Kid stuff, no worse than pulling old boys' beards or break-ing this window or shooting out that street lamp.

No one could say he didn't have a good, de-cent upbringing. His papa, Gabriele, was a bar-ber; his mother, Theresa, a seamstress, loving and kind and a hell of a cook, as his going-on-two-hundred-fifty pounds proved. Papa having a trade, and the ability to read and write English, meant a quick climb for the Capones—only a few years in the really nasty tenements.

Yet the memories of squalor stayed with young Al. He was not likely to forget the early days with the family of six (Al had three brothers) sharing two unfurnished rooms with no gas or electricity, cold water from a sink in the hall, heat from the kerosene stove Mama cooked on, and a two-holer shitter out back for the whole goddamn building.

These beginnings had been as rough as the Sands Street neighborhood, which bordered the Brooklyn Navy Yard and its bedlam. His ears rang with the clamor of shipbuilding and shipping, punctuated by the screech of sea gulls; his nostrils twitched at the smells of acrid oil, rotting vegetation and brackish seawater. The stench off the Gowanus Canal—a manmade waterway for barges, a marshy brownish scar across Brooklyn—could bring tears to a grown man's eyes, let alone a little kid. And that was the good part.

The bad? Saloons and brothels and pawnshops and gambling joints and tattoo parlors served the swaggering, drunken sailors who infested the Sands Street sidewalks, leaving gutters brimming with used lambskins and broken beer bottles. To this day, the sight of a sailor in uniform brought a bile of disgust to his throat.

Papa's profession, honest though it was, was literally a nickel-and-dime affair. For years the old man assisted other barbers and worked part-time in groceries (where his English skills were valuable) and finally was able to open his own barbershop at 69 Park Avenue (in Brooklyn—this was a step up, but not hardly Manhattan). The family took an apartment over the shop, with such luxuries as electricity and indoor plumbing and even furniture . . . and such necessities as taking on a couple boarders.

Al's memories of those years were pleasant. The new neighborhood was a mix of mostly Irish and such other nationalities as

Chinese, Swedish and German. He had grown up around all kinds of people, which contributed to him being the kind of guy who could get along with everybody. His people were from Naples and it always surprised and disappointed him when Italians fought amongst themselves, Northerners against the Southerners and the Sicilians against everybody.

Hell, he wasn't even Italian, not really. He was born here. He was American.

He'd started school at P.S. 7, near the Navy Yard, where he rubbed shoulders with the toughest Irish kids out of Red Hook and held his own, winning every fight and earning straight B's. After the move, he found himself in a Gothic prison of a school, P.S. 133, and the teachers there, Irish women mostly, rubbed him the wrong way. Nuns had taught these young broads to use a ruler on unruly knuckles and Al did not go for such shit.

That was when he began running with kid gangs, and his truancy rate went up, his grades went down, and finally one of those Irish bitch teachers slapped him and he slapped her back. What the hell—seventh grade was farther than most guys got.

Around then the family moved again, to an even nicer Brooklyn neighborhood, into an apartment on Garfield Place, a quiet residential area with shade trees and row houses. Best of all, a pool hall nearby allowed him and his Papa to spend some father-and-son time together, with the old man passing along his considerable skill at pool to a fourteen-year-old pupil who at the moment wasn't studying much of anything else.

Those were the best hours he ever spent with his Papa, who he admired, though Al sure as hell had no desire to go into the nickel-a-haircut business. Anyway, he had another guy to look up to, another "father," name of Johnny Torrio.

Moving to Garfield Place meant Al walked damn near every

day by a restaurant on the busy corner of Union Street and Fourth Avenue; on the second floor a window glittered with gilt letters: JOHN TORRIO ASSOCIATION. Often the diminutive, dapper Italian leprechaun called Little John—with his pallid face and chipmunk cheeks and mild button eyes and tiny hands and feet—would reward neighborhood lads with trivial errands that paid a generous five dollars per.

The boys who proved trustworthy earned the right to perform more difficult, demanding tasks, such as making payoffs or deliveries. Occasionally a boy rose to Little John's inner circle, as had Al, who had passed a test that few boys had.

Little John had left teenaged Al alone in the Association office, in full view of a pile of cash on the desk. Most boys presented with this temptation took it, and never did business with Johnny Torrio again. Al didn't touch the money and won his mentor's trust.

Al Capone was no fucking thief.

Little John was the father he wished he had—oh, sure, he respected Papa for making a living for the family, and a better one than most. But Torrio was wealthy and successful and fucking brilliant. Nothing in his growing-up years meant more to Al than the moments Torrio spent alone with him in that unpretentious office, teaching him the ways of business.

"Everybody wants to fight, Al," Little John would say in a musical voice unusual for an Italian, an Irish brogue of a voice, really. "But the smart man makes alliances. He picks his fights carefully. He knows what ties to make, and when to make them—and when to cut 'em, if a tie starts in to binding."

Such a reflective man, so calm, Little John was, to have come up through Manhattan's Five Points Gang, that skull-cracking, eye-gouging bunch, available for hire to those needing a strike broken or votes discouraged (or encouraged) or anyone in the specific need of general mayhem.

"There is profit enough in the rackets," Little John told him, "for all to share, in peace. You can't enjoy the proceeds when you've been murdered, Al. Even injury is too high a price to pay."

Not that the puny little guy was a pushover where it came to violence.

"I've never fired a gun in my life, Al," he told his pupil. A dainty pink hand raised as if in benediction: Pope John Torrio. "But I have no practical objections to the use of force. I just consider it a poor solution to business problems . . . if sometimes necessary."

Al already knew Little John approved of such tactics, "if necessary," since by fifteen he was one of Torrio's chief collectors of outstanding accounts, skilled in the use of fists, blackjacks and wooden clubs. But what about rubbing out a guy who's in some way out of line?

"The execution of a business rival," Little John would say, "is an unfortunate, occasional necessity in *la mala vita*."

The evil life.

The life of crime. And Johnny Torrio, behind the gilt-lettered window of his association, was running the local Italian lottery, the so-called numbers racket—criminal but not hurting anybody. His other business interests included whorehouses and gambling joints, in the very Sands Street neighborhood Al had escaped. Johnny Torrio had helped make those sailors drunken.

"Little John," fourteen-year-old Al had once asked, "*is* it evil? *Are* we evil, living this life?"

"Is your mother evil?"

"No! Hell, no!"

"Does she ask where the money you bring her comes from?"

"No."

"Does money know where it comes from?"

"No."

"Do we have anything in America without money?"

"No."

A gentle, knowing nod. "Your mother knows that a man's life at home is separate from the life he leads at work. We deal with whores in our business so that we can give a good, respectable life to the madonnas in our homes."

"They're . . . separate things? Work and home?"

"They have nothing to do with each other. Nothing. Does your mother praise you when you bring money home to her?"

"Yes! She says she's proud of her good boy."

"She is right to be proud of you, Al. I'm proud of you, too. No boy who has crossed the threshold of my association has ever had your aptitude. Can do sums in his head, calculate the odds so quick, so accurate. But it's more than that—you calculate *people*, too. How much will a man pay for a bet? At poker? At craps? At numbers? How much is ten minutes with a woman worth? Good things to know. Important things to know."

Al had been running with the South Brooklyn Rippers, but Little John paved the way for him to join the offshoot gang, the Five Points Juniors. But Al was disappointed by the piddling nature of the gang, limited as it was to petty vandalism and hanging out and smalltime theft, none of which was Al's style.

His style, really, was having a good time, and loitering on street corners with the guys was not his idea of one. Thanks to his Papa, he was the best pool player in the neighborhood and, despite his size, a hell of a dancer. The girls liked him, liked his natty style of apparel (picked up from Little John), and were frequently won over by his confident, brash manner.

Mae Coughlin he met at a dance at a cellar club on Carroll Street. The "club" was just a rented storefront with the windows blacked out where its young members, Italian and Irish alike, drank and gambled and danced with girls. Mae was respectable, a sales clerk at a department store, but she was a little older than Al, and she liked to have fun, too. Nice girls often frequented the cellar clubs.

What a nice girl—an Irish girl—like Mae ever saw in a fat Italian slob like him, Al would never know; but he wasn't knocking it. She was smart and slender and blonde and pretty, and though she lived just a short stroll from Garfield Place, hers was a world away from his.

The Coughlins lived on Third Place in a three-story house on a broad tree-lined lane in an upstanding middle-class Irish enclave. Her father worked construction and her mother was active in the church and neither was thrilled about the prospect of Alphonse Capone, trash blown over from the rough neighborhood a few blocks away, for a son-in-law.

The unlikely couple had been dating for a month when Al asked his mentor for an opinion on a possible Capone/Coughlin union.

"Ask the girl," Little John said without hesitation. "I married an Irish girl from Kentucky, and it was the best thing I ever done. We Italians like to marry young and those mick men wait around till they're thirty and miss the good opportunities. Don't make their mistake."

Still, Al couldn't bring himself to pop the question. Finally, when Mae missed her period, he knew he could expect a positive response, even from her parents.

A year ago December, he and Mae had been married at the Coughlins' family church, the impressive St. Mary Star of the Sea, near the Brooklyn docks. Mae hadn't suffered the embarrassment of going to the altar fat and pregnant, because they'd already had their son earlier the same month—Albert Francis Capone, who Al called "Sonny Boy."

The marriage came in very handy with the draft board, giving him a deferment from getting sent overseas, the war still going on at the time. And, as a new father, he did his best to make a living for his new family.

For the past several years, he'd tried the occasional straight job, sometimes to serve as a front, for example the pinsetter job Little John arranged at a bowling alley; but also real legit jobs, such as working as a clerk in a munitions factory, then as a paper cutter at a book bindery. Clerking wasn't so bad, he could exercise his brain; but that paper-cutter baloney was a big yawn, and tired his ass out, to boot.

Now that he was a married man, a father with responsibilities, Al needed real work. Good-paying work, legit or not . . . and probably not. But when he turned to Little John, his mentor gave him shocking news.

"My business interests in Chicago," Torrio said, "require my full attention."

For years Little John had been taking the train to Chicago two or three times a year; he had a cousin there, Victoria, married to Big Jim Colosimo, the cathouse czar of Chicago.

"Take me with you, Little John."

"No, Al. I need you here."

"What's here with you gone?"

"Frankie Yale. He's looking after my interests. You look after Frankie."

"Don't you trust him, Little John?"

"Sure I do. With you standing behind him watching."

And Johnny Torrio took the train west, and Al went to work for Little John's second-in-command, Frankie Yale.

Already Al knew Frankie well, and liked and respected him. The stocky, black-haired, pug-nosed, dimple-chinned Yale, only five or six years older than Al, was already a stunning success in business—owning a mortuary, a nightclub (the Sunrise Café), a laundry, racehorses, prizefighters, even distributing a line of his own cigars.

Al Capone was no fucking thief, and neither was Frankie Yale—he lent workmen money at twenty percent per week; he provided shopkeepers insurance policies; and organized unions, the local ice men, among others.

True, Frankie had a notoriously short fuse. In a heartbeat he could go from gracious don to brutal wacko. He could explode in a torrent of filthy talk and put his own brother in the hospital, for a minor perceived insult (as he did with Angelo Yale, ten years his junior).

Al had never faced Frankie's wrath—whether because Al had never given him cause or maybe because Frankie was careful not to go bughouse with somebody Al's size.

Yale maintained three headquarters—one in a Brooklyn garage that housed his booze business delivery trucks; another at the Adonis Club, Fury Argolia's restaurant; and finally at the Harvard Inn at Coney Island, on Brooklyn's south shore. The latter was where, at Little John's request, Frankie Yale gave formal employment to Al Capone.

Al's size had dictated the role—bouncer and bartender. The eighteen-year-old had the right heft and the necessary affability for that combined role—you didn't want to throw a drunken bastard out so hard on his ass that the sobered-up bastard felt resentment and did not in future return with his trade.

"You got tact," Yale would say, after Al escorted out a rowdy drunk who'd gone from problem to pal when the burly bartender slung an arm around his shoulder and walked him out, cooing threats.

"Tact," Al said, savoring the compliment, because it sounded like one; later, when he'd looked the word up in a dictionary, it meant even more.

Though the Harvard Inn was rougher than a cob, Yale—a darkly handsome, compactly muscular guy—was himself an even bigger fashion plate than Johnny Torrio, replacing Little John's crisply stylish business attire with tailored double-breasted suits whose startling colors were outdistanced by a big diamond belt buckle, not to mention pearl-gray spats over black patent-leather shoes and a wide-brimmed Borsalino, usually white, sometimes gray.

Soon Al was patterning his own attire after Yale's, which might have rubbed the hot-headed Frankie wrong, only the boss took it as a compliment. In fact, Yale took to Al, in general. Before long the bartender was a regular fixture at the Harvard Inn, doing everything from washing dishes to waiting tables under Frankie's fatherly eye. Customers who nervously paid their respects to Frankie, or avoided Frankie's bodyguard Little Augie altogether, would seek out Al, whose smiling way with serving up a foamy beer won almost as many friends as his turns on the dance floor doing the Castle Walk and Balling the Jack with the band's girl singer.

People got a kick out of seeing a big man move gracefully, and he liked the attention, the applause.

Frankie Yale also liked the way Al handled other jobs.

Such as last year, when Al happened to be at a neighborhood crap game where Tony Perotta rolled his way to a cool $1,500.

When Perotta and his new bankroll left the game, Al followed the tall, thin dice player out into the hallway and cornered him, saying, "That's a nice win, Tony."

Perotta and Al knew each other a little.

Mustached, with a snappy green fedora, Perotta said, "Thanks, Al. And what the fuck's it to you?"

"You owe Frankie Yale two thousand in markers for a game last week."

"I repeat, what the fuck's it to—"

"You know what it is to me, Tony. I work for Frankie."

"Why don't I should slip you a C-note and you work for yourself for a change."

Al shook his head. "Hand over the wad, Tony."

Tony shoved Al. "Go fuck yourself, fatso!"

The .45 automatic was in Capone's hand and shoved in Tony's belly faster than a blink.

"Hand it over," Al said.

Perotta's lip curled back like a pouty brat. "You oughta be ashamed of yourself!"

But he handed the money over.

Al put the gun back in his waistband.

Perotta was shaking his head, pissing and moaning. "Don't you think I'm gonna forget this, Capone! It ain't fair, it ain't right, I known you for a long time. I know where you and that mick wife of yours live!"

Al took the gun out again and shot Perotta in the head. The guy's mouth was open to start another bullshit sentence, but nothing came out. A spatter of blood and brains and bone on the wall hung and dripped, after Perotta slid to the floor and sat, making himself comfortable for the last time.

When Al gave his boss the money, in a booth at the Harvard

Inn that same night, Yale looked like he might for the first time really lose his temper with his favorite boy.

"What the hell's the idea!" Frankie said. "I'm not gonna get my other five hundred now, am I?"

"He had a big mouth," Al said.

"A lot of guys have big mouths!"

"This one threatened my family. The prick deserved what he got. Mr. Yale, you can dock my pay till the five hundred is clear. I'd appreciate it, though, if you spared me the twenty percent vig."

Frankie's expression hadn't been that different from Perotta's open-mouthed final one—only Perotta didn't break into laughter, like Frankie did.

"So you're willing to do a piece of work," Frankie said, "now and then."

This meant murder.

"You're the boss, Mr. Yale."

"Quit that. Quit that. It's Frankie. I love you, you big bum. I love you. You don't owe me nothin', kid, but loyalty. Got it? Sit down and let's talk about where you're headed."

Even now, Al still worked a few weeks a night behind the Harvard Inn's famous twenty-foot bar. But the job, like the bowling-alley pin-setting duty, was mostly a front. He did all kinds of things for Mr. Yale.

Such as last February, when the trouble with the Irish boys—who called themselves the White Hand just to thumb their noses at the Italians—had boiled up bad. A huge truckload of Old Grand-Dad had been hijacked, Yale's drivers beaten-up and humiliated, the truck abandoned in front of Yale's booze-truck garage.

Yale smuggled in lots of legit product from Canada, though

what had been hijacked was bootleg hooch, but of the highest order, purchased from the Purple Gang out of Detroit, makers of the finest illicit whiskey in the country.

Yale went bughouse and dispatched Al and two cronies of his, Baldy Pete Ragosta and Curly Sam Binaggio, to exact punishment.

Sitting in their booth at the Harvard Inn, Frankie and Al and no one else discussed the details.

"Here's what I got in mind," Frankie said. "We got to hurt these assholes. We got to make a real point, a definite point."

"Okay," Al said.

"They're having a Valentine's Day dance at Sagaman's Hall, this weekend."

"Okay."

"You ever been in there?"

"Few times. You'd don't have to be Irish to rent out the joint."

Frankie nodded. "Right. You know the layout? The balcony?"

"Sure. What are you thinkin'—ambush?"

Frankie nodded again but more animatedly, his black eyes glittering. "From the balcony, you'll have a view on the far side of the dance hall—all the big-shot micks'll be sittin' there. Lovett and Pegleg and Ashcan, the whole sorry bunch."

"They'll have wives and girls with 'em, won't they?"

"Your point being?"

"Nothing. Just asking."

Frankie's right eyebrow hiked. "Yeah. It's a dance. They ain't pansies. There will be wives and girls—does that offend your delicate morals?"

"No."

"I think the shooting has to be general in nature. I want you to take one of the tommyguns."

Al gestured with an open hand. "I can make sure I get Wild Bill and some of them if I use a revolver or—"

"No. It's a dance but they'll likely be heeled. You want to start our party, and stop theirs, in a hurry. Tommy's the best way."

"Just me?"

"No. You man the tommy, and let Baldy and Curly do the sharpshooting. Al, thirty seconds after the first shot, I want you fellas out of there. *Capeesh*?"

"*Capeesh*."

The party was going strong when Al led Ragosta and Binaggio through the unguarded entrance and up the stairs to the swinging doors onto the balcony. Al swung the Thompson up out from under his light-brown overcoat to open those doors with its snout, and was relieved to find the balcony empty. The three men in their long overcoats and wide-brimmed Borsalinos took positions in the dark along the railing.

The hall below was decorated with paper hearts and red and pink streamers, and red floral centerpieces, and the lights were down, for romantic dancing; but the mood was festive, laughter and hollering. A blue fog of cigarette and cigar smoke drifted and caught dancing dust motes. The hall was not packed—this was for the White Hand elite. Thirty-some people; fifteen couples or so.

The micks were passing bottles and slapping backs and some were standing beside their tables doing impromptu jigs to an Irish ditty the orchestra, up on the stage way at the far left, was plowing through doggedly.

Al's eyes took in the tuxedos and the frilly ball gowns. His wife Mae's face entered his mind, but he refused to let it linger. He'd already told Baldy and Pete to try their best not to hit the women. More than that he could not do. . . .

Al let rip with the machine gun and its stuttering roar echoed, while Baldy and Curly stood a few feet away on either side of him, at the railing, shooting fish in a barrel with their nickel-plated revolvers. From below they would be vague figures showering fire and lead. The fusillade of .45s from the tommy gun ripped open wood and flesh and paper and glass and red splashed the Valentine's Day dance, but not at all in a festive way.

The screams were strictly female. No men went for their guns, not a one, rather diving below the tables or running for exits. None of the cowards grabbed their wives or girl friends, letting the females fend for themselves. The men knew that death was raining down and the only way to survive was to get out of the downpour.

Less than thirty seconds had passed when Al and his two assistants rattled down the balcony stairs and outside to a waiting LaSalle sedan. Behind them the echo of gunfire had just faded, the screams dissolving into wails.

The death toll was modest—only three—but the list of wounded touched almost all of the thirty or so in attendance.

"We walked right in," Al told Frankie later that night, in their Harvard Inn booth. "They didn't even have guards on the doors."

"They thought they were safe," handsome Frankie said with a nasty laugh. "Like kids yelling 'king's X' . . . what heartless bastard would ruin a St. Valentine's Day party?"

Frankie had been right, Al knew; a point had definitely been made.

Now, less than two months later, tensions remained high between Yale's gang and the White Handers, but Frankie was handling it. Al had been dispatched to look after new interests and opportunities in the Roaring Forties across the river.

Today he and Frankie were meeting at the Adonis Club, a

grimy ramshackle two-story clapboard restaurant on Twentieth Street overlooking Gowanus Bay, its less than inviting rotten-eggs aroma hardly an eating place's best calling card.

The Adonis was no great shakes inside, either—its wooden tables ancient and wobbly, chairs with shredded canebacks that had torn more than one female customer's dress. The walls and ceiling were adorned with murals by an amateur artist who had found bizarre new ways to combine religious imagery with scenes of the Colosseum and Mt. Vesuvius. Al had heard drunks rhapsodizing about the artwork, staring up at the ceiling of this low-rent Sistine Chapel in awe; but only drunks.

The food, however, was wonderful. Fury Argolia, the restaurateur, served up endless varieties of salad and antipasto, and Al had put away more lasagna, baked clams, veal rollatini and calamari here than at any of the classier half-dozen Italian joints he frequented.

He and Frankie sat at a table. Al had a beer, Frankie his usual tumbler of whiskey. Frankie, typically, looked like a million bucks, his suit a mauve number with pale purple lapels, a four-carat diamond stickpin in his yellow silk tie. Class all the way.

"Wyatt Earp," Frankie was saying, his forehead tight, as if mentally constipated.

"Yeah. He's an old codger, but truth is? Don't look his age."

"He and that sports reporter took down Baldy and Curly?"

"*And* me," Al said, never one to bullshit the boss. "These guys may not be kids, but Frankie—you heard the stories about out West. Cowboys and Indians and shit. I mean, didn't that guy Wyatt Earp kill eight or ten guys at the O.K. Corral or something?"

"Fairy tales for grown-ups," Frankie said, and waved a dismissive hand. "If all this Holliday clown has going for him is a couple of rickety-old Western sheriffs, we don't have much to worry about."

"I'm not saying worry about them," Al said. "But Little John always says, 'Don't underestimate your opponent.'"

"Little John, with all due respect, is not an expert on the strongarm side of things."

"Granted. But this Holliday character, he didn't seem ill at ease with a rod, neither."

Frankie sneered. "Yeah, and he's supposed to be Doc Holliday's kid, right? The deadly dentist? Al, the joint is all decked out Western-style, ain't it?"

"Yeah."

"So it's a gimmick. Guy says he's Doc Holliday's kid. Two old boys say they're Western gunfighters. And you believe it?"

"I had the same instinct, but Frankie—Masterson's for real. It's been in the papers, lots of times. Hell, the old boy just roughed somebody up at the Waldorf-Astoria. It was in all the—"

Frankie's interrupting laugh rattled off the ceiling. "That says it all! Guy about a hundred years old, in a dust-up at the Waldorf, and it's got your attention? Al. Come on. Listen to yourself, kid."

Al sighed. "I hear what you're saying, boss. You think I don't wanna kick those coots' keisters down Broadway? Embarrassing as hell to me . . . but this is just one joint in a town full of joints. And, anyways, Holliday says he's willing to buy his beer from us, six months down the line, when his supply goes dry."

Frankie shook his head and the black eyes were hard as coal. "If this bastard has a supply of booze that'll last him years . . . I want it. I *need* it. Al, that's all we have to offer our customers, is the best stuff. We're importing it. And when we ain't importing it, we're going with the Purple Gang's topnotch swill."

"I know. I know."

"The White Hand yahoos, why do you think they're hijacking us? Because the micks are selling local brew, cooked up in cellars and warehouses and garages and goddamn fuckin' *bathtubs*! Their stuff don't got the bouquet, the body, the kick of our product, from Canada and Detroit."

Al nodded.

"If this Holliday has a supply that big, somewhere on his property or in a warehouse or whatever . . . I want it. I want to find it."

Again Al nodded. "What do you want me to do, boss?"

"Go back to Holliday's," Frankie said, and he grinned, wide enough for his gold tooth to show and catch the light and sparkle. "You made a point at Sagaman's Hall, Al—go back over to Manhattan . . . and make another one."

# Eight

JOHNNY HOLLIDAY AWOKE TO WHAT HE THOUGHT was thunder.

At least that was how the dream he was having translated the racket, as he and his father and a young Wyatt Earp rode the range on a sunny Arizona day, only to have the sky turn immediately dark and lightning-streaked, when God's war drums began to beat and the horses started to rear, needing steadying.

"That ain't drums," Wyatt said, no longer young, rather the white-mustached man Johnny had so recently met, and Johnny's father was suddenly Bat Masterson, also current variety.

Bat said, "Not coming from the sky."

"Where, then?" Johnny asked.

Wyatt, young again, pointed a finger to the earth. "Down below."

"Below . . . ?"

Old again. "You know, Johnny—*hell*."

That was when Johnny awoke, and the noise beneath him was indeed thunderous yet at once mechanical, like a hammering by a steady, swift, powerful carpenter; beside him in bed was Dixie Douglas, the girl from Tex's show that he'd been seeing—she stirred sleepily.

No telling what time it was; they'd gone to bed, as usual around six-thirty a.m., and the shades were of the blackout variety. Enough sunlight leached in to tell him it was day; but he already knew that.

As Johnny, in black silk pajamas, climbed out of bed, the noise continued and now Dixie was awake, leaning on an elbow, her dark brown eyes half-lidded, her brunette curls tousled, custard-cup breasts straining the chemise.

"What *is* that, Johnny?" Her voice was a sexy second soprano and musical, more musical in fact than when she was singing downstairs during Tex's act, where often her pitch (unlike her figure) was flat.

The thundering continued, muffled yet distinct, and she said, fear in it now, "What, Johnny? *What?*"

But Johnny didn't answer her, a voice from the doorway did: "Not mice."

Wyatt Earp, in his trousers and suspenders and t-shirt and bare feet, leaned in the bedroom doorway, his white hair sleep-askew, and in his right hand a revolver with a gun barrel that seemed endless, long as a rifle's, pointed upward.

Dixie fell back against the black-lacquer headboard, pulling the covers to her throat, half in terror, half in modesty; but Johnny knew his well-armed house guest's attention was not focused on the beautiful young chorus girl, rather the continuing, insistent, mechanically drumming sound from several floors below . . .

*. . . which was, Johnny now believed, machine-gun fire.*

Within moments he and Wyatt were on the stairs, Johnny in his loose flapping pajamas working to keep up with the old boy, as if the latter were the man of the house and Johnny the guest.

Still, Wyatt—who Johnny had insisted stay here in the brownstone—had taken time to come up to Johnny's top-floor apartment to get him, before looking into the commotion below. Whether this was out of courtesy or the desire for back-up, Johnny had no idea, and was hardly about to ask.

On the third-floor landing, Bat Masterson—more fully dressed, in his shirt and trousers and even socks and shoes (but minus his tie or suitcoat) faced them with his much smaller revolver in hand. Bat had taken Johnny up on his offer of the other guest room, when they all realized how long the night had run. Obviously Bat had flopped onto bed mostly dressed.

"I was just coming up after you two," Bat said. "That's a god-damn tommy gun!"

But as Bat was speaking, the sound finally ceased, at least for the moment.

Wyatt headed on down, with Bat trailing and Johnny close on his heels. At the main floor, Wyatt wheeled and pointed toward the office.

"Get your gun," Wyatt whispered to Johnny.

Who followed orders and retrieved his nickel-plated pearl-handled revolver from the desk drawer, then met Wyatt and Bat at the place where the elevator, kitchen door and open landing to the basement nightclub converged.

Wyatt's gun barrel, which on closer look was a mere ten or eleven inches, still pointed up; and the old boy's left hand was also up, but like a uniformed copper stopping traffic.

They could hear movement down there—not gunfire, but

heavy feet moving through clutter. And laughter. Harsh echoing laughter.

Wyatt went over and, quietly as possible, opened the cage door of the self-service elevator.

Bat whispered, "We can't—"

Wyatt shook his head.

He leaned in, adjusted the lever, and sent it back down, withdrawing in good time; while the vacant car made its noisy, mechanical way below, Wyatt slowly headed down the stairs, with Bat a step behind and Johnny, his heart pounding, one step behind Bat.

The noise of heavy footsteps in the club continued and male voices, words tumbling on top of each other, "What the hell," "Son of a bitch" and so on.

Johnny understood now: Wyatt had sent the empty elevator down to distract and mislead the intruders. . . .

The staircase took a jog and then was open to the lower floor, a banister providing scant cover, and Johnny (with the two older men out front) didn't get the view as soon as Wyatt did.

But he heard Wyatt yell, "Drop it, or die!"

Then the machine-gun fire came their way, and Wyatt was motioning and yelling, "Down," and the three men were hugging the steps as the bullets flew over them and through the wooden railing, chewing it up into scattered kindling, sending chunks and shards and splinters of wood flying, and stitching bullet holes overhead into the wall, plaster dust spraying.

More machine-gun fire followed, but not directed at them, and when the deadly chatter paused, Johnny saw Wyatt extending his arm between broken railing posts, an arm that seemed longer than humanly possible because of the endless barrel of the revolver in his fist.

Two shots from the .45 revolver reverberated through the

nightclub, two periods on the end of the tommy gun's long-winded sentence.

Next Johnny knew, Wyatt was on his bare feet and taking the stairs two at a time and rushing across what Holliday could begin to see was the ruins of his club. Bat was right after Wyatt, though circling to make sure no one was tucked away behind them for an ambush as Wyatt headed toward the entrance of the club, where the door haphazardly hung, sprung open and in ruins from the machine-gun fire that had rudely opened it.

Johnny followed Bat and Wyatt through the succession of speakeasy doors that had been similarly opened by the key of the Thompson submachine gun. Even the steel barrier onto the street hadn't stood up to it, the lock, anyway; and by the time they had made their cautious way up the stairs to the sidewalk—not caring to be sitting ducks—early morning sunshine was all they found.

The street was dead, in part because so many of these brown-stones were speaks themselves and their proprietors were also nighthawks unlikely to be up at this hour, unless they hadn't got to bed yet. But also the gunfire had chased away even the most curious of pedestrians. Too late for milk wagons, too soon for cops. When bullets flew in this part of town, the coppers waited till the lead had done them the courtesy of falling to the ground and cooling off into evidence.

Bat was saying to Wyatt, "Some getaway driver waiting out front?"

Long-barrel revolver in hand, its snout up, Wyatt nodded. "We'd spot 'em on the sidewalk, otherwise . . . unless they ducked into one of these buildings."

"Possible. Not likely." Bat's light blue eyes narrowed under the dark slashes of brow; his small revolver he too held nose up. "Surely they didn't come in this way."

Wyatt shook his head. "I think you'll see they came in the kitchen and took the stairs down."

Johnny was beside them now, a guy in black pajamas next to one partly dressed man and one almost dressed. "Why do you say that?"

Wyatt shrugged. "When we came down the stairs, you could see the front door hadn't been breeched. They wouldn't have had to shoot their way out, if they'd come in the front of the club, somehow—with stolen keys, say, or just breaking in."

"Not likely," Bat said, "they'd break in through all those doors. Too many locks to pick."

"And there might have been a watchman," Wyatt said.

Johnny rolled his eyes. "I guess I should've hired one."

"You'll hire more than one now," Wyatt said. "Let's go in and see what the damage has to say."

The damage had plenty to say.

The tommy gun had fanned around to do as much random mischief as possible—most of the chairs and tables were chopped to pieces, tablecloths shredded, the bandstand and its seats puckered with .45-caliber kisses, stage lights shattered. The plaster and the decorative touches were well-pierced, though about half of the framed Western scenes were untouched and a few of the nicknacks had survived unnicked.

Worst was the bar—the pinewood cracked and split and splintered, the picture of the nude senorita dotted with bullet holes in a diagonal stuttering slash, and every bottle on the shelves broken, shattered, bleeding liquor. The smell of it was strong, almost medicinal. The only survivors were some beer bottles in a refrigeration unit tucked away under the bar.

Clearly the bar had received the only targeted attention—the rest was random, as if some street kid had come in to vandalize the place.

"Watch your feet," Wyatt advised at Johnny's side, putting a hand on his host's silk shoulder. "Glass and wood. Maybe we better tiptoe over and—"

"*Oh my!*"

The voice was Dixie's. She was on the steps in a red and yellow kimono and red slippers, eyes wide, mouth an "O," and cuter than a box of puppies. "What have they done to us, Johnny? What have they done to *you*?"

"Just the competition, Dix," he said gently, patting the air. "Trying to cause a little trouble."

Wyatt said, "Young lady?"

"Yes, sir?"

"I'm in the bigger guest room. Would you find my shoes and some stockings, please, and bring them down? You can leave the garters."

"Yes, sir."

"And do the same for Johnny, here. . . . Bat, you're properly shod?"

"Yes," the newsman said with a nod; his sky-blue eyes were slowly sweeping the ravaged landscape.

Wyatt smiled up at the chorus girl. "Would you do that, honey? Be much obliged."

She smiled back at him. "You bet."

"Go on, Dix," Johnny said pleasantly. "Do what Mr. Earp says."

"You bet!"

And she was gone.

Dixie was a pretty girl and, in her way, fearless. How many kids off the chorus line would have run downstairs into the sound of gunfire to see what was wrong? And it wasn't that she was stupid—she was a smart girl, a secretarial-school graduate who'd done that to please her mother and then had had the gumption to leave Des Moines and try her luck in New York.

"Johnny?" Wyatt's voice.

"Uh . . . yes? What?"

"Do we need to call any certain cop?"

Johnny sighed. Nodded. "Yeah. Harrigan. Fifth Avenue station. He's a lieutenant."

Bat chimed in. "I know him. Should I make the call?"

"You're the one with shoes, Bartholomew," Wyatt said.

"Righto," Bat said, and made his way through the breakage to the stairs and headed up.

Wyatt, watching where he put his bare feet, found a table that had been knocked over but had not been shot up. He righted it, collected four survivor chairs and, with Johnny's help, assembled them in a clear, clutter-free area off to the far wall, which had received no gunfire whatsoever.

Wyatt gestured for Johnny to sit and he did; then so did Wyatt.

"Did you see them?" Johnny asked the older man.

"Same three who were here earlier," Wyatt said, checking the bare soles of his feet, having run on them through the wreckage, finding them fine.

"You saw Capone. You definitely saw Capone."

"He was the one chopping wood with that tommy gun. Those shots I fired, I threw at *him* . . . but he was halfway out the door. I looked for blood trail and didn't see any. I doubt I hit the fat fucking son of a bitch."

"Is this a . . . declaration of war?"

"It's not a love letter." Wyatt gave up half a humorless smirk. "Anyway, Capone may think the war's over. . . . Is it? Has he put you out of business?"

Johnny waved dismissively. "Not hardly. I got tens of thousands in the bank. I told you, Wyatt, this place is a gold mine."

"I was here last night. Saw you minting the stuff."

Johnny leaned in toward the older man. "And I went out of my way, not to plow much into the place knowing we'd get raided now and then. You can see the bar's just cheap pine. The tables, chairs, tablecloths, nice enough but standard restaurant fare. Nothing fancy."

Nodding, looking around, Wyatt said, "Holes in the wall, some plaster, lick of paint, good as new."

"He put me out of business, all right—for a *week*, at most. I'll get on the phone with my suppliers and carpenters and painters and . . . only, Wyatt—Capone and his boss, Yale? They *have* to know this is just an inconvenience. They *must* know. Then . . . what was the point?"

"To scare your ass out. They didn't bust up the joint with baseball bats or axes. They used firepower. The bullets that chewed up this nightclub could do a lot more with people in it."

Johnny blinked. "Would they do that?"

"They want you thinking they would. They want you thinking about how you'd like to be standing in front of a machine gun and receiving what it delivers, you and maybe your clientele."

Johnny shook his head as he surveyed the wreckage. "Hard to imagine, isn't it?"

Wyatt shrugged. "No. Gatling had a gun of such kind. I saw Indians turned to stewing meat with its ilk. I am never surprised by what one man will do to another out of greed."

"Hell, I'm greedy. Aren't you?"

Wyatt nodded. Again his eyes traveled around the shatterment. "Not this greedy."

"Then . . . should I quit? Should I sell these bastards my liquor supply?"

"Are you considering that?"

"No, but I—"

"Then don't insult your father's memory with such stupid talk."

From the stairway Bat called out: "Lieutenant Harrigan is heading our way. And our guests came in through the kitchen, all right! Forced the back door. Searched the joint, too!"

"The whole place?" Wyatt called back.

But Bat didn't answer till he'd joined them at the little pristine table. "Well, they poked around; but the kitchen, pantry in particular, got the real once-over."

Wyatt's eyes narrowed.

Bat studied his friend for several long moments. "What are you thinking, Wyatt?"

"I'm thinking this isn't about shutting Johnny down."

"Well, it's a goddamned good imitation!"

"Bartholomew, you told me yourself, these Brooklyn boys are not in the speakeasy business."

"No, they're in the business of selling their wares to speakeasies. And Johnny Boy rubs 'em wrong, because he doesn't *need* their damned wares."

"Exactly. But they need his."

Bat squinted. "Pardon?"

Johnny said, "I don't follow you, either, Wyatt."

"Think like a detective, Bartholomew—you used to be one. Think like a pink."

Johnny guessed that meant Pinkerton.

"Well . . ." Bat began, and started in mulling out loud. "They were looking for something—I mean, they didn't come in and start ripping the joint apart until they'd had a damned good look around for . . . for Johnny's liquor supply?"

"Give the man a Kewpie doll," Wyatt said, and sat back with arms folded. "And they made sure they shot up every bottle of hooch in the joint."

"I'd expect them to do that," Johnny said. "Wouldn't you?"

"Yes, but they're not federals. And in fact, they might well have brought carpet bags to steal away every bottle to sell themselves. That is, after all, their business."

Bat was frowning. "Why *didn't* they steal that booze?"

"Maybe that would have tipped their hand," Wyatt said.

Johnny still wasn't getting it. "They shot up a speakeasy. And all the liquor got killed. Isn't that—"

But the conversation was interrupted by a pair of blue-uniformed beat cops finally making the scene. Wyatt directed Johnny to show them around, and the flat-capped coppers took in the damage but asked very few questions, because Johnny had mentioned his friend Lieutenant Harrigan was on the way over from the Fifth Avenue station house.

About the same time Dixie came down with a black silk robe for Johnny as well as shoes and socks for both Johnny and Wyatt. Time was taken to put on these things, and then Dixie was sent away, and she started off without protest, possibly because she was no fan of cops, since her father, who used to beat her, was one back in Des Moines.

That police background, however, may have prepared Dixie for a sub-rosa task Wyatt gave her, namely to return his long-barreled gun to his bag. Wyatt had been holding it surreptitiously beneath the table, since the blue boys arrived, and now he slipped it to Dixie.

"My, that's a big one," she breathlessly told Wyatt, who made no comment in response, and she scampered off, holding it to her side along her leg, away from the cops who were poking around on the other side of the club.

Just then, right on cue, Lieutenant Harrigan came strolling through the various sprung doors to the club.

Johnny made introductions. Bat already knew the stocky plainclothesman, whose fleshy face was ravaged with pockmarks and whose bulbous nose had anticipated next Christmas by turning bright red already. His teeth were yellow as fresh corn though not nearly as appetizing, and his eyes were a rheumy bloodshot blue. Appearance aside, Johnny knew the man was as smart as he was venal, which meant plenty smart.

The fourth chair at the little table awaited the bulky plainclothes lieutenant. His clothing was off the rack but high-grade, a brown topcoat with black lapels, a brown derby, which he politely removed and placed like a centerpiece on the table. His hair was brown and parted in the middle and sprinkled with dandruff.

Harrigan had an affable manner, and started by telling Wyatt he'd read Bat's article about him in *Human Life* magazine, and was impressed.

"Don't be," Wyatt said. "You and I both know what police work is really like."

"We do at that, we do that." Harrigan had a gentle brogue, befitting his name, but his voice was rough-edged, possibly from too much cigar smoking. "Do we have any idea who this was, these intruders?"

"On the record," Johnny asked, "or off?"

"What's your preference, son?"

"Off."

"Off it is, then. Who?"

Johnny glanced at Wyatt to speak.

"Some characters from Brooklyn," Wyatt said. "One is a fat, well-dressed punk named Capone."

Harrigan's big head went back, his chin up, like a boxer in a fixed fight presenting his opponent with an option. "Yale's number-two man. Bartender come up in the world. Them in the know says the boyo's smart and mean."

"How mean?"

Harrigan sent his eyes for a trip around the ravaged room; when they returned, the copper smiled yellowly at Wyatt and said, "Imagine this room full of people."

Wyatt exchanged glances with Johnny, the lieutenant's words confirming Wyatt's take on this rough visit having been in part scare tactics.

Bat said, "Capone's done violence of that kind?"

"Word on the other side of the river is that young Mr. Capone's pudgy fingers were all over the Sagaman's Hall Massacre."

Wyatt asked, "What's that?"

Harrigan told him. Both Johnny and Bat knew of the brutal White Hand ambush from the newspaper coverage.

"Three dead isn't much of a massacre," Wyatt said.

"Boyo's just gettin' started," the copper said genially. "Anyways, St. Valentine's Day and all, you know how these cheap reporters like to play up such shenanigans."

"That I do," Wyatt said, flicking a glance at Bat, who smirked in return.

Johnny felt numb; the blood had gone out of his face, when he said, "A man who would open up with a machine gun, on a hall filled with men and women, why—he's capable of just about anything."

"A man," Bat said, looking across at the fractured pine bar, "who will destroy unopened bottles of real Johnny Walker and Jim Beam? *That* man will do anything. . . ."

"If you don't mind my asking, son," Harrigan said, and his smile was so broad the upper gums showed, "does this unfortunate breaking-and-entering, and the attendant harm done you, discourage you in any way?"

"No," Johnny said. "In fact, I have next week's envelope upstairs, if you'd like it before you go."

Wyatt looked briefly at Bat, and Bat at Wyatt.

Harrigan held out his palms. These were hands that had seen honest labor, but not in some time. "My boy, that is generous of you, though I am glad to wait till next Monday, if that is better suited to you."

"Today's fine. I'm still in business, Lieutenant Harrigan. This is a minor setback."

Harrigan's brow furrowed. "I just hope . . . my sincerest wish is . . . well . . ."

"What?" Johnny asked.

"You have such good friends. Mr. Rothstein. Mr. Luciano, and other Manhattan businessmen. Everything has been so . . . peaceful. If they enter into the, uh, fray with our brash Brooklyn friends, the world can become an unfriendly place. I, and my compatriots, might have to become more actively engaged. Could no longer, as the expression goes, turn a blind eye. Do I make myself—"

"Perfectly," Johnny said. "I'll handle this matter myself."

"Wonderful!" Harrigan rose, collecting his derby from the tabletop. "I do need to go through the proverbial paces. File reports and such like. The 'on the record' version of this musical comedy."

"Of course," Johnny said. "Shall I show you around?"

This took only fifteen minutes—part of which was upstairs, where Johnny saw what Bat had reported, the forced-lock on the back door—and within half an hour of his arrival, Lieutenant Harrigan (his weekly envelope tucked in an inside suitcoat pocket) had taken his leave. The two beat boys were gone, as well.

When he joined Wyatt and Bat again at the little table amid the rubble, Wyatt said, "We've been talking."

"And?"

Bat said, "Clearly what Yale is interested in is your liquor supply."

"Okay," Johnny said. "And?"

"And," Wyatt said, "he'll likely be watching when you go to replenish it—which is one reason why he broke every bottle in the joint, right now. To force that."

"He sent Capone searching," Bat said, sitting forward, "to see if your liquor supply is on the premises."

"It isn't," Johnny said.

"He's determined as much," Wyatt said. "Oh, he could come back and look upstairs; but I think Yale and Capone are smart enough to know that either a storeroom off the club itself, or a hidden one taking up a pantry in the kitchen, would be the best bet."

"Oh, I have much more of a supply than that," Johnny said.

"How much?" Wyatt said.

"I told you—five years' worth, even doing land-office business."

"Everything but beer," Bat said.

"Right." Johnny shrugged. "I'm willing to give Yale that concession, once my current supply runs out. Six months or so."

Wyatt was studying Johnny. "So where is your five-year supply? You don't have to be specific."

"Oh, I trust you, Wyatt!"

"Too early for that. When the time comes, you can say where, exactly. But generally speaking."

"Generally speaking, specifically speaking—it's a warehouse. It was part of my winnings in the big game that started this whole shooting match."

Bat said, "Shooting match indeed."

Wyatt said, "Yale will be watching this place. Waiting for you to make the next transfer of stock to the club from the warehouse. Once he knows where that warehouse is, you're done."

"You make it sound inevitable."

"It may well be. At best, it's a tricky proposition."

Bat sat forward. "Why not cut Yale in? Meet him halfway?"

Johnny sat back. "Are you serious?"

Wyatt said, "Deadly so. This is business. This isn't about whose cock drags the widest swath in the dirt. This is about money, and surviving to spend it."

"After the life you've led?" Johnny said, wincing. "*That's* your philosophy?"

"If it wasn't," Bat said, "you might be talking to Ike Clanton right now, or maybe Curly Bill Brocious."

Johnny knew the names; he knew everything a man could know, from books and articles, anyway, about these two old legendary gunfighters. Their blue eyes, scary goddamned blue eyes, were boring in on him as if they were sighting rifles.

Wyatt said, "Start buying your beer from Yale, this week. You've got bottles. He can give you barrels of draft. You'll sell both. It's good business."

Bat said, "And offer him a percentage of your liquor sales with an understanding that, when you run out of stuff, you'll buy from him."

"Tell him," Wyatt said, "that these rumors about how you have this endless supply of hooch are just that—rumors, stupid ones. Why, you'll be ready to do business with him in a year or at most two."

"But I won't," Johnny said.

"He doesn't know that." Wyatt's shrug was expansive. "All of a sudden Frankie Yale and Al Capone are just business expenses."

"Overhead," Bat said, "like that red-nose police lieutenant you just greased."

"Two years from now," Wyatt said, "Yale may be dead, maybe shot by his ambitious boy, Al. Two years can be a lifetime in a business like yours."

"And maybe the swelling his pecker has taken on," Bat said, "will go down, when he doesn't think you have five years' worth of Johnny Walker stowed away someplace, like pirate's treasure."

Johnny thought it over.

Then he said, "What do we do?"

"Call Capone," Wyatt said. "Or better, Frankie Yale. Arrange a meeting where we all sit down together. But someplace public."

"There's a dance hall on Coney Island," Johnny said. "Harvard Inn. Capone tends bar there, they say . . . and it's one of Yale's chief hangouts."

"Coney Island," Wyatt said. "Sounds like a good time."

# Nine

BAT MASTERSON HAD ONCE BEEN A REGULAR AT Coney Island, but since back in '09, when the anti-betting laws closed the three racetracks down, he'd found little to bring him to Brooklyn's notorious southernmost peninsula.

Hard to believe this tawdry playground had, within relatively recent memory, been the proud home of fine restaurants and elegant hotels, a haven where the worlds of fashion, theater and sport could meet for a gay old time. Many an afternoon he'd sat on the veranda of one ritzy hotel or another, the Brighton or Oriental or Manhattan Beach, watching the shimmer of sun on foamy blue water and pretty young women in bathing apparel splashing and laughing while he sipped sparkling champagne, as sporting types like himself mingled with the wealthy and well-to-do.

Coney Island had been the scene of so many

storied races—the triumph of Salvator over Tenny, and Ballyhoo Bey winning the 1900 Futurity, its jockey Tod Sloan inspiring George M. Cohan to write "Yankee Doodle Dandy." What days! And some of the best prizefights Bat ever witnessed (which was saying something) were held at Coney Island—for instance, the Jeffries-Corbett twenty-three-rounder, the last great bout before the bluenoses closed in.

And what had they accomplished, when it came to that, the do-gooders? Coney Island had gone from a glittering Garden of Eden to a second-rate Sodom. Cheap trolley fares and the subway extension had sealed that—a nickel ride to a gaudy Nickel Empire, where everything from hot dogs to a roller-coaster ride to a peek at a hootchie cootch cost five cents (well, maybe ten, for the latter).

This was not to say that honky-tonk pleasures for the proletariat hadn't been a part of Coney Island's appeal since as long as Bat, or anybody, could remember. For many decades now, several great amusement parks, notably Luna, set the sky on figurative fire every summer night—and, on occasion, the grounds literally so, conflagrations having given Coney Island numerous (if unrequested) fresh starts.

The season proper wouldn't begin for a month or so, and not every vendor was open as yet, some in obvious stages of sprucing up. Whether stall or pavilion, however, the majority were open for business, particularly on Surf Avenue and, one block over, the rowdy Bowery; taking advantage of good weather was a must for these capitalists, as rainy weekends would inevitably take unwelcome bites out of their official fourteen-week season.

For that matter, a good number of businesses were open year-round—restaurants and dance halls and, even in these "dry" days, certain saloons, notably tonight's destination, the Harvard Inn.

The Bowery (officially Ocean View Walk, but no one called it that) ran less than a quarter mile, packed with amusement booths and eating joints. This was Saturday night, so even pre-season the promenade was mobbed in the mid-evening noon of electric lights, which were everywhere, even draped overhead, challenging a fellow on stilts striding through, his signboard advertising Nathan's Nickel Hot Dogs. No verbal pitch emanated from the stilt-walker, who did not attempt to compete with the din of barkers spieling and the swoop-and-rattle and shrieks-and-squeals of roller coasters, or the frequent rifle shots, whistles, gongs, and music, from calliope to jazz band.

Walking along between Bat and Johnny Holliday was young Dixie Douglas, the pretty brunette chorus girl who looked to be about twelve, except for her figure, which appeared to be of age. She wore a green cloche hat and green and white polka-dot dress with white ruffly collar, the skirt just below her knees, where flesh-colored stockings were rolled up; her lips and cheeks were rouged and she had that contradictory combination Bat was seeing in young women these days, of a certain knowing innocence.

Wyatt was on Bat's other side, and seemed not to notice the ruckus around them, able to ignore the very things that Dixie was reacting to with wide-eyed wonder.

Dixie was supposedly from Des Moines and fairly new to the big city, so perhaps she should be excused for her naive sight-seer's take on the Bowery bedlam. But, hell—surely she'd been to a state fair! You would think she had never seen a shooting gallery or a penny arcade or a waxworks or a freak show or a ring toss (*"Everybody wins! Three for a nickel!"*) (what else?) or had her fortune told or her weight guessed (and it wasn't just the professionals doing the latter).

And didn't that cutie's cute button nose register the stench around them that was making Bat's eyes all but water? That sickening, ungodly mix of gun powder, Woolworth perfume, frying knishes, human body odor, popping popcorn, corn-on-the-cob, candy apples, and Shetland pony dung?

"Don't you just love the fresh salt air?" she said, her arm looped in Johnny's.

Bat traded glances with Wyatt, who lifted his left eyebrow an eighth of an inch.

Wyatt, incidentally, had earlier that day accepted Bat's gift of a new black Stetson, which he was currently wearing. The brim was not as wide as those the Earp brothers had favored back in Tombstone, but—with that homburg residing atop a bureau in a guest room at Holliday's—this lanky white-mustached gent in undertaker's black was recognizably someone who might be (or at least might have been, once upon a time) Wyatt Earp. And anyway, in this crowd, a wider brim would have got the damned thing knocked off.

His flat-topped black derby at its customary jaunty tilt, Bat was in a well-tailored gray suit, his tie a golden yellow that went well with the gold-crowned cane in his left hand. He didn't often use the cane, but considering the crowds, and the prospect of Coney Island's unreliable streets and sidewalks, he'd removed the heavy, straight black stick from the front closet in the apartment. He'd even polished up the knobby crown with a kid cloth.

This he'd done sitting on the edge of a Queen Anne chair in the living room, a Victorian space he did not usually frequent, being the domain of his wife Emma, who liked to sit in the peaceful room and do her needlepoint, which she at that moment was.

When he'd married Emma in Denver, some thirty years before, she'd been a lithe blonde song-and-dance gal he'd booked into the Palace Theater, which he then owned and operated. Now she was heavyset but handsome, a graying dignified patron of the arts whose worst habit was playing bridge for pennies, and whose best quality was never asking questions about where he was going and when he'd be back.

But seeing him with the gold-topped cane had perked her interest enough to freeze her needle-in-hand and lock her pretty blue eyes upon him.

"Why the cane, my darling? Is the old wound bothering you?"

"No, dear. I'm accompanying Wyatt out to Coney Island, and you know how that hustle and bustle is."

"Oh yes," she said, although they both knew she'd never been to Coney Island in her life. "And, of course, with that rough crowd, you are clearly keeping in mind what your friend Teddy always said."

She meant Teddy Roosevelt, but otherwise Bat didn't know what she was talking about.

His wife smiled at his confusion, the same teasing smile she'd so often shown him at the Palace on (and off) stage. " 'Walk softly and carry a big stick?' "

He laughed. "Emma, you are right again—as always."

And he'd departed the apartment with no further inquiry from her, although she had (for the twentieth time or so) inquired as to when he'd be bringing Wyatt around for a "decent meal," as if the restaurants in New York were not up to the fare of their colored cook, Alberta (and, truth be told, they often weren't).

At Holliday's, Bat had witnessed the discussion between Johnny and Dixie as to whether or not the latter would join the former on this trip to Coney Island.

"Oh, Johnny, *please*! I've heard about that magical place since I was a little girl!"

Bat—thinking Dixie still was a little girl, and that describing Coney Island as "magical" was worthy of argument—had glanced at Wyatt, whose expression gave away nothing. They were standing near the foot of the stairs on the main floor.

Johnny—looking eerily like (a healthier version of) his father in a cream-colored suit, a pastel blue shirt and a darker blue tie with diamond stickpin—was preparing to put on a dark brown snapbrim fedora. He seemed appalled to hear Dixie make this suggestion; she was in the green polka-dot dress, clearly poised to go along.

"Dix," he said firmly but not cruelly, "that's ridiculous. In the first place, it's a business meeting. In the second—"

"Bring the girl along, John," Wyatt said.

Bat's head swivelled to see if Wyatt were foaming at the mouth or otherwise displaying symptoms of dementia.

But Wyatt seemed calm.

Dixie was clapping and saying, "Goodie, goodie," while Johnny approached Wyatt, apparently to get his own close look for symptoms.

"Wyatt, you can't be serious," the younger man said. "This is much too dangerous for Dixie."

"Are you intending to fire her?"

"What?"

"When you've refurbished and reopened—are you intending to fire her?"

"Why no! Of course not!"

"Then you intend to continue employing her as an entertainer in a speakeasy—a speakeasy that was recently shot to pieces."

". . . Well. Yes."

"Then your protective instincts for her only go so far."

"That's not fair!"

Wyatt put a hand on Johnny's shoulder and spoke softly; Dixie couldn't hear but Bat could. "Bring her along. Her presence makes it less likely our hosts will get lively."

"You really think so?"

"I asked for a meeting with Yale in a public place on a Saturday night. *His* public place. Dixie will fit in just fine." His eyes went past Johnny and he granted the young woman a smile as he raised his voice to say, "Glad to have you along, Miss Douglas!"

She was figleafing a small beaded bag to herself. "Oh, Mr. Earp—you're such a gentleman!"

Bat muttered, "I was just about to say that myself."

Wyatt said to her, "Dixie, thank you for that sentiment. You look beautiful."

She beamed at him.

"But I need a moment with Johnny and Mr. Masterson. Would you wait here?"

She nodded, and Wyatt led Bat and Johnny into the latter's own office.

Wyatt gathered them into a huddle near the desk. "Johnny, I do feel we're not facing any great danger, otherwise I wouldn't suggest bringing Miss Douglas along. But feel free to overrule me—"

"As if I could," Johnny said with a smirk, "at this point. You think there's any dissuading that girl?"

"No," Wyatt admitted. "She has a child's will and a woman's wiles. But I do think we need to take precautions. Bartholomew, I note the cane, which tonight may serve as a club."

Bat nodded.

"And I assume you have your revolver. In your pocket?"

Bat patted under his arm. "Holster."

"Excellent tailor job. I didn't spot it. Johnny, you've seen my revolver—the best tailor on the planet couldn't disguise that."

"It does have a singular snout," Johnny said with an admiring smile.

"Could I borrow your nickel-plated job?"

Johnny lifted it from his suitcoat pocket. "Frankly, Wyatt, I was planning to—"

"Thanks," Wyatt said, taking the weapon and depositing it in his own coat pocket.

"Am I to go bare naked?"

"Do you have another piece?"

Bat said, "Yeah, Johnny—you know the old saying, physician heel thyself?"

Johnny frowned to himself momentarily, then said: "I do have something at that." He began to slip out of the suitcoat, saying, "Be with you in a minute," clearly wanting some privacy, and Bat and Wyatt exited the office.

For a few minutes Wyatt and Dixie chatted, Wyatt informing the girl that he'd grown up near Des Moines himself, in nearby Pella, and she mentioned how lovely the tulips were there, this time of year, and he said yes they were. Then he asked her if her people were farmers and she said no, her father was a policeman.

"That was my trade," he told her, "off and on."

"Oh. Do you like to hurt people?"

"No."

"Well, Daddy did."

Wyatt nodded, once. "Maybe he hurt them when they were causing trouble, or had it coming."

Bat was struck by how lovely and sad her smile was when she replied, "Well, I never."

Johnny emerged from the office, straightening his suitcoat and in particular snugging the left sleeve. He planted himself a few steps from where Bat, Wyatt and Dixie were congregated, and opened his arms in presentational fashion.

"Anything show?" he asked Wyatt.

"No. What caliber?"

A smile twitched. Bat had seen the smile before, or at least its predecessor: a nasty little thing, on Doc Holliday's slightly scarred upper lip.

"You'll find out," Johnny said, "if it comes to that."

Wyatt took a step and placed a hand on the younger man's shoulder. "We're not looking for trouble. That's why this sweet child's coming along. We're a friendly delegation."

"I understand that. But the last delegation these animals sent came 'round with a tommy-gun calling card."

"Noted." Wyatt tossed a thumb at Bat. "I've asked Bartholomew to do our talking. He and words are well-acquainted."

Johnny frowned. "But, Wyatt—it's my place. . . ."

Bat wasn't sure Johnny meant literally his place—the club—or his rightful role. Not that it mattered.

"Son," Wyatt said, "Bartholomew could talk a nun out of her habit."

This remark seemed a little rude, in front of a lady, but Dixie's big bright brown eyes showed no sign that its meaning had registered. Or that it hadn't.

Wyatt was saying, "Bat'll talk, we'll listen and watch. Agreed?"

Johnny took a deep breath, swallowed it, said, "Agreed."

"How are we traveling? Do you own a car?"

"I do, but we'll take the subway. Short walk, then forty-five minutes and we wind up right at Stillwell Avenue station."

"That's good?"

"Right across from Nathan's hot dog stand."

Dixie clasped her hands. "Oooh, can we eat there?"

They had.

And now that that delight was history, the delights of Frankie Yale's Harvard Inn remained to be savored. On a corner of sorts—numerous dark narrow alleys bisected the Bowery, leading to the ocean, or perhaps disaster—the grand-sounding dive inhabited a modest one-story clapboard affair with an electric sign—perhaps significantly, with bulbs burned out spelling HAR—D INN, but with its front windows blacked out.

"Oh dear," Dixie said, still on Johnny's arm.

Alarmed, Johnny glanced at Wyatt. "Are we really taking this angel into that hellhole?"

"Yes," Wyatt said. "And bringing her back out again, wings and all."

Wyatt opened the door, and Johnny with Dixie, and Bat just behind, followed him inside, where they were met by the bouquet of sawdust and spilled beer, and trundling up to them came a heavy-set fellow in black trousers, white apron, white shirt and black bow tie.

The greeter was none other than their old friend, young Alphonse Capone.

He grinned at them, his teeth large and almost white, his lips obscenely reddish-purple; despite the dim light of the saloon, his dark eyebrows over the slightly bulging gray eyes and that bulbous yet flattened nose and the slightly acned chin all added up to a nastier, more ugly countenance than Bat had perceived during their meeting in Johnny's office Friday night. Perhaps it was the absence of the garish but expensive apparel, the Borsalino hat and the tailored purple suit and silk tie and diamond stickpin. As a greeter-cum-bartender in apron and bow tie, Capone was just another thug, albeit an obnoxiously grinning one.

"Mr. Yale will be with you shortly," Capone said, upper lip

curling the smile into a patronizing sneer, as he gestured with a
fat palm toward an empty booth, a little off to the left side near a
door marked EXIT.

Capone walked them over and gave Dixie a frankly fresh eye.
"Didn't expect you boys to bring your own talent along. What's
your name, doll?"

Johnny said, "Don't talk to her."

Capone reared back, his smile becoming a frown but remaining amused. "Is she deaf and dumb? Pretty little lady can't talk
for herself?"

She said, crisply, "I'm with Johnny."

Capone gestured grandly at the booth and its RESERVED card.
"Well, honey, everybody makes mistakes. What can I bring you
to drink?"

"We're not thirsty," Wyatt said, and tossed his Stetson on the
tabletop. Johnny's fedora and Bat's derby followed.

Capone shrugged and winked at Dixie and lumbered off.

Bat sat nearest the exit; Johnny, with Dixie next to him, had
the other outside seat. Between Dixie and Bat sat Wyatt, surveying the place; but Johnny's eyes were on Dixie, who was
frowning.

"Are you are okay, Dix?" the young man asked her. "We can
leave. Wyatt and Bat can—"

"We'll stay," she said. "What a horrible man."

"That's Capone. He's the one who shot up the club."

"He's evil. What an awful liver-lipped creature."

"You'll get no argument from me."

Bat took a look around himself.

The crowd at the Harvard Inn was not particularly collegiate—
its name was, after all, a stupid joke of Yale's, which Bat doubted
was the proprietor's real name. A group of chippies in garish

make-up and short skirts and rolled-up stockings (who might have been parodying Dixie) sat at a row of tables along the left wall just the other side of the Earp party, past the exit. They were dime-a-dance girls, possibly prostitutes; but the place wasn't a brothel—the one-story facility didn't provide space. Tickets were bought at the bar, opposite, an endless affair, twenty feet, anyway, the most impressive thing about the long, narrow joint.

A small jazz combo on the bandstand was playing a sluggish "Avalon" and the fairly good-sized dance floor—twenty by forty, easy—was packed with a mix of working-class couples and guys with tickets for the dime-a-dance dolls. All were dancing so close it was damned near sex standing up.

Three bartenders were working the long bar, with Capone sometimes serving off a well-balanced tray, sometimes greeting and seating new customers, and the other two making the drinks in tea cups—a lame deception, Bat felt, as beer was being openly sold in foaming mugs. Bat counted eighteen stools and six spittoons at the bar, and the rest of the green-plaster-walled place was packed with small tables, mostly couples, with barely enough space for Capone and a couple other waiters to get by.

Capone's role was unique—he seemed popular here, joking and chatting with customers, a number obviously regulars. He presented a jovial front and had a certain theatrical presence.

Bat was no stranger to saloons, but to him this kind of dive held no appeal. What an outrage that a gutbucket like this could thrive openly, while the great watering holes remained shuttered, like Shanley's or such stellar hotel bars as the Metropole or the Churchill or the Knickerbocker. A nightclub like Holliday's was one thing; but the Harvard Inn was no better than the roughest barrelhouse on the plains. Christ, the goddamned Lady Gay was better!

Funny that the Lady Gay should jump into his mind . . . or maybe not. The Harvard's dime-a-dance girls were not so unlike Mollie Brennan, and this sawdust-and-suds-scented slophouse was just the sort of dump to suit a besotted bastard the likes of Sergeant King of the Fourth Cavalry.

And, to be frank, it was just the kind of seedy, noisy saloon the twenty-one-year-old Bat Masterson might have frequented. . . .

By the summer of '75 in Sweetwater, Texas, Indian scouting had slowed way down. Most months Bat had little else to do but pick up his paycheck at Fort Elliott, and gamble and drink and generally frolic at the Lady Gay and other such joints. Though he'd skinned buffalo and killed Indians, he wasn't yet wise in the ways of the world, and when black-haired, blue-eyed Mollie said she loved him, Bat believed her, even though the wench with the hour-glass shape sold her dances (and probably more) to any scout, soldier or cowboy who swaggered in (and staggered out of) the Lady Gay.

Funny thing was, a run-in Sergeant King had with Bat's old buffalo-hunting compadre, Wyatt Earp, probably lit the fuse. . . .

King was a burly, brawling loudmouth, a mean drunk but a brave gunfighter who had initiated, and survived, any number of barroom battles with fists and/or guns. Perhaps ten years older than Bat, the sergeant was such a hardcase that he would arrange his furloughs around when he could accompany cowboy friends to trail towns to help them "hoo-rah" the main streets. Which was to say shoot them up, restricting the killing to dogs when possible but leaving no survivors among street lamps, hanging signs and store windows.

That summer, a few days before the Lady Gay incident, King and his cowboy buddies, in search of a little such fun, came to Wichita, Kansas, where Wyatt was on the police force. King and the cowboys had barely started having a good time when Wyatt Earp strolled around a corner to find the sergeant with a sixgun in his hand and an unsteadiness in his feet.

Wyatt, of course, strode up to the son of a bitch, yanked the weapon from King's mitt, tossed it in the street, and slapped him while simultaneously removing a second gun from the soldier's belt, tossing it also in the street. Wyatt responded to King's complaints by clubbing him with the barrel of a .45 Colt, and dragging the semi-conscious brute by the scruff of the neck to jail. King was fined a hundred dollars but left town in a thousand bucks' worth of bad mood.

Though he'd seen the burly sarge around Fort Elliott, Bat didn't know King to talk to, though he was aware of the man's reputation as a gunman and brawler; certainly he was not aware that Sergeant King considered black-haired, blue-eyed Mollie Brennan, hour-glass shape and all, to be his personal property.

So when the sergeant and six other cavalrymen, all well-lubricated, came roaring into the Lady Gay that summer night, pushing through other soldiers and gamblers and buffalo hunters and dancehall girls, Sergeant King was distraught to find Bat and Mollie dancing and getting along famously.

Bat didn't even see King draw.

Mollie did, and threw herself in front of her dance partner, taking the bullet meant for Bat in her stomach and collapsing to the hardwood floor as other patrons scattered and the next bullet smashed into Bat's pelvis.

As his legs went out from under, Bat nonetheless drew his Colt and fired at King; hurting, maybe dying, Bat was no less a crack shot, and his target was King's heart, and he did not miss.

The sergeant fell in a bleeding motionless heap; Mollie was bleeding and moaning and would be dead within minutes. The six soldiers who'd come in with King advanced on the fallen Bat, to finish him, but were held off by Bat's English-born friend Ben Thompson, who'd been running the Lady Gay's faro table, which he hurtled gun-in-hand—the soldiers may have outnumbered Ben, but they didn't try him: he was the only man in the West more dangerous with a gun than Wyatt.

The West.

How bitterly ironic that an incident like that one, a drunken sergeant taking the life of a poor saloon girl and Bat killing the son of a bitch, whose bullet narrowly missed making Bat a god-damned eunuch, that such a shabby, tawdry tragedy would fuel Bat's legend, a legend he admittedly traded upon every day here in New York.

As for the West, whenever he was asked, he would say he never wanted to see it again, or see anybody from those days; to hell with the West and everybody in it.

And yet here he was beside Wyatt Earp, and glad to be, enjoying the company of his old friend, even if this shabby saloon brought back the wrong kind of memories.

Wyatt tapped Bat on the arm. "Wake up, Bartholomew—that's Yale."

Capone was coming over with a stocky but muscular-looking character in a gray double-breasted suit with black lapels and a gray shirt with a black silk tie with a diamond stickpin. His black shoes were mirror-polished and a handkerchief in his pocket was also black—where the hell did a person find a black handkerchief, anyway?

Most startling was a big jewel-studded belt buckle—good God, were those diamonds?

A black-haired, dark-eyed, oval-faced individual with a pug nose and dimpled chin, Yale stopped at the booth and smiled, just a little, and nodded toward Dixie, saying, "Miss . . . gents. Don't get up."

Wyatt and Bat exchanged glances—who was planning to get up for this guy? What, crawl out of this booth?

Capone got his boss a chair and Yale sat with his hands resting on his thighs; the hands bore two heavily jeweled rings each, including a massive apparent-diamond pinkie ring.

"Whiskey," Yale said to Capone.

Capone nodded, then asked the group, "Sure you don't want to wet your whistles?"

"We're sure," Wyatt said.

"Suit yourselfs."

Before he left, Capone winked at Dixie and licked his lips. Bat saw Johnny stiffen with anger, but nothing was said.

"Thank you for coming," Yale said. "You know who I am. I've seen you around sporting circles, Mr. Masterson. You must be Mr. Earp."

Wyatt nodded.

"And I'm Holliday," Johnny said quickly. "This is Miss Douglas, who's an entertainer at my club."

Yale's eyes narrowed. "I thought you had that Guinan broad—"

"Miss Douglas is in Miss Guinan's chorus line. Miss Douglas is a personal friend. She wanted to see Coney Island."

Yale half-smiled—not quite a smirk—and said politely, "Hope you're not disappointed, Miss Douglas. . . . Is it all right to discuss business in front of the young lady?"

"I said she was a personal friend," Johnny said, perhaps a tad too touchy.

Yale patted the air with a palm. "No offense meant. Anyway, I hear the feds raided your place."

"*You* raided my place," Johnny said. "Your fat flunky 'raided' my place."

Wyatt gave Johnny a look, and Johnny swallowed and nodded.

Bat sat forward and said to Yale, "That's the past, Mr. Yale. We're here to discuss a future business relationship."

Yale's forehead frowned while his lips smiled. "The past, the future . . . kinda sounds like the present-day got lost in the shuffle, there."

"We're here," Bat said, "on your turf, to pay you respect. You're providing an important service in this Prohibition period—your reputation for good beer and superior liquor is well-known on the East Coast."

Capone was back with a tea cup for his boss. The big man threw a wink at Dixie before he strutted off in time to the little jazz band playing, "Look for the Silver Lining."

"Who am I to argue?" Yale sipped his whiskey. "But my understanding is, Mr. Holliday here has a bottomless supply of quality liquor. Why would he need *my* services? In fact, it is I who am interested in doing business with Mr. *Holliday* . . . in purchasing that supply."

Bat began, "Mr. Yale . . ."

Yale pressed on. "Mr. Holliday here is in the retail business—I am not. I supply wholesale product to the likes of Mr. Holliday and his fellow retailers. My suggestion is, Mr. Holliday stick to his business, and I will stick to mine . . . and, in accordance, we will do business with each other."

Johnny was breathing hard.

Bat said, "We have a . . . similar view. We would like to begin purchasing beer from you more or less immediately."

"We can do that," Yale said with a nod.

"And as for the liquor, we will pledge to do business with you, on an exclusive basis, when Mr. Holliday's supply runs out."

Yale frowned. "My understanding is his supply is considerable."

Bat shrugged. "Hard to say. The marketplace has its demands. And a sophisticated citizen like yourself, Mr. Yale, is well-versed in how rumors get out of hand. Our best estimate is . . . a year or so."

"A year or so."

"In the meantime, Mr. Holliday will pay you a ten percent premium on all the liquor he sells, until he begins buying from you."

"No."

Bat cocked his head. "It's a fair offer, Mr. Yale."

"He sells his supply to me. He stays in retail. I handle the wholesale."

"Mr. Yale, Johnny's not wholesaling his liquor to anyone; he's merely supplying himself."

"Way I see it, he's *wholesaling* to himself. That trods on my toes, business speaking."

Bat glanced at Wyatt; Wyatt nodded. Johnny was frowning.

Bat said, "Twenty percent, Mr. Yale. For doing nothing but being patient. A year, perhaps a shade longer . . ."

"No." He turned his dark eyes on Johnny. "Can't you speak for yourself? You're no goddamn kid. You're as old as me, for Christ sake!"

Johnny's mouth opened but Wyatt shook his head at the younger man, and Johnny said nothing.

Bat said, "Twenty-five percent, Mr. Yale. And this is on top of buying beer from you. There's plenty for everybody here."

Yale said, "A year's supply of high-grade booze? I'll give you five thousand for it. First and last offer, Holliday. Take it or—"

"Leave it," Wyatt said.

A dark eyebrow arched. "Oh, you're getting into it now, Grandad?"

"We came to do business," Wyatt said. "We didn't come to be robbed."

Yale studied Wyatt for a long time—maybe thirty seconds, which seemed an eternity.

Then Yale sipped his tea cup of whiskey. And said, "I need to make a phone call."

"Fine," Wyatt said.

Yale scooted his chair out, rose, and quickly walked toward a doorway between the bar and the edge of the dance floor.

Bat said to Wyatt, "I thought Yale was the top of the ladder in Brooklyn."

Wyatt's shrug was barely perceptible. "Well, he's checking with somebody. And I don't think it's his mother, wife or priest."

Shaking his head, a steaming Johnny said, "Twenty-five percent? That's highway robbery!"

"May be the price of doing business," Wyatt said.

The jazz band was well into "A Pretty Girl Is Like a Melody" when Capone came swaggering over. Was he a little drunk?

He leaned a pudgy hand on the tabletop. "Pardon my being so impolite. I think I was dazzled by the young lady's beauty. Did I remember to ask youse if you wanted anything from the bar?"

"You did," Wyatt said, "and we don't."

"Anybody? Anything? Boss says on the house . . . How about you, sweetie?"

Capone was leaning past the seated Johnny, almost putting his face in Dixie's.

"No," Johnny said. "And back off."

Capone leered at Dixie, then at Johnny. "Why don't you let

her talk for herself? These dames are gonna get the vote, 'fore you know it. She oughta get started usin' her noodle."

Wyatt said, "Mr. Capone, I think you're needed at the bar."

Capone ignored that. He leaned in farther and his thick lips were inches from a recoiling Dixie's face. "Honey, I been in love since I saw you come swayin' in the door. I been meaning to tell you—you got a real nice ass . . . and I mean that as a compliment."

Johnny was out of the booth and Capone pulled back; the big man did seem a little tipsy.

"She's with me," Johnny said. "Apologize."

"What the fuck?"

"Apologize and go away—before you get hurt."

The bullnecked Capone roared with laughter, throwing his hands over his head in hilarity, then bringing them back clawed. "Who the hell's gonna hurt me, punk?"

With a straight-arm left, Capone knocked Johnny against the corner of the booth, hard, and was drawing back a big fist when Johnny's right hand went to his left sleeve and something shiny caught the dim light and glinted and winked and the blade flashed once, twice, three times.

And Al Capone was stumbling backward, his eyes huge and filled with surprise and rage and pain.

Three gashes, almost perfectly parallel, the top one widest, shed tears of blood down his left cheek and upper neck.

Capone's left hand clutched the wounds, scarlet oozing between his fingers, and he yelled, "You prick!" and he was advancing on Johnny, knife or no knife, when Bat came out of the booth and cracked Capone a good hard one on the back of the skull with the gold crown of the cane.

People were screaming and scurrying, and Capone was on the floor, on his knees, blood everywhere—on Capone, on the floor, and on the five inches of steel of the knife still in a stunned Johnny's grasp.

Then Wyatt was out of the booth on Bat's side, and Dixie on Johnny's, and, taking time only to grab their hats, they took the nearby exit out into an alley that led them onto the Bowery again and soon back to the Stillwell Avenue station.

They'd ridden fifteen minutes in shocked silence before Wyatt said, "Where'd you get the knife, John?"

"It was my father's," Johnny said.

Dixie, looking dazed, her complexion as white as blistered skin, clutched one of his arms with both of hers and pressed against him in the subway seat.

Johnny was saying, "My mother gave it to me. . . . Even the scabbard was my daddy's."

He showed it to them, an aged brown leather sheath with two straps affixed around his left forearm shirtsleeve. Probably the knife that slashed Ed Bailey in Fort Griffin.

"Your mother would be proud," Bat said dryly.

"Well, his father would be," Wyatt said.

Which was the last any of them said for quite a while.

# Ten

THE LAST THING FRANKIE YALE NEEDED RIGHT now was this Holliday thing turning bloody, and on his own goddamn turf.

Didn't he have enough on his goddamn mind? Any day now those fucking White Handers would retaliate for the Sagaman's Hall shooting. He'd dispatched young Capone to handle the Holliday matter and other potential speakeasy accounts in Manhattan's Midtown, in part to get the kid out and off the front line; but also because Capone was a smart boy who could think and talk, able to reason with people when possible, yet could put the muscle on them when need be.

But for all his size and commanding manner, Al Capone was still just a big enthusiastic kid, horny and ornery and hot-headed, God love him.

Frankie, a mere six years older than Al, could relate. Hell, he knew his reputation was built on his own bad temper; he'd put guys in the hospital with his bare hands (including his brother Ange) and he'd put his share on a slab, too, though these dozen kills whispered about, that was inflated. If he'd kept proper count, the number was closer to nine, though that of course did not include hits he did for money or favors.

More important was his standing in Brooklyn as a gracious type of big shot—that time when thieves robbed a poor deli owner in town, Frankie replaced the cash; when a fish peddler got his pushcart knocked over into splinters by a runaway horse, Frankie gave the old guy two C's, and told him to get his own horse; when two freelancers tried shaking down a popular hatcheck operator at a restaurant that wasn't even Frankie's, why, Frankie personally pounded the piss out of both the interloping pricks.

He was especially proud of how he'd helped Nick Colouvos, who ran the Mount Olympus Restaurant in downtown Brooklyn. Nick had come to America with nothing, started out washing dishes, worked up to chef and finally saved enough to open his own place.

But on one visit to Mount Olympus last summer, Frankie noticed Nick wasn't his usual cheerful self.

He took Nick aside and asked what was wrong and the little man broke down crying. In back of the restaurant Nick admitted there was trouble at home.

"The wife?" Frankie asked.

"No, no, Mr. Yale, everything's fine with my Maria. It's my daughter . . . you remember little Olympia, you gave her twenty dollars, her last birthday?"

"Yeah. She turned eight." Nick and Maria had a beautiful kid, face of an angel, flowing auburn curls. "Kid's always smiling, always laughing."

"Not no more," Nick said. "She's been crying and won't say why. Won't eat a bite. Hardly sleeps and, when she does, she wakes screaming from the nightmares."

"You take her to a doc?"

"Finally we did, yeah, but the doctor, he says Olympia, she has nothing wrong with her. It's a phase she goes through, he says. But Maria and I, we can tell something is not right."

Frankie knew at once what to do. "Nick, you know Mary Despano?"

"Sure. Everybody knows Mary. She's a saint. Her husband dead for two years, in the flu epidemic, she still respects him, wearin' nothing but black."

"Yeah, well she's got a real way with kids, Mary does. These kids will tell Mary things they wouldn't tell their own mother or a nun or nobody."

"You think Olympia . . . but Mr. Yale, my daughter doesn't know Mary, except maybe a little from church."

"Never mind. Look, Nick, I got pockets full of these Annie Oakleys for out at Coney Island."

"Annie what?"

"Annie Oakleys—free tickets. Merchants out there, we treat each other good. So you loan me that kid of yours for a Saturday afternoon, and Mary'll take her on rides and buy her cotton candy and ice cream and you watch, your kid'll open up to her like a flower blooming."

Which was exactly what happened.

And when the solemn Widow Despano reported her findings to Frankie, he let loose a torrent of obscenities that would have turned Mary's face ghostly pale if she hadn't already been that way.

Frankie called Nick and said he knew why Olympia was crying

and having nightmares . . . but he couldn't tell Nick till next Sunday.

"Why next Sunday, Mr. Yale?"

"No questions. Just have Maria prepare her best meal, but make sure your daughter, make sure *none* of your kids, eats with us. I'll have Mary take Olympia, and your two boys, too, back out to Coney for more fun."

"All right, Mr. Yale . . . but I don't understand."

"You will soon enough. And there's one more thing, very important. . . ."

That Sunday, Frankie went to the Colouvos apartment in a brownstone on Clinton Street. Nick met Frankie at the door and escorted him into the living room, where Maria and Nick's brother George, who had the apartment just above them, were already seated. After some small talk, Maria excused herself to put the finishing touches on dinner.

Soon Frankie, Nick, brother George and Maria had put away a wonderful meal, including roast leg of lamb with all the trimmings, followed by Turkish coffee and baklava. Finally little jiggers of *ouzo* were served.

Frankie took a last sip of his, then turned to Nick and said, "I have bad news . . . for you, Nick, and for you, Maria. Nick, your brother George is the reason Olympia's been having nightmares."

Nick cocked his head as if he hadn't heard right. Maria's expression was blank, or maybe stunned. George was looking at the tablecloth, as if memorizing its lacy pattern.

"You want to tell them, George, or should I? About how you lured their little girl down to the cellar, promising her chocolate, and then raped her? And told her you'd kill her if she ever said a word?"

George froze in terror, then jerked to his feet, but before he could run, Frankie had the .45 revolver out and pointed at him.

"Sit down," Frankie said. "It ain't polite to leave when somebody's talking."

Maria was weeping, her hands over her face. Nick was on his feet, eyes popping, but saying nothing. George, slowly, sat down.

Frankie put the .45 on the table and pushed it over to Nick. "As much as I would like to kill this *disgraziato degenerato* brother of yours, I am not a selfish man. I would not deprive you of the honor."

Nick, his face white, his eyes wide with shock and sorrow, said, "My . . . own . . . brother?"

"I know. It makes me sick, too."

"I mean . . . you want *me* to . . . to kill my own brother?"

Frankie gave Nick a hard look. "I know you're a gentle fella, a peace-loving man. But I went to a lot of trouble to find out what was troubling your daughter, and I didn't go to all that bother to have this sick bastard escape punishment. But it's not my place to mete it out. It's yours."

Nick stared at the gun on the lacy tablecloth.

George was trembling. George was crying.

Nick's hand reached in stops and starts for the weapon. Finally the revolver was in Nick's hand.

George, cringing in fear, blurted: "Adelphi, *mou . . . oyi!*"

"You are no longer my brother," Nick said.

"Nick, please . . . please. I did a sick thing because I am sick! But I am still your brother!"

Nick's hand quavered as he trained the gun on his mother's other son; and his voice quavered, too, as he said, "I am ashamed and humiliated that you are my brother. If Papa was alive, he would kill you himself. But he is gone, so I must."

Frankie sat back, folded his arms, and smiled just a little as Nick squeezed the trigger, twice, both shots entering George's left temple, as the man had turned his head away as if that would help. Twin spurts of blood ruined the tablecloth and preceded George dropping wound-side down in the remains of his baklava.

Maria began screaming, but Frankie settled her down and made it plain that the job right now was the same as after any Sunday dinner: clearing the table.

Frankie helped Nick dispose of the body, putting the man's blanket-wrapped brother in the Colouvos family sedan, which they drove to the New Jersey ferry and conveyed their human garbage to a weedy, illegal dumpsite.

A phone call from Nick a week later made all of the trouble Frankie had gone to worth it. In the sedan and on the ferry, Nick had been pretty glum. But now the restaurateur was his old ebullient self, reporting that his daughter was talking again and smiling just as before. Even eating again, and no more nightmares, since "Uncle George went back to the Old Country."

Nick said, "You are a very fine man, Mr. Yale, and I am proud to call you my friend."

Such considerate, high-class behavior had made him beloved in Brooklyn.

He thought of himself not as a common criminal, but a successful businessman, and what some called "protection" he considered insurance, and what others called "kickbacks" he considered fees. He owned a mortuary, which was a business that never went out of fashion and which was useful, where certain of his other business interests were concerned. He owned race horses and pieces of boxers and his two nightspots, the Harvard Inn and the Sunrise Café, just around the corner from his big brick house on Fourteenth Avenue, out of which the mortuary operated. For the new booze business, he had a fast fleet of boats, for pick-up, and a garage full of trucks, for delivery.

Of all his enterprises, though, Frankie got the biggest charge out of the "Frankie Yale" cigars manufactured right here in Brooklyn. To show how legitimate he was, he put his own picture on the box; wasn't a tobacconist in town from whose shelves Frankie's image—jet-black hair parted on the left, square handsome face, stiff white collar and black necktie—didn't beam. He didn't gouge the public for this fine smoke, either—twenty cents per, three for a half-buck.

Of course it had been hard to market a new product, however fine quality the item, and a few windows and arms had to be broken, to get the smokes their proper shelf space all over the borough. That had led to hard feelings, which was the only logical explanation for the cigars being nicknamed "stinking Frankie Yales," an insult that his boys didn't know had got back to him.

But he had the class to shrug that off; he knew that little people were naturally jealous of big men. Anyway, beating up on shop owners was one thing, pounding on customers was another. So what if some guys with their taste in their ass dismissed his cigars as cheap, bad smokes? The tobacco shops were meeting their monthly minimums, weren't they?

Frankie Yale considered himself an American success story. Born Francesco Ioele in the poor province of Calabria, he'd come over at age eight and spent his young days in the Five Points junior gang, just having fun and fooling around, like kids do. He'd first done time when a poolroom fight got ugly—he'd been surprised himself, how much damage the fat end of a pool cue could do to a human head—and another for carrying a firearm. He had a bunch of arrests for thefts, but luck and pay-offs helped him avoid any convictions. In fact, as an adult, he had no convictions whatsoever.

Still, he might have gone down the wrong road in life if he hadn't met Theresa. No question, married life had changed him. Hard to believe a respectable businessman such as himself had once been nothing but, let's face it, a cheap hoodlum.

In these last few years Frankie Yale had accomplished so much— he had taken over the insurance action on twenty-some pier operators and shipping firms, who'd formerly paid protection to those White Hand bastards. And his superior product in the liquor business had put him way out front of the White Handers, who'd been reduced to hijacking Yale's trucks, so weak was their own bathtub product.

Plus, South Brooklyn's small businessmen were also availing themselves of his protective services, and warehouse heists and hijacking and loan-sharking were filling the Yale coffers nicely, as well. And his stable of strong-arm boys he could contract out when politicians needed backup, or industrial outfits needed strikebreakers.

Maybe he was getting spoiled; maybe things had been going so smooth, he was turning fat and lazy. Maybe to fight such slothful urges was why he'd declared war on the White Handers—they were, really, the only major obstacle to his controlling the Brooklyn rackets. And maybe that was why he'd ventured across the river, into Manhattan, to expand his booze business.

No question Al had fouled up the Holliday play. What started out a little problem was now a big fucking mess. Frankie could put it down to two kinds of growing pains—a business, expanding by leaps and bounds so much that Frankie maybe gave too much responsibility to a kid like Capone; and a kid like Capone, whose dick swelled up to where he didn't have brains left to lay off a business rival's doll in the middle of a goddamn peace parlay.

But why did the shit have to hit the fan at the Harvard Inn last night, when Johnny Torrio was in town?

Little John, these days, was a mostly silent partner, trusting Frankie to run the Brooklyn end while Torrio took care of their Chicago action. But from the sound of things, Chicago was heating up, prompting Torrio's second Brooklyn visit in three months.

Down the street from the Adonis Club, in the office of the garage where Frankie kept his bootleg delivery trucks, he and Little John sat and talked. Young Capone would be here soon and the Holliday matter discussed. For now, however, Torrio was filling Frankie in on the state of affairs, Chicago way.

Behind his desk, Frankie swivelled his chair to look at Torrio, who had the seat of honor just beside him. The ornate, expensive chair—mahogany and plush maroon cut-velvet and lushly padded— stuck out like a fancy sore thumb amid the scratched-up, serviceable wooden furniture of Frankie's otherwise strictly functional office.

The chair had been in Frankie's living room for years, till his father-in-law suffered a heart attack and died in it, after which Theresa told Frankie to get rid of "the unlucky accursed thing." Rather than let the fucking junkman have it, Frankie brought the chair here, where he used it to honor certain guests, like Torrio . . . or sometimes to spook other ones ("Don't get too comfortable—my father-in-law croaked in that son of a bitch!").

Also in the room was Frankie's squat, muscular bodyguard, Little Augie, standing by the window onto the alley, keeping watch, suitcoat unbuttoned, butt of a shoulder-holstered .45 auto handy. Between the White Handers and the Holliday's screw-up, you couldn't be too careful.

Torrio, in the fancy chair, sat with an ankle resting on a knee, exposing money-green silk socks; his beautifully tailored suit, downplaying his small potbelly, was a lighter shade of green while his silk necktie was emerald, in color, the stickpin emerald, in reality.

Frankie almost smiled—they called Little John a fucking Italian leprechaun, and this afternoon, he looked the damn part.

His voice soft, mellow, almost soothing, Little John said, "I trust your friend Augie completely, so I know he won't be offended if I ask you to ask him to take his position on the other side of that window."

Augie had not heard that, apparently. He had the ability to pay no attention at all to business conversations, but Frankie relayed the request, which of course wasn't a request, and soon the two men were truly alone.

Frankie, whose navy suit was every bit as well-tailored as his partner's, complimented Little John on the cut of his clothing.

"Maxwell Street," Little John said with a gentle smile. "The material, the craftsmanship, is comparable to anything in Manhattan and comes close to England. And they give you a hell of a price, down there."

"So Chicago has its points."

"It does indeed. I only wish I could say the same about my uncle."

Frankie shifted in his chair, frowning. "I thought you and Big Jim were gettin' along famously?"

Torrio's round pallid face turned grave. "We were. I've made him rich beyond his limited imagination."

Frankie knew Little John had, in just a few years, doubled the revenues on Big Jim Colosimo's whorehouse business, from the classy House of All Nations down to the sleazy buck-a-fuck Bedbug Row, and all the steps between.

"I've made him so rich," Little John said, "he's like a big fat spoiled house cat." Little John's expression saddened, as if he were about to report a death in the family; perhaps, in a way, he was.

"Big Jim is resisting getting into the booze business, Frankie—money in the street, and he won't bend over."

Frankie chuckled without humor. "And then there's his new wife."

Little John frowned, something he rarely did. "Yes. The man isn't even really my uncle, anymore—not since he threw my sainted aunt over for the *new* Mrs. Colosimo. Something has to be done."

"Say the word. I'll do it myself." He gestured toward the otherwise empty room, specifically to the empty chair opposite his desk. "Maybe that's the answer with young Alphonse—get him out of Brooklyn and into Chicago, where he can help you with your former uncle."

Little John said nothing, his dainty hands folded in his lap, his mild blue eyes unreadable.

"Premature," he said finally. "But I wanted you to know my situation. And that I may need your assistance."

Frankie put his hand on his heart. "You have it. Whenever you need it."

A knock at the alley door prompted Frankie to call out: "Yeah, what?"

Little Augie leaned in. "Kid is here," he said.

"Send him in."

Al Capone came in, his big white Borsalino in hand; he was wearing a white Palm Beach suit, very natty, which went well with the large white gauze bandage on his left cheek and upper neck. His shoes were black and white, mostly white.

He looked sheepish. "Mr. Yale. Mr. Torrio."

With a sweeping gesture, Torrio said, "Come and sit, Al. And we'll discuss this."

The big kid lumbered over and deposited himself onto the hard wooden chair that had been placed opposite Frankie—with Little

John seated in the ornate chair to Frankie's left, the kid was facing his two surrogate fathers at once. To the left was a wall with the window onto the alley, a few framed pictures of Frankie with local politicians and celebrities hanging crookedly, and a couple filing cabinets; to the right was a wood-and-windows wall onto the garage with the trucks, where a few mechanics in greasy coveralls were doing maintenance.

Capone sat there slumped, his chagrin apparent. "I apologize for what I done," he said glumly.

"How many stitches, Al?" Little John asked.

"Thirty-eight."

"How many scars?"

"Three." A thick finger indicated. "One about four inches, two below that are two inches each. I'll always have 'em, the doc says. On my face."

"Any concussion from the cane blow?"

"Naw. Just a goose egg." He touched the back of his head, delicately. "Hell of a one, though."

Little John nodded. "Your cheek—does it hurt, son?"

"Naw. Well, yeah. But not as bad as my pride."

"Did you learn anything?"

"Hell, Mr. Torrio. Lots of things."

Frankie said, "How about starting with not shitting where you fucking eat?"

"That's one," Capone admitted.

"And not putting the moves on somebody else's twist, particularly when that somebody has come around, invited, for a business meeting?"

Capone swallowed. "That's another."

Frankie sighed. Shook his head. "You know what disappoints me most, Al?"

"No, Mr. Yale."

"You're a married man! A recently married man, with a beautiful young wife at home. And a beautiful young son."

"I know. I know."

"And in public you go around waving your cock at cooze? Is that dignified?"

"No, Mr. Yale."

"You want a little on the side, aren't there places for that? Where you can have whatever you want on the house? Would I deny you any of the women that work for us?"

"No, Mr. Yale."

"You should be ashamed."

"Yes, Mr. Yale."

"Well, *are* you?"

"Yes, Mr. Yale. Ashamed, yes. Real ashamed."

Frankie heaved a sigh, then glanced at Torrio, who shrugged a little. Boys will be boys.

Capone swallowed and said, "Just the same, we got to do something. I been disrespected. I been . . . what you call it, humiliated." He sat up. Chin up, too, a move that tugged the bandage. "More than that, Mr. Yale, Mr. Torrio—I been fucking assaulted. I can't stand for that. *We* can't stand for that."

Little John studied his old pupil. Shook his head. Sighed wearily. Said, "Haven't I taught you anything, Al? You make me sad."

Crushed, Capone was turning the Borsalino around in his pudgy hands as if he were driving a car, wildly. "Mr. Torrio—what? I . . . how . . . ?"

A small forefinger raised on a dainty hand. "Business first. Pleasure later."

Frowning, Frankie said, "Al may have a point, Johnny. Word is all over town that Holliday and these fucking old codgers, Earp and Masterson, cut my best boy up in my own joint. It looks bad. It looks like shit, is how it looks. Hard to maintain discipline when—"

"Business first," Little John cut in, this time the words directed at Frankie. "You . . . we . . . are in the business of supplying liquor to speaks all over New York and New Jersey. Holliday has the biggest and best supply of pre-Prohibition liquor in the city."

Frankie waved that off. "Hell, J.T., it's a lousy year's worth. That's a lot of hooch, sure, but not enough to suffer *this* kind of insult—"

"Don't you have enough on your hands," Little John interrupted sharply, "with the backlash you're facing from these White Handers?"

The words were an indirect rebuke—the Sagaman's Hall ambush had been Frankie's idea alone; he had not cleared it with Torrio, whose style it clearly wasn't.

"J.T., I'm just saying, why chase a year's worth of liquor, when these people won't do business? We take them down, and maybe we find their storehouse, along the way."

"Taking them down is the second step," Little John said. "The first is snagging that liquor . . . and you are wrong, Frankie, about the treasure at stake. Where did you *hear* it was a year's supply?"

"Well . . . uh . . ."

The Neapolitan leprechaun's eyes twinkled. "From *them*, by any chance? . . . Frankie, I know where Holliday acquired that supply, it was in a poker game, and I know who he won it from, and I am telling you that the liquor involved would represent five, perhaps six *years'* worth of the best product for the biggest of speaks."

Frankie thought about that. "That is a lot of product for our wholesale business. . . ."

"Yes it is."

"We could water it down and stretch it here to Sunday."

Torrio nodded. "Or sell it at a premium to our most discriminating clients."

"Lot of product," Frankie said. "Lot of possibilities. . . ."

Capone cleared his throat.

Their eyes went to him.

"With all due respect, Mr. Torrio . . . Mr. Yale. I have *some* say in this. It was me who—"

"Fucked up," Little John said.

Capone blinked; almost looked like he would cry.

Frankie had to grin; the times Little John used such language wouldn't tic off the fingers on one hand.

"Okay," Capone said, sitting on the edge of the hardwood chair, his face flushed around the white of the oversize bandage, "but I was the one whose puss that prick cut. I'm the one who's gonna get called 'scarface' for the rest of my goddamn life. I got a *right* to settle that score. He has to die, Mr. Torrio. Johnny Holliday has to fucking *die*."

Torrio raised his hand in Pope-like benediction. "I would not deny you that. Only the 'when' is up for discussion, the 'why' and the 'what' are understood. Our Sicilian friends have a saying: 'Revenge is a dish best served cold.' Al, my boy, I wouldn't dream of denying you the pleasure of dining in that fashion. But before any fine meal, first . . . something to drink, eh?"

"And what is it comes before pleasure?" Frankie said to Capone.

Whose sigh was deep, making his cheeks, including the bandaged one, quiver.

"Business," Capone said.

"Business," Frankie confirmed.

"Good," Little John said, and he settled back in the plush chair and tented his tiny fingers over the mound of his belly. "Now, Frankie, Al . . . tell me how you're going to find, and take, all of that nice liquor for us."

# THREE

# MONKEY WITH THE DEADWOOD*

*gambler lingo for:* cheat;
literally, using discarded cards

# Eleven

THE WEEK FOLLOWING THE CONEY ISLAND INCI-
dent proceeded quietly, not counting the construction and carpentry work on the brownstone's
basement level, as the pieces of the nightclub got
put back together. Life was calm and pleasant, in
its way, Wyatt thought—as within a fort under
siege, in the lulls between Indian attacks. About
the worst you could say about the experience was
the smell of fresh, wet paint filtering up from
downstairs got a mite pungent.

Since the club was not open for business, Wyatt
kept regular hours, rising at six a.m. and going for a
morning constitutional, taking breakfast at a diner
several blocks from the brownstone. Sometimes
he indulged in an afternoon stroll, and he often
took dinner out, as well, at various restaurants
within easy walking distance. Exercise and eating
were in part an excuse for reconnaissance—these

normal activities allowed him to keep track of how well and closely they were being watched.

And they were, on all sides. Yale was deploying three shifts of at least four cars, and whether anyone was maintaining surveillance from windows across the street, Wyatt had not yet determined. But the front of the brownstone, as well as the openings of the four-foot-wide utilities easement behind it, were being watched. So was the passage off West Fifty-third that led to that easement.

Yale was not so bold, or foolish, as to post Capone in any of the parked cars, not that his number-two boy would demean himself with such flunky's work. But Wyatt did recognize both the curly-haired and bald hoodlums from Capone's first visit to Holliday's, in separate vehicles, on several occasions.

Tempting as it was to brace these boys, or perhaps seek help from Johnny's bent cop pal Lieutenant Harrigan, Wyatt let these sleeping watchdogs lie.

At Wyatt's insistence, Johnny brought in several of his harder-boiled employees to live on-site for the time being, which meant the other guest room was converted into a sort of barracks. The brownstone's new residents included two burly bartenders, Harry and Fred, the latter a veteran of the Alaskan Gold Rush, though Wyatt didn't remember ever running across him in those parts; bulky Lou, the downstairs doorman; a bald waiter-cum-bouncer named Gus, a former wrestler who'd tired of taking dives and preferred a job where he regularly won any matches; Franz, another waiter with bouncer abilities, an ex–German infantryman with terrible scars and a grateful manner for being accepted in his new homeland. A Negro porter named Bill was a veteran of the same war as Franz, and despite having served on opposite sides, the two had become great friends, and in fact none of the white men complained about sharing quarters with Bill.

All of these saloon and restaurant workers declared themselves comfortable with firearms, when asked, and Wyatt inquired of Bat as to where five or six rods might be picked up for the happy little barracks brothers.

"We can get off cheap," Bat said. "I do business in guns all the time with a cubbyhole pawn shop around the corner from the *Telegraph*."

They'd been sitting, alone, in the otherwise deserted dining room of Holliday's having some mid-morning coffee.

"Bartholomew," Wyatt said, "why would you be doing business in guns, at your advanced age? Isn't that lady's revolver you pack enough to prove your manhood, when the subject comes up?"

"My age," Bat said, "may be advanced, but I'm still five years younger than you. As for guns, well, somebody's always coming around wanting to buy one off me."

"Why would somebody do that?"

Bat smirked. "Because idiots are always looking for souvenirs. 'Do you still have your six-shooter from the Old West? The one with all those notches on it? Tell me, is it twenty-three notches, or twenty-four?' "

Wyatt chuckled, sipped his coffee. "All the badmen you gunned down, Bartholomew, I can see it would be hard to keep track."

To Wyatt's knowledge, Bat had wounded any number of opponents, but only the late and unlamented Sergeant King had earned a notch.

"Well, of course I tell them twenty-five," Bat said, after a coffee sip. "And then the dubs usually want to buy the damned thing . . . so I say, come back tomorrow about this time and I'll have it for you."

"Hope it's a good price, for you to give up so precious a museum piece."

"What I do is, I send my copy boy around the corner to the pawn shop, have him buy any old cheap Colt, and then I take my pocketknife and carve twenty-five notches on the handle . . . and sell it for a C-note to my admiring public."

"Fools and money need parting," Wyatt said. "But we need good working weapons. Smaller pieces that the fellers can put in pockets and such, but with stopping power."

Bat waved a hand. "I'll take care of it. I have a standing discount."

Wyatt gave his old friend a sly smile. "How many of these notched guns have you sold, anyway, Bartholomew?"

Bat shrugged and smiled back. "I think we're at a baker's dozen."

As the week progressed, with no retaliation from the Yale/Capone camp—and with the Holliday's staffers armed—Wyatt ventured out for more than a meal, on a few occasions. Bat stopped in every day, usually more than once, but had to keep afternoon hours at the paper as well as take in various sporting events for his column. This included several prizefights and, notably, the Withers Stakes at Aqueduct, which Wyatt could not resist attending; Man O' War won, and so did Wyatt, and not just at the bettor's window: the brownstone and its inhabitants had survived an afternoon without him.

To repay all the time he was taking up with her husband, Wyatt gave Bat's wife Emma an evening at the Masterson apartment, where his thoughtfulness was repaid with a delicious meal of roast beef and brown potatoes and various trimmings. Emma smiled and flirted with Wyatt, which he didn't mind, and Bat didn't seem to, either—it brought out the pretty girl of the past in the heavyset matron of the present.

And Emma did not question it, when Wyatt said he might

need to impose upon her for Bat's continued company in the days to come.

"I know William prizes your friendship, Wyatt," she said, embarrassing both men as they all sat in a frilly, fussy living room that seemed an unlikely hideout for an old buffalo hunter such as Bat. "And I'm not about to stand in the way. Just look after him—you know how impulsive my William can be."

While Wyatt couldn't bring himself to call his old deputy "William," he did restrain himself and used "Bat," not "Bartholomew," in Mrs. Masterson's presence.

Midweek he'd called home, his second call of the trip, having checked in with Sadie early on to confirm his safe arrival.

The connection was a good one, little crackle or pop on the line, and it was as if dark-haired, dark-eyed Sadie were standing there talking to him.

He could almost see his wife's eyes flash, and not with affection.

"'Katherine Cummings,' is it?" she said, her husky, musical voice long on the husk right now, and short on the music.

"What, sweetheart?"

"Don't 'sweetheart' me, Wyatt Earp. Don't pour me vinegar and try passing it off for champagne. She called wondering if I had heard from you. She wants to know if you're helping her son."

Wyatt—alone in Johnny's office, at his desk, using the phone—closed his eyes and shivered. So Kate Elder had called the bungalow, and now Sadie knew that Doc Holliday's woman—with whom Wyatt had his own history—was on the one hand his client, and on the other had dropped by the Earp residence when Sadie wasn't around. . . .

"Sadie darling—"

"Don't 'darling' me today, Wyatt Earp. I won't be lied to!"

"I didn't lie. Her married name is Katherine Cummings."

"Sin of omission, then. Something else interesting she shared—you said she paid you 'several hundred.' More than once in our conversation, which I will have you know was entirely civil, she said she certainly hoped she was getting her five hundred dollars' worth. Five hundred dollars!"

Wyatt leaned an elbow on the desk and covered his face. "Sadie, no use arguing. I didn't tell you because I needed a good stake for this trip. And I didn't say my client was Big Nosed Kate because I knew damned well you'd have conniptions."

Silence on the other end.

"Sadie?"

Finally: ". . . well. Any time I rate a speech like that out of you, I guess I can forgive you a couple of sinful omissions."

"Nothing sinful. Small omissions. But Sadie, listen to me, Kate's son has a real gold mine going out here. He calls it a second Gold Rush, and he's right."

Briefly, he filled her in, leaving out only the Coney Island affair, since he knew she didn't like fights involving knives. But Sadie was well up to hearing about a saloon getting busted up, even if it did involve machine guns.

"We'll be reopening soon," Wyatt said.

" 'We?' "

"Well, the boy needs me. He's got nerve but has much to learn. And, anyway, I think this joint is ripe for gambling—some cards anyway, and maybe down the road a casino layout."

"Wyatt—listen to yourself. We have a life in California—you have your detective work, and then there's our Happy Days mines. . . . You're not of an age to run a saloon anymore, and anyway, it's illegal!"

"Sadie, our diggings haven't given us much but bored looks for the past three years, and you damned well know it. I've hit a rich vein of silver out here—"

"Now it's *silver*. Before it was gold."

"Well, it is a golden opportunity. Damnit, woman, this could be the last chance I ever get to . . . to really strike it big."

"Last chance *you* get?" Her voice mingled indignation and hurt feelings. "What about me, Wyatt? What about us?"

"When things settle down, I'll bring you out here. We've seen our share of big burgs, but New York is all of 'em wrapped up. You will love it out here, my darling child."

She groaned. "Things *are* bad. When you wheel out 'my darling child,' I know I'm in for a horse-manure bath."

"Sadie . . ."

"So, Wyatt, if 'Katherine Cummings' calls again, what shall I tell her? That the five hundred she paid you to talk sense to her wayward son, and get him of the speakeasy business, has bankrolled you into a partnership with him? That you hope to expand past illegal hootch into illegal gambling?"

"For Christ's sake, woman, tell her nothing. Lie if need be."

"Well, the sinful omissions are pilin' up like poker chips, aren't they? Wyatt, you finish up out there and come home. You've had three calls from Bill Hart. Your last chance to hit it big isn't playing cowboys and Indians in the Wild, Wild East—come west, old fart, and sell your life story to the movies, why don't you?"

"Sadie . . . I have to finish up here. I'll call you next week."

"Well, why don't I just sit here by the phone, then, and wait for that delightful gesture."

". . . How's Earpie doing?"

"Your dog misses you more than I do. Wyatt. . . ."

"Yes?"

"Try not to get killed."

She said goodbye and he did, too, and hung up. The door onto the hallway was open and he wished he'd closed it before making the call; even from just his half of the conversation, embarrassment would not be at a shortage.

Absent the restaurant's chef and his assistants, Dixie—with the help of Bill the porter—had been doing all the cooking. Wyatt doubted your average chorus girl could handle pots and pans and stoves the way Dix did, but not all chorus girls were from Iowa. He made sure to compliment her, and even accompanied the kid to a grocery store several blocks away, pleasant bodyguard work at that.

Once, carrying a brown bag of groceries for her, he said, "What made you want to go into show business?"

"I was in plays in junior high and high school," she said, also carrying a brown bag. In street clothes and without the jazz baby make-up, she just looked a human, an attractive one, but a human.

"And you won beauty contests, I reckon," he said.

"Yes. One came with a screen test. I left town with a big fuss about me, all sorts of ballyhoo. So I just *can't* go back."

"Would you like to?"

"No. Not really. But I'm not very good, am I?"

"Hell, child, you're cute as a box of kittens."

"Yeah, and just as talented."

"What about that screen test?"

"I took it. A little studio on Long Island. Producer tried to make me in his office. I turned him down. Studio did me the same service."

Wyatt liked the girl—she wasn't an ambitious witch, which was what you found if you scratched the powdered surface of most show-business femmes. Just a nice smalltown kid knocking around the edges of the big city, coasting on her looks.

He was having a cup of coffee in the big white modern kitchen while she was starting to get lunch ready for the brownstone's residents, beef stew, when a milkman made his delivery through the back door.

The milkman, a redheaded character in his twenties with freckles exploding all over his puss, wore a black cap, white blouse and black trousers. The cap and the back of his shirt both had stitched DROSTE DAIRY. He came in and helped Dixie load up the icebox with ten cold-sweating quart bottles with wire-fastened heavy-paper caps out of his big wire-and-wood case. Helping Dixie load was probably not part of his job, but the answer to his helpfulness likely lay in the goofy smile he wore, and the way his eyes didn't leave some part or other of her body.

"Where's your horse?" Wyatt asked the redheaded boy, knowing the four-foot easement behind the building would not exactly accommodate a milk wagon and its steed.

The kid grinned; his teeth were not the color of milk. "Aw, Bessie's over on West Fifty-third. There's a warehouse driveway over there I can leave her in, while I cut down the passageway. This brownstone's my only delivery on Fifty-second, in fact it's the only building we deliver to in the fifties."

"Why's that?"

"Well, it's Klingman Dairy territory."

"Then why don't we get our milk from Klingman?"

Suddenly the redheaded kid looked nervous. "You'd have to ask Mr. Holliday that." Then, to Dixie, he said, "Have Mr. Holliday let us know when he wants his regular deliveries started back up."

Then the redheaded kid departed, lugging his case—now

filled with clinking empty bottles—and Wyatt sat thinking as he slowly finished his coffee, while Dixie cut carrots.

Wyatt asked, "Dix, why does a delivery boy delivering milk remind a customer to ask if he wants delivery service started again?"

"I don't know," she admitted. She was cutting celery now. "That's at least one more 'delivery' than I can make sense of."

"Me too," Wyatt said.

On Friday afternoon, just a little under a week since the "raid" (as Frankie Yale had put it), the club was its old self, none the worse for wear with the exception of a few paintings and nick-nacks that had as yet to be replaced, and the lingering odor of fresh paint.

Texas Guinan dropped by to check out the progress; she had stopped in last week and saw the club at its shot-up worst, and was very pleased to see her domain recognizably itself again.

She was wearing a dark blue dress with tiny white polka dots, simple but clinging nicely to her generous figure, with only a couple of strings of pearls to hint at her stage persona. A big beaded handbag was slung over her shoulder, and a cloche hat could not contain her wealth of blonde curls.

Hands on her hips, pirouetting to appraise the joint, Tex said, "Well, the little elves have sure as hell done their work! How's our young cobbler feel about it?"

Wyatt alone was down here keeping her company—the carpenters and painters had cleared out, and "cobbler" Johnny was upstairs talking to his chef, who had stopped by for the first time since the shooting.

Wyatt, in a black coat and trousers and white shirt and string tie, gestured to a nearby table with checkered cloth and chairs, and they sat. The basement club was naturally cool.

"Johnny's pleased with the place," Wyatt said. "Nobody gouged him, and look how we're back to normal."

Her mouth was smiling but her eyes weren't. "Are we? Back to normal?"

Wyatt twitched a frown. "Then you know about what Johnny did to that kid Capone?"

"Of course I know about it."

"Little Dixie told you, I suppose."

Tex's laughter echoed in the empty club. "Hell, Wyatt, everybody in *town* knows! Winchell put it in his column—didn't name names, but certain blanks ain't that tough to fill in."

"I suppose not."

She leaned forward, her eyes narrowing. "I just wanna know if it's safe to bring my girls in here. Me, I'm a grown-up woman, and I can take care of myself. But most of those girls, well, they may now and then advance their careers on their backs, but in their way, they're still kids, innocent kids, and I don't wanna see 'em get hurt."

"Me either."

Tex froze for a moment. Then her eyelashes batted, as if she were whipping him with them. " 'Me either?' That's all you have to say, after I ask you a question twice as long as the goddamn Gettysburg Address?"

"I don't think they're in any danger."

She sighed. He enjoyed what the sigh did to her breasts under the white-dotted blue cloth, but tried not to make it obvious.

She said, "Why don't you?"

"Why don't I what?"

"Think they're in danger! Wyatt, stop looking at my tits and concentrate. Are my girls at risk here?"

His eyes met hers. "No."

"My God, I oughta get that dentist Johnny down here!"

"Why?"

"Getting anything out of you is like pulling goddamn fuckin' teeth!"

"Sometimes your language is less than lady-like."

"Is it, really?"

He gestured. "Capone came around and shot up the place well after closing, when no customers or staff were around—he shot things, not people."

"That was before Johnny carved his fat face up."

"True enough. But Capone is not the boss—Yale is. I watched Frankie Yale close, and he strikes me a businessman. Remember, he was embarrassed, too, by Johnny cutting that pudgy hood."

Tex nodded, her eyes knowing now. "You were on Yale's turf."

"Right. We made him and his top toughie look weak. Not good for him in his business."

"So . . . as a businessman, why hasn't he retaliated?"

Wyatt sighed. He looked at the stage, which was dim, but the lights above had been replaced and were ready to shine.

"If he wants to do Johnny monetary damage," Wyatt said, "he'll wait for our renovations. Why shoot up a place that's already shot up? No, Holliday's is clean as a whistle again, and ready for destruction."

"Wyatt, you really know how to put a girl's mind at ease."

"You're not a girl, you said it yourself, you're a woman full-grown, and I got no intention of putting your mind at ease. You deserve the truth, Tex, and you'll get it."

"Thank you. I appreciate that."

He rose and she watched as he prowled the edge of the nearby dance floor, walking, thinking, talking.

"If vengeance was all," Wyatt said, "Capone would have struck by now—not at this place, but at Johnny. Or maybe at me, and then there's Bat, who clobbered him. No, I figure Capone's boss is thinking like a businessman. Restraining Capone, and himself."

She frowned, shaking her head. "Can Yale still want to do business with Johnny? After that bloody farrago at the Harvard Inn?"

Wyatt said nothing. He trusted Tex, but he didn't know if Johnny had made her privy to the existence of his extensive liquor supply.

"Sit down!" she ordered. "You're making me nervous."

He sat.

"Goddamnit, I just want to know my girls are all right, coming back here. That's all."

He pointed a finger ceilingward. "Dixie's still here."

Tex raised a pencilled eyebrow. "That's because she and Johnny are an item, and she's probably best protected with all you big strong men around." The latter had a lilt of sarcasm to it, but also the ring of truth.

"My understanding," Wyatt said, "is Johnny's treating your girls just fine. He's kept them on the payroll, hasn't he?"

"Yes, well that's all fine and dandy, but that's not Johnny being a philanthropist. Every girl on my line but Dixie is either in the *Follies* or *Scandals* or *Vanities*, you know—this is a second job for them; they come over here after curtain."

"But not Dixie . . ."

Tex rolled her eyes. "Wyatt, you've seen her dance. You've heard her sing."

"Well, uh . . . I've never heard her sing a solo."

Tex batted the air. "Brother, Dixie's always singing solo! Very few of the notes she hits have anything to do with what the other girls are singing."

"Then why did you hire her?"

Tex raised a forefinger. "First, she's one of the cutest kids in town, and no healthy male in the audience will give two diddly damns about her dancing or her singing as long as they can take in the gams and the cute bottom and that girl-next-door kisser."

Wyatt shrugged; she had a point.

"Second," Tex said, holding up another finger, a rude one, "I didn't hire her—Johnny did. We held auditions, and I advised against hiring her, but Johnny had that look you boys get—you know, the one with the open mouth and the popped eyes, like any moment you may start drooling or bust out crying or both?"

Wyatt, wondering if he'd been looking at Tex's bosom that way, asked, "Then Dixie doesn't have a future in show business?"

"She has a big future, sleeping with guys like Johnny who hired her because they're thinking below the belt. Look, a kid like Dix will marry the boss someday, and that's the way of the world since the Big Guy booted Adam and Eve outa Eden. But the way things are going, she won't marry Johnny, because Johnny is gonna wind up dead."

"A possibility," Wyatt said.

"And I don't want my girls to wind up prematurely deceased, neither."

"Can't blame you."

"Plus . . . I gotta level with you, Wyatt. I got offers. I got good offers to go other places and make a fool out of myself in public for good money."

"Better money than Johnny's giving you?"

"Yes. A lot better. You should see what Larry Fay's waving at me."

"Tex, I don't want to see what any man is waving at you. Anyway, isn't that guy a hoodlum?"

She blew out a burst of indignant air. "Ain't speakeasies illegal?"

"Is that what this is about, Tex? Better offers you're getting?"

Her chin crinkled with anger, and she jumped to her feet and leaned across the table and glared at him, so close he could barely keep her in focus. "Hell with *you*, Wyatt Earp!" She slapped the table. "I put this joint on the map! I deserve more than that! And I don't mean money!"

Wyatt backed up, displaying palms of surrender. "Whoa there, Tex—you deserve the best money you can get for your talents. I don't like seeing you drop Johnny when he's down, but—"

She moved away from the table and crossed her arms over her bosom and now she was the one prowling the edge of the dance floor. "I'm *not* dropping Johnny! I just want to know you will do your utmost to protect my girls!" Then she looked right at him. "You and your big goddamned gun, Wyatt Earp! Will you *protect* us?"

"Sure," he said.

All the air went out of her and she began to laugh, not a laugh that echoed, this time, rather a soft one that was the cousin of crying. She staggered over in a graceful dancer's way and deposited herself on his lap.

She put her arms around his neck and she kissed him on the mouth, leaving half of her red lipstick behind.

"We had fun once, Wyatt," she said.

"We did at that."

"You weren't half bad for an old boy."

"You weren't half bad for a young girl."

"I wasn't that young."

"Well, I was that old. I was then, and I am now, an old married man . . . only when we got together, Tex, I was on the outs with Sadie."

She raised her chin, gazing down at him. "I heard you just had a fight with her."

"Johnny told you that?"

"I have my spies. You argued on the phone, the other day, didn't you?"

". . . Might have we did."

She kissed him again. Her tongue flicked at his. She ground on his lap a little and got the desired result. He put his hands on her breasts and they were soft and pliant and yet firm.

"Let's take the elevator up to your room," she said.

". . . No."

"Why not? You're married, not dead. . . ."

He kissed her, just a little one, then took her by her waist and set her on her feet on the floor, and stood.

She looked him up and down and gave him a dirty smile. "That your gun, Wyatt Earp, or are you just glad to see me?"

"Either way," he said, and waggled a scolding forefinger, "I don't shoot unless I mean it. I *am* a married man, and anyway, I got my mind on other things. We better agree to be friends, here and now. I don't need distracted."

She shook her head. Hands on her hips again, she said, "You can't blame a girl . . . a grown-woman, either . . . for trying."

"I enjoyed the attempt. You might try again. Maybe I won't feel so noble, once I got less on my mind, and been away from home long enough to work up a real appetite."

That made her laugh, an echoing one this time, and she took his arm and they went upstairs where Johnny was in the dining room with the chef, a Greek named Nick, almost unrecognizable out of his kitchen whites and into a gray suit. Across the hall, in the front room, the assorted waiters and bouncers were playing poker for nickels and dimes, the air blue with cigarette smoke.

Nick the chef nodded, and smiled at Wyatt and Tex as they approached, then got up and left.

Wyatt held out Tex's chair and she sat and then he did, next to Johnny, saying, "Ol' Nick looks happy."

"He should be. I doubled his salary."

Wyatt said, "What do the boys in the service call it? Hazardous duty pay?"

Johnny, whose coat was off and the sleeves of his white, tie-less shirt rolled up, looked haggard. He'd been working hard.

"He deserves the pay hike anyway," Johnny said. "He's damn good, got laid off at Rector's. Still. . . . You know, some joints rent out their restaurant action as a concession. Maybe I oughta consider that. Hatcheck, too."

"Maybe," Wyatt said. "But let's start with my concession."

"What's that?" Then Johnny remembered, and said, "Room across the way. Yeah, we're all set. It's another two C's for Lieutenant Harrigan."

"Cheap at half the price," Wyatt said.

Tex, not following any of it, asked, "What are you putting in, Wyatt? A couple two-dollar hookers?"

Wyatt rubbed his hands together, as if the restaurant were about to serve him up a meal. "I'm going to give these New York boys the rare honor of losing money to Wyatt Earp playing poker."

"Strictly legit," Johnny said, raising a forefinger.

"I won't need to cheat the clientele you attract," Wyatt said. "You'll notice your staff's already turned the front room into a poker den."

Texas said, "It's your game, Wyatt?"

"Yes. Five card draw. I deal every hand, but I also play."

"Brother, does that give the house the odds."

"Nobody's going to hold a gun to anybody's head. Johnny's bankrolling me, and he gets fifty percent of all action."

Johnny said to Tex, "If it goes well, we may put in more, up-stairs."

Tex's eyebrows went up. "Fine, but don't you go giving away my girls' dressing rooms! And if Wyatt suggests a concession where men get to pay to come *watch* them putting on and taking off, well, Johnny, you just take a pass on that one."

Johnny laughed out loud at that and Wyatt smiled so hard he damned near showed some teeth.

"Monday night, then?" Tex asked the proprietor, rising. "Back in business?"

"Back in business," Johnny said.

With that, Tex took her leave. Both Wyatt and Johnny watched her go, which was always a worthwhile expenditure of time.

Alone with Johnny, Wyatt asked, "You've got everything you need to re-open your speak with one small exception—liquor."

"I know," Johnny said, and sighed. Shook his head. "With Yale watching our every move, it's a problem. If he backtracks to my liquor stockpile, I'm finished."

"How did you handle it in the past?"

"I transported it personally. I didn't even use any of my boys here from the club, not till I got back from the warehouse and needed them to quickly unload."

"How did you transport the hootch?"

"I just loaded up the back seat of my flivver with cartons and threw a blanket over it. Once every week or so has done the trick, fine, so far."

"This warehouse, Johnny—nobody knows but you where it is."

"That's right."

"I notice you haven't told me where it is."

"Wyatt, if you want me to tell you, I'll tell you."

"It may come to that. Let me ask you something, Johnny—why don't you use Klingman's Dairy?"

A slow smile preceded Johnny shaking his head and laughing, gently. "Boy, you don't miss much, do you, Wyatt?"

"More to the point, why do you use Droste when everybody else in the West Fifties uses Klingman?"

Johnny held up a hand, then got up and closed off the double doors of the dining room. He also checked the push-doors into the kitchen, appeared to be satisfied the room was secure, and returned to his chair at the table next to Wyatt.

Leaning in close, almost whispering, Johnny said, "Ronald Droste is a good friend and a good customer. Over on Warren Street, in the city's dairy-wholesaling district, he's a butter-and-egg wholesaler . . ."

"One of Tex's 'big butter-and-egg' men."

"Righto. He also has a dairy, and services several parts of Manhattan, but not this neighborhood. The reason he has one of his boys make a long run over here is that Ronald isn't just delivering milk to the restaurant—he's also delivering beer."

"I thought you had a six-month supply of bottled beer."

"I do. That's what Ronald's delivering, in dribs and drabs—he's been good enough to give me space in a modern refrigerator he installed in his dairy's basement, to keep eggs fresh."

"Those wire-and-wood boxes have false bottoms?"

"That's right."

Wyatt chuckled. "So that's what that milk kid meant by 'starting regular deliveries back up'. . . . Johnny, is the warehouse you're using, for your treasure trove of liquor, in that same part of town?"

Johnny reared back. "How the hell did you know that?"

"I didn't. Figured you'd be somewhere on the West Side, and

maybe this pal of yours, Droste, rents warehouse space to you, too."

"Well . . . actually . . . yeah, he does. I kind of, well, lied when I told you I'd won the warehouse in that same poker game I got the booze in . . . sorry. My God, is it that obvious? . . . What's on your mind, Wyatt?"

Wyatt fished a cigar out of his inside coat pocket, a nice quarter's worth of smoke that he lit with a flourish and a smile.

After blowing a ring, he said, "Do you think your butter-and-egg buddy could spare me a milk wagon? And a horse?"

# Twelve

THE HORSE-DRAWN MILK WAGON THAT MADE ITS leisurely journey from Warren Street to West Fifty-third, on this crisp, almost cold Spring morning, was unusual in several respects, only one of which might have been noticed, and only then if someone were really paying attention.

To the casual observer, what the clipping-clopping bay was pulling was just any other delivery wagon, although Droste Dairy had the most modern such in the city, a white metal body with red-and-black lettering and four equal-sized rubber tires. A glance might give the impression that a square squat truck had broken down and was being towed away by a horse; but the intended effect was to make the vehicle blend in better with the modern automobiles with which it mingled, though few were around at so early an hour, dawn having just broken over the concrete cliffs of the city.

Most milk wagons included one man and one horse, but here a second (apparent) dairy employee rode behind the man at the reins. That it was doubly manned was one of the unusual aspects of this particular milk wagon; another was that it wasn't making any deliveries. . . .

Of course, the vehicle might be on its way to a specific route, which was the case, although the "route" in question included but a single stop.

And the driver was older by decades than the typical milk-man, though few would look past the black cap and white jacket and black trousers. No one would guess the slumping figure, guiding the reins with casual authority, was Wyatt Earp.

This was not a buckboard affair, as the driver sat on a pad-ded bench within the largely enclosed wagon; but, modern automobile-style wheels or not, the ride was old-fashioned rough, often over bouncy brick. What few autos were out this time of morning often pulled around with a honk of their horns, drivers frowning and sometimes cursing—nothing better told the tale, Wyatt thought, that the day of horse-drawn wagons in this automotive age was drawing to a close.

Wyatt had been a teamster at age sixteen, driving freight wag-ons between California and Arizona. In those days, he and his brother Virge had had their share of scrapes with Indian raiders and highway bandits. And hauling this liquor-laden milk wagon through an early-morning ghost town of a big city brought back old feelings, including that tingle of anxious excitement he'd learned to control, back then . . . and, oddly, relish.

Moving down main thoroughfares and side streets alike, guid-ing the bay—he'd asked for a young, strong steed and this one fit the bill—Wyatt was taken back to not just freight-hauling days, but to the years when he and his brothers would ride with shotguns up top of Wells Fargo stagecoaches, rattle-clattering through canyons, wondering who was watching from above, and did they wear feathers or a black hat with mask, and was an ambush in the offing . . . ?

The long-barreled Colt .45 rode on the bench beside him; and squeezed in back with the crates of liquor was Bat, also wearing a dairy delivery uniform of black cap and white jacket and black trousers. Bartholomew was crouched back there, actually sitting on a crate, the small revolver tight in his fist, held alongside his leg, his chin set in its bulldog way. Part of the back was open, so Bat's eyes were at the rear while Wyatt's were everywhere else.

The nub of the plan had come to Wyatt all at once; the execution took some thinking, even some ciphering. But everything revolved around the simple fact that though the brownstone was being watched, its residents could come and go at will, never picking up a tail.

As they sat alone in Holliday's dining room, Wyatt had explained to Johnny.

"Yale's boys are staking out the building," Wyatt said, "because they want your booze supply. You'll get one load of liquor, unimpeded . . . but then they'll trail your delivery man back to the warehouse, and heist it all."

"And if they pull that off," Johnny said, arching an eyebrow, "I'll be out of business . . . and Capone will be free to get even."

"Oh, Capone doesn't want to get even." Wyatt gestured with his lighted cigar, making a smoky trail in the air. "You won't just get your face cut up, though it might start that way. He'll kill you. You know that don't you, son? You need to know that."

Johnny said nothing. After a moment, he merely nodded.

"But right now," Wyatt said, "you are not on top of their list—your booze trove is. Now, you know I've ventured out any number of times, as have others, since these dark clouds rolled in. And I believe that I . . . and even you . . . can come and go as we please, and not pick up a shadow."

Johnny's eyes narrowed. "How is that helpful?"

Wyatt explained what he had in mind, then said, "But first I need to see the lay of the land—the warehouse with the liquor, the dairy where you store the beer."

Wyatt and Johnny had gone separately, over an hour apart, each man finding a street corner and picking up a taxi, but only after exiting the brownstone to walk in opposite directions.

They met at a small corner restaurant three blocks from Droste's Dairy, and sat in a hard-wooden booth and consumed corned beef and cabbage and near beer, while Wyatt determined to his satisfaction that no one was watching them. In their suits— Wyatt's dark brown with white shirt and darker brown tie, Johnny's pinstriped gray with an eggshell-blue tie against a pale gray shirt—they might have been two businessmen ending their day with talk of work, and a meal.

But Wyatt was not attempting to hide, and had even worn the black Stetson Bat had provided; and Johnny, too, sported a Stetson, a gray one with a black band, worthy of his late father. The point was not to slip a shadow but to spot one.

And no shadow was there to be spotted.

"My intention," Wyatt said, over a slice of apple pie, "is to go out for a walk the evening before . . ."

He meant before the day of delivery, but was keeping his conversation elliptical.

". . . and to bunk in with Bartholomew. Around four a.m., he and I will catch a cab over to Warren Street, pick up our conveyance and our apparel and load up the goods, make our delivery and head back to Warren Street."

Johnny, smoking a Camel (having passed on the pie), was indeed following this. But he asked: "What about our regular weekly delivery?"

He meant the beer the dairy was clandestinely bringing around with the milk.

Wyatt swallowed a nice tart bite of pie. "That can and should go on as before. What Bartholomew and I deliver will be the hard stuff."

Johnny sighed smoke. "It's risky, Wyatt."

"That's why Bartholomew and I are worth the ten percent of your weekly gross we agreed to."

The younger man sat forward in the booth. "That's more than fair, but why don't I come along and back you up?"

Wyatt pushed his empty plate aside and tossed his fork on it with a clatter that emphasized his response: "No. Me leaving in the evening and not showing back up till the next day, that just means the old man got drunk or maybe lucky. You are the proprietor of Holliday's, the owner of the house. You staying out all night raises questions."

"I don't know that I agree. Young men can get drunk or lucky, too, you know. Happens frequently in this town."

Wyatt shook his head. "Johnny, this will be a weekly procedure, for the foreseeable future. You start disappearing one night a week, and even the thickest of Yale's thugs would begin adding two and two and coming up with something damned near four. No."

But Johnny was frowning in concern. "Jesus, Wyatt, I would feel like hell if anything—"

"Something happens to me, son," he said with a shrug, "I've had a life. You are just getting a jump on yours."

His forehead tensed. "Well, damnit all . . . at least let's make your cut fifteen percent of the gross."

Wyatt bestowed the boy a rare grin. "That one I'll let you win."

The dairy wholesaling district was part of a fruit and produce center called Washington Market, close to the river and harbor. The Droste Dairy housed itself in half a dozen boxy, unremarkable-looking buildings amid warehouses and five- and six-story brick structures with oversize windows and stone and marble facades that not so long ago had been considered skyscrapers.

The buildings may have dated back to the middle of the last century, but the interior of Droste's was clean and modern. A tour (conducted by Johnny's friend Ronald Droste himself) was quick if impressive; this seemed more a plant than a dairy by Wyatt's estimation—no cows on the premises, the raw milk arriving in ten-gallon cans from over a thousand farms in five counties, an army of white-clad workers weighing, testing and pumping the stuff through sanitary lines to refrigerated tanks. A pasteurizing room followed, and machines washed glass bottles, filled them with milk and capped them, rollers conveying bottles to a loading dock.

Odd to go from this modernization to the stables, and its familiar dung aroma, where, with the stable master's help, Wyatt picked out the young bay.

The warehouse Johnny rented was in the next block, nicely away from the hubbub of the dairy. Two big inwardly swinging steel doors would, when the time came, allow the milk wagon to be ridden within; but for now Johnny used a key on a side door, constructed of the same heavy steel.

The interior seemed small—no, not small: it was after all a warehouse, and an empty, cavernous one at that. But the exterior of the brick building had appeared much larger. This Wyatt made out thanks to a single yellow security light glowing over the door of a small, empty office visible thanks to its glass-and-woodframe walls; the warehouse had scant windows, and these were high and boarded over from within, keeping any other illumination out.

Over by the door, Johnny clicked-on some high overhead lights, bright bulbs in conical shades that threw pools of light, and Wyatt understood the size disparity between inside and out.

At the left from where they'd entered, one "wall" was wooden, not brick, and painted a flat black. Johnny strode across the cement floor, cutting through circles of light with his long shadow trailing, his footsteps echoing like gunshots. Confidently he found an inset rope loop, a handle that he yanked, hard, as he stepped back using his full weight and swung open one of two massive doors that comprised the false wall, the bottom edge scraping the cement and complaining about it.

"Shit," Wyatt said.

Crude though it might be, the word Wyatt uttered was infused with awe; because no pirate ever saw a cave so brimming with bounty, no bank robber a vault so piled with loot. . . .

Stacked halfway to the ceiling, taking up what must have been a third of the warehouse's space—and damn near all of the concealed space behind the false wall—were wooden crates. Hundreds, no—thousands of them. Stamped on these crates were legendary names from that ancient time, months ago, when liquor was legal. . . .

BOOTH'S.

JIM BEAM.

SEAGRAM'S.

OLD FORESTER.

DEWAR'S.

OLD GRAND-DAD.

OLD CROW.

Other words, of great yet simple poetry were similarly stamped here and there on rough pine sides: GIN; BOURBON; SCOTCH; RUM; RYE; WHISKEY; and (best of all) PURE RYE WHISKEY. Even where wood was emblazoned black with the names of distilleries—HAYNER, BROWN-FORMAN—the stark words resonated, familiar yet foreign, like hieroglyphics in the just-unearthed tomb of a pharaoh.

This section of the warehouse lay in darkness, the conical lights above minus their bulbs, a precaution against illumination leaching under the false wall when the outer light switch was thrown. An unintended result was to shroud the cache of liquid gold in a near darkness that made a mirage of it.

Johnny, hands on his hips, was grinning. "It does take the breath away." His voice echoed a little.

"Does at that," Wyatt said.

Gesturing to the towering crates like an impresario presenting a star attraction, the younger man said, "I've worked it out on paper, done the figures: at my present rate of business, this represents almost six-years' product."

"I believe you."

Johnny motioned for Wyatt to follow him past the slant of the door and inside the cloister of crates, and Wyatt did so in the quiet, respectful manner of the devout, right down to taking off his hat.

Wyatt, like most gamblers, had a mind for math, but he couldn't work out just how much this trove would be worth to the right buyer.

He strolled around the squared-off area of stacked cartons, surveying the brain-boggling hoard of liquor. The wooden boxes were not stacked in a massive block, rather in rows two crates deep, aisles—Wyatt counted six—providing access. Two sets of metal portable steps were available to aid in plucking boxes from the top.

Coming around from behind, he returned to the younger man's side.

"How many?" Wyatt asked, his voice so church-hushed it didn't echo.

"Give or take? Four thousand."

*Four thousand crates of top-level pre-Volstead liquor.*

". . . Johnny, we may be going about this wrong."

Johnny eyed him with curiosity and surprise. "Why? A different plan spring to mind?"

"No. The plan is sound. But seeing this stockpile in all its glory. . . . How well do you know this Rothstein character?"

Johnny shrugged. "Nobody really knows him. He's the sort who seems friendly, but has a coldness about him. I've played cards with him, many times—he was there the night I won all this."

"I bet he hated losing it."

Johnny grinned. "My take is, Rothstein hates losing, period. But he's a sort of silent partner in Holliday's."

"To what extent?"

"A modest monthly pay-off. He mediates problems, and fixes Tammany Hall when need be. I think he's the single reason no shooting wars have started in Manhattan—he's got ties to every hoodlum faction and works at making sure nobody gets too greedy."

Wyatt nodded toward the towering crates. "Wouldn't he be interested in this?"

"Sure. And he could probably afford a hell of a price. He carries a big fat bankroll on him; to him a hundred grand is pocket change."

Wyatt nodded. He stared at the boxes of booze. No small wonder that Frankie Yale coveted this stockpile.

Then he said, "Here's a thought. Why don't you sell this boodle to Rothstein, grab that little brunette by the hand, and go set up shop pulling teeth somewhere?"

Johnny grinned and shook his head. "You can't be serious . . ."

"Am I laughing? That little Dixie doll loves your scrawny ass, and if she were any cuter, I'd marry her myself. My God, she cooks, she sews, she makes good conversation. The only thing she can't do is sing and dance, which of course is what you have her doing."

Johnny's mouth was open, but no words were coming out. This torrent of advice had blindsided the younger man.

"None of my business," Wyatt said, stiffly, "but as your father's friend, I took the liberty."

"Wyatt . . . Dixie is . . . she's dear to me, but I'm just starting out. You said it yourself—just getting a jump on life. Maybe . . . maybe five or six years from now, when I have a stockpile of cash not booze, I'll settle down to a quiet life. And maybe I'll take Dix with me. Maybe even take up dentistry again, like my late father. But, right now—"

"All this booze, it looks like treasure to you."

"Yes, of course it does! Why, are you immune?"

"Hardly. Fills my eyes up with ideas." Wyatt turned to Johnny and put a hand on the boy's shoulder. "I still like money. I still aim to get rich. But a man needs a partner."

"Well . . . we're partners in this, Wyatt. You and I. And Mr. Masterson, of course."

Wyatt scowled. "I'm not talking about that kind of partner, son. I'm talking about somebody who can keep you warm at night and I don't mean a horse and I certainly don't mean an old walrus like me."

Johnny seemed astounded by this continuing onslaught of words from Wyatt, who generally parceled them out.

And, frankly, Wyatt didn't know what had got into him; and, suddenly—rarely for him—he felt embarrassed, his face red, flushed. Coming into contact with this storehouse of pre-Prohibition liquor had made him drunk, somehow, and he hadn't even cracked a bottle.

Johnny swallowed. Then he asked Wyatt a question, and going over it in his mind later, on several occasions, the older man could not understand how this query came to flow out of the talk come before.

What Johnny asked was: "What was my father like?"

And without pausing for even the briefest beat, Wyatt said, "Loyal."

This, as it turned out, was the only further conversation about the younger Holliday's father the two men ever had; but, on reflection, Wyatt felt he'd covered the subject more than adequately.

They got down to business.

Wyatt paced a small area as he asked, "How many crates of booze a week do you go through?"

"Around ten—I've been sticking a dozen in the flivver, under blankets, and run it over to the club, first of every week since we opened. I've never had to make the weekly run earlier."

Looking at the cement floor as he paced, Wyatt said, "We'll want to vary the day. We'll start with Monday, then jump around, Wednesday next time and then Friday and such like." Now he stopped and looked at Johnny. "That in mind, do you think we need more than a dozen crates?"

Johnny thought for a moment, shook his head, said, "No. A dozen is fine. I'll give you a list of how many boxes of each variety to take—we sell twice as much gin as bourbon, for example."

Wyatt, pacing again, rolled his eyes, and said, "To each his own. Judging by the milk wagon . . ."

The two men had checked one over thoroughly at the dairy.

". . . twelve cartons should pack in there without difficulty."

Johnny nodded. "I should think so."

"We won't have the luxury of those false-bottom milk carriers your beer's delivered in."

"Couldn't we transfer everything into boxes, or bags . . . ?"

"No." Wyatt planted himself before Johnny, stood with arms folded, his expression stern. "That's at least as suspicious as crates, and anyway I believe we can do this unobserved, going in the way your regular milkman does."

The following Monday, before dawn, Wyatt had returned to the Washington Market with Bat. To most of New York, this was still Sunday night, the wee hours; but the area around Warren Street bustled with farmers and dealers and their trucks of perishable product. This was a sort of Times Square of produce, as freight cars disgorged their contents and fruit and vegetables were moved and stored and boxed and stacked. The vehicles coming in and out, backing up, pulling forward, sent lights here and there, a combined glow that provided illumination for frantically paced farmers, truckers, tally-keepers and inspectors.

Amid all this moved Wyatt Earp and Bat Masterson, in black business suits and Stetson and derby respectively, creating no notice. In Ronald Droste's outer office, they traded their business attire for milk-delivery uniforms; and soon had hitched up the bay to the empty auto-like wagon. Within minutes they were to the warehouse, Bat using the keys Johnny provided to swing open one of the big metal doors for Wyatt to guide the horse and wagon within.

Wyatt had warned Bat, but no description did the storehouse of wooden liquor crates justice. After a good minute of shocked admiration, Bat joined Wyatt in loading up the milk wagon with an assortment of crates numbering twelve. So quickly was this accomplished that the bay didn't even have time to leave behind a road apple or two; and the sun was not up when they began their journey back to West Fifty-second.

Or to be more precise, West Fifty-third.

As the milk wagon clip-clopped by, Wyatt unobtrusively noted the parked-at-the-curb black Ford containing the curly-haired hoodlum who'd accompanied Capone that first night, slouched hatless behind the wheel, with a skinny sharp-nosed fedora-sporting companion, in the rider's seat. The vehicle was half a block down the street with a good view on the narrow passageway that cut between the warehouse and another building and led to the utilities easement behind Johnny Holliday's brownstone.

The curly-haired hood was literally asleep at the wheel. The sharp-nosed one barely acknowledged the passing milk wagon, his narrow face a study in put-upon boredom. With the casual skill of an experienced teamster, Wyatt worked the reins and coaxed the bay into backing the wagon into the warehouse drive-way, at a slight angle that actually cut across and blocked the adjacent passageway to the easement and the brownstone.

Wyatt steadied the bay, then climbed out of the wagon, casually monitoring the men in the parked Ford, who appeared to be paying them no notice.

The unloading was quick and precise.

Neither Wyatt nor Bat actually participated in hauling the crates down and out of the rear of the vehicle—both stood guard back there, not visible from the street, revolvers in hand, Wyatt's long-barreled Colt .45 and Bat's short-snouted Detective's Special .38.

On cue from the brownstone, down the passageway, came a little team in workclothes and caps, bartenders Fred and Harry and bouncers Franz and Gus and Bill the porter, and the bouncers unloaded crates and the bartenders and porter carried them away, taking four quick trips to do it.

When the last sight of Gus's behind disappeared up through the kitchen door, Bat returned in back of the now-empty wagon, and Wyatt—the gun held just behind him—got up inside and shortly was guiding the horse and wagon past Frankie Yale's sentries, one still slumbering, the other still bored.

As they made their way through the city canyons, Wyatt could only wonder if he and Bat had been lucky, on this first trip. Yale's boys were tired and sloppy at this early hour, but maybe that would not always be so.

Still, they had made their first delivery, without incident. Nothing remained but to return the horse to its stable, the wagon to its garage, and trade their milkman duds in for their own clothes.

At Bat's insistence, he rode with his old friend in a taxi to Jack Dunston's for scrambled eggs and Irish bacon.

"Wyatt," Bat said, chowing down, "I have to thank you. I haven't felt this alive since the Dempsey/Willard bout."

"Let's hope, Bartholomew," Wyatt said, biting off the end of a strip of crisp bacon, "that we feel alive after the next week's delivery, as well. . . ."

# Thirteen

OLLIDAY'S HELD NO GRAND RE-OPENING, AND OF course was not in a position to advertise. But hints in various newspaper columns by the likes of Runyon, Winchell and a certain Masterson fueled New York's version of the Pony Express— the rumor mill—and on Monday night, when the club started up again, business boomed, as good as or better than a Friday or Saturday night.

The violence done to the establishment had only added a luster of danger and mystery in a trade already inherently exciting, thanks to its illicit nature, not to mention the newness of the speakeasy experience itself with its peepholes and passwords and subterranean locales. Patrons could be seen touching the patched walls, trying to detect where the infamous machine-gun holes had been, and often succeeding.

Wyatt, Johnny and Bat sat ringside, and shook

many hands, even signing some autographs for the usual crowd of bankers, rich businessmen and sports stars and their fur-draped jewel-bedecked wives (or not wives). But kids in their twenties seemed in more abundance than before, skinny giddy girls with bobbed hair and babydoll make-up and short skirts, boys in tuxedos in search of a wedding cake to climb onto.

Texas Guinan would have seemed in rare form if Wyatt hadn't been familiar with her unstinting brand of bawdy showmanship. In the process of refitting the nightclub, Johnny had granted his star one embellishment by way of a spotlight operated from the back wall.

So when she swept onto the stage, where the seven musicians were playing her on with a jazzed-up rendition of Victor Herbert's "Sweethearts," her strings of pearls swinging, Tex was in a blazing circle of light that made her brand-new flame-red taffeta dress and red satin slippers sparkle. Her marcelled platinum blondness was topped off by a fire-engine-red Stetson glittering with diamonds (or not diamonds).

When she brayed "Hello, suckers!" the avalanche of laughter she generated indicated she had been greatly missed, and also that this crowd was already half blotto.

"Three cheers for Prohibition!" she yelled.

Newcomers were confused, but regulars only laughed, even before she tagged on, "Without it, where the hell would I be?"

"*Nowhere!*" a score of audience members shouted.

"You're damn right!"

She climbed up on a stool already waiting for her and began singing in her appealing throaty way a special piece of material: "*'Hello sucker' is my nightclub salutation to one and all . . . I mean it to say, hello, pal—aren't we all alike after all?*"

Tex had put together an almost entirely new show during the

break so thoughtfully provided by Frankie Yale and his boy Capone, with new costumes for the six showgirls, including tiny rhinestone-flocked flesh-colored wisps mostly hidden by big lace fans. The latter routine hadn't been previewed for Johnny, and Wyatt sensed young Holliday was not pleased—not out of any sense of propriety, but because everybody was getting a glimpse of his Dixie, both north and south of her Mason-Dixon Line.

Wyatt was in the club, and not up in his new domain—the front room converted to poker den—to pay respects to Tex on opening night . . . and to allow her to inform the group of his new venture. Later tonight, upstairs, he would say hello to some suckers himself.

Right now, watching Tex and her "little girls" do their work was a real pleasure. Some of the established bits remained, such as the popular "Cherries" number; but a new one that had the shapely girls singing a silly, racy song about having two eyes (pointing to same), two ears (pointing to same) and on down their anatomies, went over particularly well, invoking "woo woo's" and whistles. A nonsense refrain—"*And she knows her onions!*"—was quickly picked up by the partying crowd.

As usual, Tex threaded through the tables rubbing bald domes and handing out noisemakers, making flirty fun of the men and coyly complimenting the women on their own onions, with a police whistle added to the mixture when she deemed things were getting out of hand. By the end, a snowball fight with the audience (felt snowballs had been passed out) concluded a raucous show.

Tex came out for a bow and got a "great big hand" for not just her "little girls" but the boys in the band, outrageously telling the crowd, "The union won't let me pay these mugs a proper wage—they can hardly make ends meet—little kids at home starving—rent overdue—so let's pass the hat and help 'em out!"

And, five-buck cover charge forgiven or perhaps forgotten, the well-oiled audience passed the hat and filled it with dollar bills.

Wyatt sat in awe of the woman's audacity. *Nicely done, Tex*, he thought. *Nicely done.*

As this was in progress, Tex took the opportunity to further try out her new toy, having her spotlight cast upon the audience, introducing celebrities, starting with boxing champ Jack Dempsey, who half stood and waved shyly, and various actors and actresses, all of whom milked it and took elaborate bows—stage giant John Barrymore, movie star Pearl White, *Follies* sensation Peggy Hopkins Joyce—and finally the white light hit the ringside table where Wyatt, Bat and Johnny sat.

"Meet the boss man, ladies and gentlemen—Johnny Holliday!" she called out, waving her red jeweled Stetson. "His pop was Doc, a dentist you may have heard of, which may explain why the drilling this joint got a few weeks ago didn't bother him none!"

This got laughs and applause, and Johnny stood and lowered his head in a dignified little bow and sat back down.

"You may already know the best sports columnist in town . . . I'm sure he's the best, because he told me so. He knew Johnny's poppa way back in towns like Dodge City and Wichita, and has a certain reputation for handling shooting irons himself. Manhattan's own . . . *Bat Masterson*!"

Bat got up and waved and grinned and enjoyed the attention.

Wyatt dreaded what was coming next. He hated attention and public notice and fuss; he despised being known for the past when the present was where he was currently doing business. But to *do* business, he had to put up with this goddamned nonsense; a man had to play the cards he was dealt, and fame was his only ace. . . .

"And this spindly gent, my children, is the man who walked

away from the O.K. Corral gunfight without a scratch, the Lion of Tombstone himself . . . *Marshal Wyatt Earp!*"

He stood in the white glare and forced a smile and nodded once and waved once and plopped down again. The applause echoed off the walls like Capone's machine-gun fire, and a good number of these New Yorkers tried to whoop like Indians and holler like cowboys and it was sillier than the "onions" song.

"Wyatt," Tex said, as the din died down, "is our guest here at Holliday's, and will be for . . . well, until either the Clanton Gang or old age catches up with him, we don't know which!"

That got laughter and scattered applause and Wyatt forced another little smile. Being a good sport took its toll. But then the white beacon swung back onto the stage and Tex, and he was out of the literal spotlight.

Finally Tex delivered the pay-off: "And we have something new here at Holliday's—for those of you who'd like to sit down with a legend, Wyatt's hosting a friendly game of cards in just about fifteen minutes. Upstairs across from the dining room."

That first night, and the rest of the week, brought land-office business to Wyatt's little venture in the former music room of the main floor.

About half the size of Johnny's office, Wyatt's poker lounge was dominated by the round green-felt table with half a dozen captain's chairs, his own covered in padded black leather. The only other furniture was a red-and-black brocade sofa against the right wall, as you entered; a row of shuttered windows, at left, was to the dealer's back. A fireplace, to the dealer's left, remained unlighted, the only heat generated by an elaborately gilt-framed nude oil of a voluptuous, mostly undraped damsel, hanging over the mantel and suitable for behind the bar in Dodge's Longbranch. A dome-style lighting fixture over the table provided a nice, soft yellow glow that complemented gold-and-black brocade wallpaper worthy of a San Francisco bordello.

Just outside the room, whose double doors stood open, bouncer Gus kept watch, keeping track of who got the next open chair by giving out numbers. Usually two or three chairs were taken and held early on, by real gamblers, with the tourists and dilettantes staying just long enough to have the honor of playing at Wyatt Earp's table (and losing a few hundreds dollars for the privilege).

Wyatt himself was the banker, as well as the dealer, and occasionally a customer questioned the house dealer participating fully in the play.

"Not the house's game," Wyatt said. "It's my game, and always my deal. Mine will be the only ante, which means lots of free rides for the rest of you. And no one has to play."

Plenty did.

Chips were five dollars a white, ten a red, and twenty-five a blue. Ante was a red chip. Raise limit was one hundred dollars and no side bets allowed. A friendly game, with stakes just low enough for the suckers and high enough for the gamblers.

The game was strictly draw. Wyatt knew that many of his brethren considered five-card stud the most scientific poker game, and he'd played his share—seven-card stud, too, less scientific by miles but full of action with chips piling sky-high in pot after pot.

But Wyatt had always preferred draw, because his approach was to play people not cards. True, the draw—and the betting going on before and after—provided the only clues to the other players' hidden cards. But their faces, and the pattern of their play, normally gave Wyatt all the information he needed.

And if he occasionally had to give himself a card off the top or bottom to help out the odds, this he might do, sparingly. He preferred to play according to Hoyle, but sometimes a streak of bad luck needed a boot in the seat of the pants.

Such tactics proved unnecessary at Holliday's, that first week, at least. The natural advantage of the dealer's chair, added to the shoddy playing of most who sat down with him, put Wyatt up well over two thousand by Friday, even after paying Johnny his share. With his and Bat's fifteen percent of the club's gross, Wyatt could be rich in a matter of months.

And this raised a question he and Bat had pondered at length: just how long could the Holliday's gravy train roll?

Earlier that very evening at their ringside table downstairs, before Johnny joined them, Bat had sat shaking his head, saying, "This boy thinks there's five or six years in this club, Wyatt. You know that's wishful thinking."

Wyatt nodded.

"At some point, the law's going to shut this place down, next time a reform mayor comes in," Bat went on, "or some honest federal is going to slap on a padlock. Sure, Johnny can relocate, but has he factored in having to do that once or even twice a year?"

Wyatt shrugged.

"And I won't deny," Bat said, "I get a sort of charge out of riding shotgun—I mean that in a figural way, since all I'm packing is what you insist on calling a 'lady's revolver,' but it'll shoot a bang-up hole in a man. . . . What was I saying?"

Wyatt raised an eyebrow.

"Oh! Yes. I admit riding along with you, as if we're delivering a silver shipment, well, it brings back old memories and it's better than bourbon, almost. But do you really picture us making these, shall we say, milk runs, once a week, for the next five years?"

Wyatt shook his head.

"And surely at some point Yale and that fat-assed hard case Capone are going to get tired of waiting and watching and *do* something."

Wyatt held up a hand, gently, an apologetic traffic cop. "Bartholomew, Yale has his own problems with the Irish White Handers. He and Capone could be dead in some ditch tomorrow morning."

Bat nodded.

"And furthermore," Wyatt said, "in just a year that kid can get rich, and so can we . . . and then maybe we can talk sense to him. He's not ready to listen to reason."

"If I were him," Bat said, "I'd sell that battery of booze to one of Yale's competitors, those White Handers perhaps, or maybe some Manhattan bootlegger, brokered by Arnold Rothstein. Be a lead-pipe cinch."

"A good idea, but as I said—he's not ready."

Bat was shaking his head, not disagreeing, rather expressing frustration. "He oughta grab that little chorus girl and go make little Johnnies and Dixies somewhere. Son of a bitch has a dental degree, and—"

Wyatt raised the palm again, because Johnny was approaching to take his seat with them, which of course ended that line of conversation.

Bat's thinking, as was often the case, paralleled Wyatt's own. He may have seemed argumentative to his old friend, but the truth of it was, Wyatt was relieved—he knew, when the time came to move Johnny out of the speakeasy business and back into teeth-pulling, Bartholomew would be at Wyatt's side.

Even in the poker lounge, Bat served as Wyatt's fill-in, much of the time. Bat tended to hang around Holliday's till near dawn drinking, eating, conversing, enjoying his celebrity, but never taking a seat at the poker table—that was for the customers— except to spell Wyatt when he needed a bathroom break or a bite to eat or a step out into the fresh air for a cigar.

Occasionally celebrities other than Bat sat at the green-felt table. His old friend from Alaska, Wilson Mizner, lately making it big on Broadway as a playwright, took a chair and kept it, about every other night.

A lanky, cheerfully dissipated character with thinning dark hair, sullen eyes, long nose and disgusted twist of a mouth, Mizner invariably wore a tuxedo and sat with his head cocked to one side, as if straightening it were too great an effort even to consider. This man had been a miner, con man, hotel manager, rich widow's new husband, songwriter and even prizefight manager— when his fighter Stanley Ketchel was shot and killed by a jealous husband, manager Mizner said, "Somebody count ten over him— he'll get up."

Mizner played well, and won frequently, but his dry, wry witticisms tended to throw other players off their game, so Wyatt welcomed him.

"I love to gamble," Mizner said, after taking a particularly bad beating from Wyatt. "It's the only sure way of getting nothing for something."

Sportswriter Al Runyon ("Damon" to his readers) played occasionally, but usually only for an hour or two; unlike Mizner and most other players, the bespectacled, thin-lipped, gray-complexioned dude did not order drinks from the cute cocktail waitress in blue satin and red satin sash, who made regular rounds of the little lounge. But he did send her for cup after cup of coffee, and whenever Runyon was at the table, half of the blue floating smoke had been generated by his cigarette upon cigarette.

Runyon played conservatively and sometimes broke even but usually lost. He said little, though once he'd said to Wyatt, "Try me at gin rummy sometime."

Wyatt, who smiled more when he was dealing than otherwise in life, smiled and said, "No thanks."

Heavyweight champ Dempsey sat at the table that first night, drinking moderately and playing indifferently, displaying none of the intense snarling force he brought to the ring. The swarthy lad struck Wyatt as a big good-natured brute with his mop of blue-black hair, narrow eyes, palooka's nose, and easy grin; his suit was louder than a brass band, yellow with black pinstripes and a red and yellow necktie. The kid was easygoing, giving autographs and chatting with anybody—in fact, Dempsey was a distraction at the table and Wyatt was fine with him leaving after an hour, the boxer three hundred bucks the wiser.

On Friday night, with his poker lounge a great success, Wyatt faced a complication that had not come up before. Guardian of the gate Gus was suddenly leaning over Wyatt and asking, "Can a woman play? I have a woman here who wants a number."

Wyatt glanced toward the open double doorway and saw a distinguished-looking well-preserved matron in a white muslin frock with tiny red dots and a white sash, white stockings and white shoes but with a black straw bonnet framing a pretty powdered face with dark blue eyes, red bud of a mouth and a long, distinctive but not unattractive nose.

As in Big-Nosed Kate.

Wyatt's long suit in cards was his poker face, but on recognizing Johnny's mother, not safely in Arizona but dangerously poised in this Manhattan doorway, his poker face went bust.

Wyatt smiled and nodded.

Kate smiled and nodded.

But the chill from the cold of those dark blue eyes damned near made him shiver.

"Give the little lady the next open chair," he said.

"But Mr. Earp, there are seven numbers ahead of her."

"Next open chair, Gus. Seat her in the dining room, see she gets whatever she wants to drink, and tell her she'll have a place here soon."

Within half an hour, Kate was seated next to Wyatt at the table. Her conversation was friendly and polite, though her presence unsettled some of these men—most of whom were none too happy that these upstart women seemed about to get the right to vote—and the action was dampened for a time.

But Kate knew her poker, and while the table talk became less masculine, the playing didn't. By four-thirty a.m., three hours after Kate had taken a chair at Wyatt's table, she was up four hundred dollars.

She cashed in her chips, gave Wyatt an icy smile and, in her thickly charming Hungarian-goulash way, said, "We must talk."

An hour or so later, Wyatt dealt one last hand—he never allowed games to go past six a.m., and this was a tad early; but he wanted to talk to Johnny, who proved not to be in his office. Wyatt tried downstairs.

Tex's last show had gone on at five a.m. and was winding down. The club no longer packed, the revue took on a pleasant intimacy; a few guests were asleep in their seats, even though the jazz band blared away, waiters and bartenders standing in the dim light like figures in a wax museum.

Bat was still at ringside but at a different table, and Johnny was with him; both were having coffee. Bat, as much a night creature as any other bat, seemed chipper. Johnny, however, slumped on his elbows, head in his hands, his cream-color coat wrinkled, his tie loose, the flesh trying to melt off his haggard face.

So. The boy knew.

Wyatt leaned in and curled a finger.

Johnny looked up at him and rolled his eyes and nodded. Wyatt followed the younger man, who staggered up the stairs, drunkenly, though Wyatt doubted the club owner had had a single drink.

In the office, Johnny fell into his padded swivel desk chair and Wyatt lowered himself into the red leather one opposite.

"Were you expecting this family reunion?" Wyatt asked.

Johnny shook his head and kept shaking it as he said, "No, God, no. She just showed up, something like two a.m. I've barely spoken to her. She just gives me this terrible stiff smile."

"How did she get in?"

"She told Lou at the door she was my mother."

"That would do it."

"Then she got Bill to carry her bags up to the guest room."

"Next to mine? Bully."

Johnny started shaking his head again. "I have no idea what she's doing here, why she even thought to come. We'd argued about this in person, and over the phone, and I thought it was settled. And now here she is, under my roof, to hound me and drag me down."

"That's a mother's prerogative."

"And it's a son's to ignore it. Wyatt, you have to talk to her. You knew her before I was born! She'll talk to you, I know she will."

Wyatt tasted the inside of his mouth; it wasn't pleasant. "I know she will, too."

If Johnny had leaned any farther over his desk, he'd have fallen across the thing. "You have to convince her it's too dangerous, her being here. What if Yale's boys knew she was here, and snatched her, and—"

"Enough," Wyatt said. He stood. "I'll deal with this in the daylight."

Johnny nodded to the window behind him, where the sun was slanting in the cracks of the blinds. "It's daylight now."

"And it still will be after noon. I believe she went up to bed, hour or so ago."

His eyes widened; they bore a red filagree. "You saw her? I mean—you've already *spoken* to her?"

"She came and sat at my table."

"Your table! And played?"

"And won. Making this my worst night. I'm only up a few hundred. Your mother can play cards, Johnny. You didn't inherit *all* your skills from your daddy."

Johnny stared at nothing, his mouth slackly open. "Ah, hell. I don't need this."

"Nor do I." Wyatt walked to the door, paused, said, "When we're all up, early afternoon say, we'll deal with it," and exited.

But Wyatt did not go immediately up to his room. He unlocked the front door and went out onto the small porch and smoked a cigar.

By God, even knowing it would be there, the broad sunlight was a surprise, after the endless night of the club; and the toilers of the city, on foot and in automobiles, were scurrying to their daily work. Real life getting its start, now that the imaginary world of the speakeasies had shut down.

He tried to make his mind sort through what needed saying to Kate; but he was too dragged out to get the gears turning. A night of poker was mental work, after all, and he was no spring chicken. He needed his damned sleep.

So he went inside and up the stairs to his guest room. Put on the blue silk pajamas Sadie gave him for his birthday, two years back, and got himself between the cool sheets and under the warm covers. The troubles he had, from Big-Nosed Kate to Carved-up Capone, were no match for how worn out he was: Wyatt Earp went right to sleep.

When the door opened, he heard it but fitted it into a dream he was having, of Sadie and him working the Happy Days mine and finding a rich vein of gold. Somebody opened the door in the dream, which made no sense because he and Sadie were in a cave, but then it was a dream and didn't have to make sense. . . .

He opened his eyes and a beautiful young woman was outlined by sunlight at the mouth of the cave, the silhouette of her slim figure clear under a sheer nightgown.

When he came fully awake and sat up, leaning on his elbows, the woman in the nightgown wasn't young though she was still beautiful, even at sixty; and she left the door half-open as she padded over in her bare feet and sat on the edge of the bed and stared at him, the blue eyes no less lovely for the near darkness. Nor any the less accusative.

"You were always a bastard, Wyatt Earp," Kate said.

Not a whisper but at least she wasn't shouting—on this floor, no one would be around but Kate in her guest room and Wyatt in his. Or rather Kate in his. The rest of the brownstone's second floor was given over to dressing rooms, and Tex and her chorines were long gone by now.

Her dark lustrous hair was curling down around her shoulders, very girlish. For a woman her age, Kate had weathered the ride just fine, though certain lines around her mouth and eyes were carved deep, not so much with years as with concern.

And anger.

"You as well as anybody, Kate," he said softly, "ought to know I'm no hero."

"But I thought I could trust you!"

"Why?"

She thought about that, couldn't find an answer and, in a quavering voice, said, "Out of loyalty to that boy's father, at least, you should have done right by him!"

Wyatt sat up straighter. He engaged her eyes. He said, "I am doing right by him. And he's no boy."

"He's my boy!"

"He's your son. I think of him as a 'boy' sometimes myself, but he's a man, well in his third decade. When I was his age—"

"You were a murdering son of a bitch!"

". . . No argument."

"You took my money!"

"I'm prepared to give it back. I can do that with interest, Kate."

Her upper lip curled in contempt. "You think that will satisfy me? Return on my dollar?"

He put a hand on her shoulder and she shrugged it off furiously. "Kate, Bat made your argument. I heard him. He made it well. And the 'boy' would have none of it."

She crossed her arms over her bosom. "I thought he'd listen to you."

"And he has. I'm helping him make a success of this place. And I am encouraging him . . . and when the time is right I will encourage him more . . . to walk away from it."

She snorted a laugh. "You have a funny way of showing it. There was no gambling here before you! You took advantage of the situation to—"

"I did. When I saw the situation, I decided to help Johnny make the best of it. I believe the day will come, perhaps a year from now, when he and that young girl of his will—"

"That little tramp!" Her eyes and nostrils flared and the upper lip curled back again. "I saw her go upstairs to him! She's *sleeping* with him! Is she living with him? In *sin*?"

Wyatt just stared at her.

Then he began to laugh.

She slapped him and it rang like a gunshot and stung like hell.

He grabbed her arms, firmly, not to throttle her, just to get her damned attention, and prevent further slapping.

"Kate, you were a whore when I met you. Christ, my brother James was your pimp! Save your self-righteousness for somebody who hasn't bedded you for money."

Her chin trembled and she swallowed and said, "Can't a . . . can't a mother . . . a mother want *more* for her son? Want better?"

He let go of her arms and took her into his. She began to weep, not a retching cry, merely a soft sobbing. He patted her back and whispered into her ear, "Sure a mother can want more. And should."

Then he held her away from him enough to look into her moist eyes.

"Kate, it's too early for him."

She was trembling all over now, her eyes confused. ". . . early?"

"I been where he is."

"Wyatt, I . . . I don't understand."

"Kate . . . it's . . . it's something I'd rather not put words to."

Her chin tightened and so did her lips. "You owe me, Wyatt. *Tell* me. Talk about it, whatever it is, goddamn you."

He took a breath. Let go of her. Turned away and said, "He lost a wife and child."

"I know. Who do you think told you? I know he did."

Now he looked at her. Hard. "So did I, a long time ago."

She said nothing, but her face changed. Softened, losing years.

"It was a journey back that took doing. And only I could figure it out. Do you understand, Kate? I think he and that sweet kid from the chorus, someday they'll have a normal life. A life more normal than you and I ever had. But Johnny needs to make that journey himself, in his own way. I mean to help him. But I can't take the trip for him. And neither can you. Not even his mother. Not even his father, were he here."

"Oh, Wyatt," she said, and threw himself into his arms, "Johnny would listen to you! I know he would!"

"No . . . no."

She kissed him, hard, a kiss salted with tears, and it was desperate and yearning and not half bad. His pecker was just getting interested when he pushed her away, gently.

"Kate, Kate . . . I'm a married man, who loves his wife, even if she probably told you enough on the phone to get you worked up and out here like this."

Now she was embarrassed, head hanging, and muttering apologies as she got to her feet and padded out, closing the door behind her.

Wyatt got back in bed; he could use a few more winks. Kate Elder was a fine-looking woman, for sixty; but he'd be goddamned if he'd give in to her charms, not when he'd turned away a younger gal like Tex.

"Sadie," he said, "the things I do for you."

Took forever getting back to sleep.

Three minutes, anyway.

# Fourteen

THE RAIN HEIGHTENED THE SMELLS OF WASHING-
ton Market, fruit and fish and produce sheds
and the nearby river adding to a damp, slightly
rank bouquet. Buildings dating before the Civil
War, with their arched doorways, elaborate cor-
nices and sculpted lintels, offered up their dirty
brick and stone surfaces to the storm, but to no
avail: even a hammering downpour couldn't
wash away years of grime.

By nine a.m., these streets would be crammed
with traffic, even in weather like this, and the
retail shops a block over would have no shortage
of buyers for their radios and fireworks and garden supplies and sporting goods and who knew
what all.

But before dawn, the shops were dark, the
streets owned by the trucks of farmers and haul-
ers. Few of the men in caps and workclothes

bothered with slickers as they loaded and unloaded in the shifting, rain-stippled glow of headlights, though their pace seemed even more frantic than usual, as the noise level of squawking fowls and yelling humans and slamming crates combined with the rumble and shriek of freight cars and the mechanical roar and squeal of trucks backing up and lumbering forward, to lend competition to the thunder that God was hurling around like He owned the place.

Through all this, Wyatt guided and coddled the bay, soothing the steed, taking it easy with the reins so that the animal didn't get spooked by the lightning flashes and celestial whip cracks. New York's two most unlikely milkmen were glad to be within the metal cab of the Droste Dairy wagon; still, enough water was making it in that Wyatt covered with newspaper the long-barreled Colt .45 on the bench beside him.

Back behind, Bat and his little revolver were dry as toast, but the thunder had an unsettling way of echoing within the wagon, and the spattering of raindrops made a steady overhead tap dance, not quite deafening but damned distracting.

They made their steady, leisurely way in and around the trucks and the men scurrying in the street, sometimes getting an irritated glance at their splash of hooves, as if people belonged there more than any lousy milk wagon. Just a few blocks down the warehouses took over, with no activity to speak of, though the Washington Market din continued to compete with the thunderstorm.

Soon Bat had hopped out, finally getting well and truly wet as he unlocked the big doors and swung one open, and slipped inside as Wyatt guided the bay into the vast warehouse, the horse's clips and clops on the cement providing counterpoint to the drumming rain on the roof, which echoed through the empty space in relentless, monotonous rhythm.

Bat closed them in and walked over to the massive false wall, wet footsteps following him, found the rope handle in the indentation in the wood, and swung open half of it. As usual Wyatt positioned the horse with the back of the wagon to the opening, and the two water-dripping men in black caps, white blouses, black trousers and white work gloves began selecting crates.

Wyatt selected one of the two sets of portable metal steps to allow Bat to climb up and take crates off the first row, but from the other side, in the first of six aisles within the formidable collection of crates. Each tier of wooden boxes was a good nine feet tall, so using the steps was a necessity. Even at his six feet plus, Wyatt couldn't have easily plucked one off the top; and Bat was almost a head shorter.

The procedure—this would represent their third delivery in as many weeks—took longer than Wyatt had expected. The crates of each variety of liquor tended to be stacked together—all of the Scotch, all of the bourbon, and so on—so the two men had to move the wheeled steps around, here and there, working off a shifting shopping list Johnny had provided.

They did not transfer each crate directly to the rear of the wagon; instead, they hauled each clinking crate out into the open area past the aisle, and then would finally load up for delivery. That neither man was a kid anymore, and that both had their share of sciatica, did not speed the process.

Today was Friday. They were, as Wyatt had suggested, varying their delivery, avoiding a pattern. First had been Monday, then Wednesday.

Business continued to boom at Holliday's, the week nights steady, the weekends wild. Yale's people continued their watch, even now with the third week since re-opening almost over. And Wyatt's own bankroll, while in no danger of rivaling Arnold

Rothstein's, was growing steadily. His net thus far approached ten thousand dollars.

Even the women were behaving themselves. On his most recent phone call to Sadie, she had agreed to come out at the start of June, if all still was going well. Tex, hearing this, laid off on the flirting, though their friendship continued apace. Johnny and Dix remained a happy little cooing couple. And, best of all, Kate had spent only two days at the club, having come to reluctant terms with her son's chosen path, even accepting Wyatt's return of her five hundred plus the expense money and a hundred-buck self-imposed penalty, before heading back to Arizona.

Wyatt had not been privy to Johnny's conversations with his mother, but Doc's wife and son were openly affectionate by the time she left. This was in part due to a small conspiracy involving all concerned, to keep Mama from learning of the threat posed by Yale and Capone.

Had Kate known about the incident at Coney Island, and all it entailed and connoted, Doc's better half would no doubt still be around . . . and on the warpath.

These thoughts had just trailed through Wyatt's mind as he set a case of Scotch atop another of gin when a thunderclap shook him . . .

. . . only it was no thunderclap, rather the metal doors of the warehouse being flung wide and hard enough for them to slam ringingly against the walls.

Bat was just approaching with a crate of whiskey in his gloved hands as Wyatt, yanking the long-barreled Colt from his waistband, moved forward only to see and hear one dark sedan sweep in, and then another, new shiny rain-pearled black Fords that screeched to sudden, angular stops.

The bay reared and whinnied, head flung side to side, nostrils flaring, eyes huge and afraid, front hooves pawing, striking the air, as the curly-headed Capone crony in a black rain slicker and rain-dripping black fedora slammed shut the big metal doors and the bald one (though his black fedora concealed that baldness) jumped out of the nearest Ford, on the rider's side, a tommy gun in hand.

"Take cover," Wyatt said, and Bat—who had already set the crate on top of others put aside for loading—ducked back into the nearest aisle.

"Over there!" the bald guy said, cradling the tommy gun under his right arm and pointing at Wyatt with his free hand, his thin upper lip peeled back over his teeth in a sick, satisfied smile. The curly-haired hood was on the run, a big automatic in his mitt as he rushed to join his pal, and both drivers were climbing out, a skinny one and a squat one, making it four hoods in black fedoras and matching slickers, and everybody had guns.

So did Wyatt, of course, but he didn't fire his, not yet—he slipped behind the small pile of set-aside crates, and assessed the situation. Only half of that fake wall exposed them, and the nervous horse was blocking that space, though not for long, Wyatt figured: the severely spooked animal was no longer rearing, but seemed ready to run, despite the lack of an exit, probably heeding its instinct to return to its stable.

The snorting, neighing horse moved headlong toward the curly-headed hood, who got spooked himself and started firing at the oncoming animal. The bay took the shots in the head and neck and instantly went down in a thousand-pound pile, taking the wagon with it in a sickening thump of horseflesh and ear-rending crash of metal and wood.

This put the dead, fallen animal in the way of the intruders, half-barring the opening onto the storehouse, and in the following few moments of confusion, Wyatt yelled to Bat, "Lay some fire down!"

Bat, in the first aisle, up the portable steps, leaning on the top row of crates, poised like the defender of a fort, began shooting his revolver at the intruders, whose first reaction was to scurry out of the way, but for the driver of the second Ford, the skinny sharp-nosed character who caught one in the knee and, as he was doing the resultant awkward dance, took another in the head, leaving a bloody mist behind as he stopped dancing and fell.

A hood yelled "Bastards," just another sound among the many, the rain continuing its own artillery onslaught, thunder adding occasional cannon fire.

At the same time, Wyatt had run from behind the pile of crates to that fake half-wall, that big open door giving their adversaries a view of them and the liquor repository, and as Bat's bullets flew overhead, the sharp cracks standing out like hail in the rainstorm, Wyatt—slipping a little in the horse's blood but maintaining his footing—put his back against the wooden door and reached one hand around and grasped its handle, that inset loop of rope, and with his other hand gripped the door's edge and pulled it shut, fingers of his other hand keeping hold of the rope, so that it squeezed through the space between the shut doors; then, as Bat's gunfire ceased, Wyatt hooked the rope over a handle on the inside of the other door.

And ran back to his pile of crates.

The two men, temporarily at least, were shut inside—the dead animal, the fallen wagon, one dead hoodlum, and three live (heavily armed) ones on the other side of the massive wooden doors.

The hoods were yelling at each other in the outer warehouse, unintelligible echoing, as Wyatt joined Bat in the aisle and said, "Is there a way out?"

Bat, still at the top of the metal steps, revolver in hand, quickly scanned the possibilities. "Those windows, maybe?"

A high row of painted-out black windows were on the rear wall.

"Even with these steps," Wyatt said, "we can't get up there—and anyway, it's a story-and-a-half drop."

From his perch, Bat surveyed the walls. "No door," he said, though they'd already known that.

Something, a shoulder probably, smashed against the juncture of the doors, straining the loop of rope.

Wyatt aimed down the long barrel at where the doors met, but above the rope-wound handle, and on the next ramming, fired off a round, wood chips flying.

"Shit!" somebody on the other side said.

Moments later, like a nasty parody of the hammering rain, the machine gun ripped into the doors at that crucial juncture and chunks of wood flew and the rope took a hit but held on by a few threads.

The tommy-gun fire let up—Wyatt figured the shooter was changing magazines—and he said to Bat, "You're fine right there," and scrambled around to the third aisle, where awaited the other set of metal steps, which he positioned just down from Bat to the left, and climbed and took his post at the top of the fortress of booze.

Another thunderous flurry of lead was unleashed on the doors and more wood flew and the rope threads were obliterated and two men came shouldering through, doors bursting open, the pair of hoods making way for the bald machine gunner who came in blasting, stitching bullets across the upper half of the first wall of crates, wood splintering, bottles cracking, liquor leaching.

Bat, trying for another head shot, managed only to take the

machine gunner's fedora off, revealing his pink fleshy dome; but it scared the son of a bitch, and as the shooter backed up, losing his footing in the bay's blood, bumping against the dead horse, a wild spray of slugs sent his two cronies scurrying in opposite directions as he literally slipped back into the outer warehouse.

Despite the slapstick of seeing the one thug slip-sliding and the others ducking their own boy's bullets, this had served to send the adversaries deeper into the storehouse, the curly-haired hood going to the left of the stacked crates, the squat joker to the right. From his position Wyatt saw each man streak by, and took a shot at both, twisting to do it, not succeeding with either round.

Confident Wyatt would watch his back, Bat kept his eyes on that opening, which yawned fairly wide now; the machine gunner was out of sight, either snugged on the other side of one big door, or crouched down using the horse carcass and overturned wagon as a barrier behind which to reload and cogitate.

In the meantime, in his own aisle, Wyatt had shoved the steps closer to the rearward row of crates, and climbed up them, and crawled onto the two-carton-deep stack to lie horizontally, belly down, and get a view of empty aisle four. Carefully, with some difficulty—not wanting to stick the .45 in his waistband even for a moment or two—he managed to drop down into that aisle, land-ing nice and soft.

He moved to the left, staying low, the long barrel of the gun in his right hand making of his very arm a rifle. Silent as a Sioux, he made his way to the end of the aisle, hurtled around to aisle five with the weapon ready to fire . . .

. . . but aisle five was empty.

He repeated the process, but headed right this time, and came around into aisle six, only to find it empty, as well.

This meant the two hoods had to be between the last wall of crates and the rear wall of the warehouse itself. Nowhere else for them to be.

He moved along aisle six, slowly, haltingly, pausing to listen.

Gunfire had, for an unsettling full minute or more, given over performance privileges to the pounding rain. Loud as the declamatory downpour was, with its punctuation of thunder, he could hear something else, somebody, *somebodies*, whispering.

With the position of his adversaries established, Wyatt smiled grimly to himself.

With some reluctance, he shoved the .45 into his waistband, and he reached up, as if surrendering, his hands finding the top crate on the stack.

And he shoved.

The two crates, butted against each other, went for a ride to come down hard on the two unseen men, whose cries of surprise and pain took any doubt away about their location, emphasized by the clatter of crates on concrete, and Wyatt emptied his Colt into the pine wood and the bullets crashed through, breaking glass, wasting liquor, and, judging by the howls, finding their intended targets.

Quickly he reloaded—his milkman's left jacket pocket was filled with cartridges—and came around to see what he'd accomplished.

Under the two broken-open crates, with shattered bottles of Scotch spilling fragrantly onto the floor, the two hoodlums lay. The squat character had a bullet in the head as he lay sprawled face-up atop the curly-headed one, who was wounded, arm and gut for sure, though the fat thug and the two busted crates and the scattered liquor somewhat obscured the view.

"Son of a bitch," the curly-haired hood muttered.

Wyatt wasn't sure whether this was an insult or merely an expression of displeasure, and didn't ask, before shooting the man in the head.

"Two down!" Wyatt called.

"No sign of Baldy!" Bat called back.

Bat and Wyatt could only speculate how this exchange had fueled the remaining hood—perhaps he was outraged or saddened, learning of the demise of his co-workers; or maybe he didn't like to have his hairlessness bandied about in so loose a manner.

At any rate, Wyatt had barely peeked out of the aisle when the tommy gunner came bounding through the gaping opening, into the storeroom, screaming as if he were on fire, but he was the one laying down fire, opening up with that tommy in sweeping, frenzied arcs.

Bat ducked back so quickly he came rattling bump bump bump bumping down the metal stairs and landed with no grace whatsoever on his ass; and, simultaneously, Wyatt dove back into the nearest aisle, number five.

The sounds this last man was generating—from his own warparty screams to the insistent barrage of bullets to the crack and crunch of splintering wood and the shattering glass of bottles—formed a mad symphony of destruction and rage, and Wyatt, with his own .45 up against a weapon that could spit .45 slugs back at him at a rate of fifteen hundred rounds a minute, wondered if his time had, at last, come.

He was not afraid; he had never been afraid in a gunfight, and his coolness, his steadiness, remained the eternal ace up his sleeve. So he told himself not to let a little noise unsettle him, and slipped out of the aisle and around behind, where the two dead hoodlums lay in a pool of bloody liquor and scattered pine.

As the mechanical chatter of the tommy continued counterpointing the bald bastard's banshee wail, along with the sad sound of shattering glass and snapping wood, Bat—wishing to hell he knew where Wyatt was, and what his friend was up to, but not daring give away either of their positions—got to his feet in the aisle and did his best to sort out where exactly the cacophony was coming from.

The shooter seemed to have moved from the doorway and off to the left. My God, the wood was flying! So were shards of glass, and the liquor gave off a pungent, medical aroma laced with cordite that in such quantity, not to mention circumstances, downright stank.

Bat was crouching, sensing that he should move left, when the tommy gunner appeared at the mouth of the aisle at left, and bullets went flying Bat's way, as the shooter's screechy scream went up a note or two, and Bat dove as if the floor were an inviting pool, which it wasn't, unless wood and glass and booze was your idea of inviting. . . .

Bat crawled around the corner into the next aisle and then was on his feet, running, hoping to come around and get the guy, but the gunner anticipated him, and the shrieking son of a bitch unleashed another hail of bullets, and Bat hit the floor and rolled, no wood or glass or liquor in this aisle—yet. When the gunner got through, though, there'd be plenty. . . .

And then the shooting stopped.

The son of a bitch was out of ammo.

Bat cut back around aisle three, to blindside the bastard, but Wyatt's gunfire, from the rear wall, drove the gunner back toward Bat.

Again Bat scrambled down an aisle, this time heading toward the rear wall, where Wyatt had been.

The machine-gunning started in again—must not have taken

the boy long to shove a new magazine in—but at least the scream-ing had stopped.

Only that was bad.

Good for the ears, but bad every other way, because the more out of control the gunner was, the better their chances were. If the hood had his mind clear and his deadly purpose in focus, then Bat and Wyatt had real trouble; after all, they were seriously out-gunned by this bird. . . .

By now the entire stockpile of liquor had been sprayed with bullets, and as the noise of cracking wood and breaking glass continued, the world of the warehouse, this section of it anyway, became a stench-ridden, booze-sodden, wood-chunk-cluttered obstacle course.

And when Bat got to the rear wall, he found the ghastly re-mains of the other two hoods, but no Wyatt.

Then he realized the relentless pummeling of gunfire was coming his way. He dropped to his knees, getting them wet in spilled liquor, using the two fallen hoodlums and the broken crates littering them for cover.

How desperate this was, Bat had scant time to consider, though he knew that chatter-gun could chop right through his modest man-wood-and-glass barricade.

When the bald gunner rounded the corner, still spraying slugs, Bat took aim and fired twice, and the guy, not hit but star-tled, pulled back, letting up on the trigger.

Bat had him now, and he fired . . . only he didn't fire, he squeezed the trigger, all right, but the hammer fell on an empty chamber.

He was out.

"Even little guns need bullets," the gunner said, his eyes wild, his smile rabid-animal crazed.

The son of a bitch was laughing when he fired . . .

. . . only *he* didn't fire, either, his trigger bringing only clicks. He was out, too.

Bat was scrambling to reload when he heard the footsteps.

Wyatt's steady footsteps.

The bald hoodlum, in the process of pulling another drum-like magazine from a pocket of his slicker, had eyes showing whites all round and a wide open but silent mouth as he swivelled to face Wyatt Earp.

"Big gun," Wyatt said.

The guy was shoving the magazine in.

"But empty is empty."

The thunder of the long-barrel .45 rivaled anything the sky could summon, and the force of its impact shattered the bald head like a melon, splashing the bricks nearby with red and pink and gray matter, none of which was of any further use to the hoodlum, who fell like a cut-down tree, the machine gun clattering to the concrete a moment later.

In seconds Wyatt was at Bat's side, helping him to his feet.

"Will you live, Bartholomew?"

Bat was checking himself out, hands roving over his milkman's uniform. "Any nick I have's from broken glass. Mostly I'm going to hurt in the morning, from all this running and jumping."

"You're not a young man, anymore."

"And you are?" Bat's eyes went to Wyatt. "What's that?"

"What?"

"On your ear?"

Wyatt touched his left lobe. His fingers brought back blood. "A little graze."

Bat roared with laughter; it struck Wyatt damned near as hysterical as the dead gunner's shrieking. "Don't tell me after all these years, you finally took a bullet!"

Wyatt raised a blood-dabbed forefinger in warning. "Not a word."

They took stock of their situation.

First, they checked the street, to see what attention had been attracted; when, in the outer warehouse, Wyatt opened the side door, and stuck his head out, he got a faceful of rain and the heavens roared at him.

No sign of anyone or anything.

He wandered back over to the fallen horse and the overturned wagon and the dead skinny hoodlum, the first casualty of the gunfight.

"Damned waste of life," Wyatt said.

Bat was approaching. "What, that dead son of a bitch? Why the hell should we care?"

"The horse."

"Ah. Yes. You do have a point, at that." Bat's hands were on his hips as he continued to assess things. "Wyatt . . . not taking into consideration the four stiffs that need attention, we're in a nasty spot."

"I know."

"That bald jackass splattered his bullets all over Johnny's booze stockpile. Why, the boy'll be lucky to salvage a fifth of it."

"He'll be lucky to salvage a fifth."

Bat sighed. "How the hell did this go wrong?"

Wyatt shrugged. "Somebody made us, hauling 'milk.' Following us back would have took 'em only as far as the dairy. So I figure they staked out your place and followed us here."

"Goddamn." Bat gave another bigger sigh. "We let Johnny down. Well and truly we did."

Wyatt shook his head. "No. Odds were against us from the start in this game."

"I suppose."

He put a hand on his old friend's shoulder. "Bartholomew, what with no sign of the coppers, I'd suggest we dump the bodies, and go request that Johnny's friend Droste come collect his horse and wagon."

Bat nodded, and jerked a thumb toward the ruined fortress of booze. "And maybe have his dairy crew clean this place up, and see if any of the soldiers in those crates survived."

"Yes."

Yet another sigh came from Bat, who then scratched his head. "Well, Johnny still has his club, anyway. He's not out of business by a long shot. All he has to do is arrange to buy from—"

"Who, Yale?" Wyatt said, frowning, his head back. "Think, Bartholomew. With Johnny's liquor gone, nothing stands in the way of Capone taking his revenge."

The blood drained from Bat's face; the pale blue eyes turned sorrowful. "Christ, Wyatt. Young Johnny's a dead man. Unless . . ."

"If there's an 'unless,' I'm pleased to hear it."

Suddenly Bat was grinning; he gestured to the nearby corpse. "Who says *we* killed these bastards?"

"I seem to recall doing it."

"Yes, but who's the wiser? Those four stiffs aren't talking, not any more than that poor dead bay." He shook a friendly finger in Wyatt's face. "Remember this: Yale and Capone have their hands full, across the river, right now—there's a small war growing bigger and bigger by the day."

Wyatt's eyes tightened. "The Irish gang? Those White Handers?"

"Exactly. Who's to say *they* didn't do this? In fact, if we handle the disposal right, namely Brooklyn way, they could be the prime suspects."

Wyatt drew air in through his nostrils. "You're the New Yorker. Have a spot in mind?"

"I know a perfect place along that lovely stink hole, the Gowanus Canal." Bat gestured to the two Fords. "We'll load both buggies up, two 'riders' each—ditch the cars with the garbage, and find our way back to Manhattan."

Wyatt was nodding, liking it. "So the Irish get the credit . . . and, since nobody knows the liquor supply's been smashed, Johnny's still in the clear."

Now Bat was nodding. "Yes! And he could make a secret arrangement with his friend Rothstein, for one of these Manhattan bootleggers to supply Holliday's, and—"

"No," Wyatt said, holding a palm up. His voice was as sharp as one final gun crack in the echo-ridden warehouse. "Such a secret would be impossible to keep. Over time, anyway."

"Yeah. Yes, damn it all, I suppose you're right. My God but Johnny's going to take this mighty hard."

Rain drummed and echoed in the warehouse.

Again Wyatt's eyes narrowed. "Would Rothstein be interested in buying Johnny out, you think?"

"What, the club itself? The building, and the business with it? Possibly. But, Wyatt—where does that leave Johnny? Hell, where does it leave us?"

"Alive," Wyatt said. "If we play our cards right."

# Fifteen

AL CAPONE MIGHT HAVE BEEN DOING ANYTHING on this cool clear spring night, from spending time in his Brooklyn apartment with Sonny Boy and Mae, to playing pool at the Adonis Club, even to bartending and bouncing at the Harvard Inn, which didn't stand on ceremony where the Lord's Day of Rest was concerned.

What he had not expected was sitting down for a friendly game of cards at Holliday's with the man who fucking scarred him, plus Wyatt Earp, Bat Masterson and assorted others.

The odd turn of events started yesterday afternoon, when Frankie Yale summoned Al to his office at the garage.

"You heard about Baldy and Skinny Sal?" Yale asked.

The usually immaculate boss had a rumpled aspect Al had rarely seen—dark hair unruly, eyes bloodshot, even his expensive wardrobe (black suit with white pinstripes and black shirt with white tie) looked slept in.

"Yeah, fuckin' shame," Al said and shook his head sympathetically, even though he didn't have any respect for nobody who let themselves be snuck up on. "Goddamn tragedy. Both with wives and little kids."

Four of Yale's top rods—Baldy Pete, Curly Sam, both Sal's (Fat *and* Skinny)—had been found shot in the head, execution style. Along the canal. Yesterday afternoon. By some strolling couple who called the coppers.

"Goddamn Irish sons of whores!" Yale said, so excited spittle was flying. He beat a fist on his desk and papers rattled and his blotter jumped and pencils and pens danced. "Lousy lowdown mick cocksuckers!"

The boss obviously considered the killings retaliation by the White Hand for Al busting up that Valentine's Day Dance. (Al, whose wife Mae was Irish after all, took no offense at such ravings, considering Frankie's reaction understandable in the circumstances.)

Sitting in the battered wooden visitor's chair opposite Yale, who was rocking in his swivel chair behind the big desk, Al said, "But Curly and them were in Manhattan. Keeping their eye on that speak. Could Holliday and those two old Wild Bills done it?"

Yale batted that away. "The only Wild Bill I smell in this is Lovett! Him and Peg Leg caught our boys flatfooted in Manhattan and hauled their asses over here and murdered them, just outright cold-blooded *murdered* them! Them micks are *animals.* . . . You're lucky *you* weren't along for the ride!"

Curly and Baldy had been at Al's side for the Sagaman's Hall ambush, so he could see his boss's point.

"So, then, Frankie—what's our next move?"

"With the micks? Let me worry about that. *Your* next move is to accept an invite to play cards at Holliday's."

Al winced. "What the hell is this, boss—some kinda gag?"

Yale shook his head. "No gag." Yale's black eyebrows rose. "What would you say, I told you I got a call today . . . from Arnold Rothstein his own self."

This sat Al up straight. "Jesus. Since when do we do business with the Manhattan money king?"

"Since now, if we're lucky. If we wanna make our move into Midtown, it behooves us keep him happy. He sees himself this, this, this big . . . peacekeeper or some such. Rothstein does business with Holliday, and if we ever should want to do business with Rothstein, he suggests we consider letting certain bygones be bygones."

"Fuckin' easy for him to say," Al said, touching the puckery pinkness of his ravaged left cheek.

"Listen, Rothstein is the pawnbroker, hell, the broker *period* for anybody working the wrong side of the street. This is a unexpected overture, from the guy, and with the shit soup we're swimmin' in over here, right now, I ain't about to shrug it off. *Capeesh?*"

"*Capeesh,*" Capone said reluctantly.

Yale gestured with an open palm. "At Holliday's request, you're invited to a private game, Sunday evening, at his club."

"Game? What the hell kinda game?"

"Poker. We talked about Earp workin' gambling in at Holliday's, didn't we? Little room on the first floor?"

Last week Yale had told Al about Earp's poker game, setting the stage for a full-scale casino to follow.

"Yeah, boss, sure. And I can see it, Rothstein wanting us all one big bunch of happy clams. But, why do they want *me* there? Why not you?"

Yale shrugged. "We were both invited. I declined for me, 'cause of this business crisis. I accepted for you, 'cause you are my number-two man."

Al smiled big; still hurt a little, when he did that. "I really appreciate hearing that, boss. Sure as hell do." His eyes narrowed as he slid to the edge of his hard wooden chair. "Is this some kind of, what do you call it . . . negotiation? Rothstein as the go-between 'tween the two unhappy parties?"

"No. That might come later. This is strictly a social evening. High-stakes game, Rothstein says."

"High stakes is right, if I get hit behind the ear."

Yale ignored that, saying, "You can take the black Caddy. Buy-in is a grand. Here." He slipped an envelope out from under his blotter and handed it across to Al.

Who reached for it, took it, thumbed back the flap and flipped through three grand in hundreds.

Yale smiled, though in his current frame of mind it was clearly an effort. "Win or lose, kid, it's all yours."

"Uh, thanks, boss. Maybe I could use a night out at that."

Yale shifted in the swivel chair. "What Rothstein said . . . how'd he put it? . . . It's a 'gesture' on Holliday's part. *Friendly* gesture. Mainly, they want to make sure you don't still want to kill his skinny ass."

"Well, I do still want to kill his skinny ass."

"Well, goddamnit, Al—make 'em think you *don't!*"

Al sighed. Sat back. "Who goes with me?"

"Nobody. No bodyguards, no back-up. Part of the ground rules. Even Rothstein will be naked."

Al was back on the chair's edge again. "Boss, you can't expect me not to go heeled!"

"Nothing was said about hardware. They just don't want a

bunch of gorillas standing around and some little misunderstanding turns into a crossfire. You can go heavy. Just don't overdo."

As it turned out, guns were the first matter of business, when Al came through the doorway at the top of the brownstone's front steps. Bat Masterson rolled up without a how-do-you-do and started frisking him, even taking the liberty of slipping a hand into Al's right side suitcoat pocket and lifting out the .38 revolver, and handing it quickly to Texas Guinan, who was playing hostess.

Al gripped Masterson's wrist, though the gun had already been passed to the blonde broad, looking gaudy as a carnival midway in that red sparkly low-cut gown.

"No," Al said.

Masterson's smile seemed genuine enough but his light blue eyes had an iciness. "Sorry, Al—it's just like Dodge City or Tombstone. Gotta check your shooting iron at the door."

"I only have the one with me," Al said, letting go of Masterson's wrist and holding out his hand, palm up, "and I'll have it back. Now."

"If you won't play by the house rules," Masterson said, and the smile turned as icy as the eyes, "we'll have to ask you to leave."

"Then I'll have to leave. I ain't gonna play Daniel in your damn lion's den."

"Your choice."

Al leaned in till the two were almost nose to nose. "Listen, old man—if you was in my house, all alone with me and my boys, would you go in without your gat?"

Masterson drew in a breath, thought for a moment, let it out. "No. No, I wouldn't. . . . Tex! Give him back his piece. . . . Come in and join us."

Then, gesturing in a "come along" fashion, he headed through nearby double doors that stood open.

Texas Guinan handed the .38 to Al, who traded her his Borsalino for it, then broke the revolver open to check the cylinders and found the bullets all there.

"Thanks, honey," Al said to her, and she smiled at him, lots of teeth and fluttery bedroom eyes, bosom half out of her dress and not a bad bosom at that, for a frill pushing forty. "I hear you put on a real good show."

"You'll have to catch one of my shows sometime, sugar," she said.

She took him warmly by the arm and walked him a short distance into the little front room filled mostly with a big round green-felt-topped poker table. Every chair but the one with its back to an unlighted fireplace with a painting of a naked broad over it was already filled. Nobody rose when he entered, but everyone nodded and said hello.

Johnny Holliday, seated dead opposite that open chair, turned to look at Al and say, "Glad you decided to come around. Welcome."

The cocky guy, half-turned in his chair, stuck out a hand for Al to shake, which he did.

"I ain't one to hold no grudge," Al said. And gave his host a great big friendly smile.

In his mind, Al pictured himself slashing that thin, pretty blue-eyed puss with a razor, blood flying, strips of skin flapping. But instead he ambled around the table to the empty chair and settled in.

He recognized all but one of his fellow players, a lanky bored-looking ghee immediately to Al's left, who introduced himself as "Mizner," and wore a tux, looking a little like a head waiter.

To Capone's left was Earp, in undertaker black and a black string tie, the whiteness of the man's mustache and hair in the grooved, pale face making a striking contrast with the dark attire. For an old goat, Earp had a kind of commanding air about him.

Next to Earp was that sportswriter peacock Damon Runyon, in a green suit with a darker green necktie with emerald stickpin and lighter green suspenders against an even lighter green shirt. Maybe the dude thought all that green would attract money. Deadpan, in wirerim glasses, the columnist had a cigarette drooping in his thin lips, a tray nearby with two cigs already crushed out. This oddball had introduced himself to Capone at a fight at the Garden, and they'd spoken a few times since, though truth be told Runyon had a way of making you do all the talking.

Next to Runyon, and right across from Capone, was their host. Johnny Holliday wore a cream-color suit with a pastel yellow shirt and a rust-color tie with a diamond stickpin. He had a smirky way that was already getting under Al's skin, though he'd said nothing disrespectful and, tell the truth, seemed friendly, or anyway that was the front he was putting on.

Beside Holliday was Masterson, who wore a dark gray suit and a black bow tie, and was wearing his derby at a tilt, the only man at the table in a hat. Al would gladly feed that fucking derby to the old man, patrons at the Harvard Inn having reported this geezer clubbing Al with his cane, after that smug prick Holliday cut him.

Finally, next to Masterson, was Arnold Rothstein, a mild-looking prematurely gray character of maybe forty, with a bland oval face and a gray pallor, though his eyes, dark brown and shining, spoke of smarts. His suit was a nice enough brown job, but was maybe off the rack, and his bow tie was the same dark brown as his eyes. Nothing impressive about the guy, on first look, a small, slim if paunchy character; that this was the city's Great Go-between seemed not just unlikely but impossible.

Could this milksop *really* be the guy politicians went to, when they needed something from gamblers or gangsters? Or who the so-called underworld called on to line up protection from prosecutors and judges and cops?

Crazy as it seemed, Al knew this to be straight.

When doing business in Manhattan, Al had the habit, like so many of his peers, of stopping in at the best deli restaurant in Manhattan, Reuben's at West Seventy-second and Broadway. Rothstein made an office out of the place, and Al had seen him there, had had the so-called Big Bankroll pointed out to him. Runyon hung out there, too.

Al got his wallet out and bought a grand's worth of chips, whites twenty-five dollars, reds fifty and blues one hundred.

"Two hundred raise limit," Earp said. "So you know, I'm dealing, but I'm also playing."

Al raised an eyebrow. "That's a new one on me."

"Sorry nobody told you the rules before you went to the trouble of stopping by, Mr. Capone. Hope you didn't waste a trip."

"No. I came to play. What's it, five-card stud? Seven?"

"Draw," Earp said.

Al grinned. "You talking guns or cards?"

Earp's smile was a cut under the white mustache, giving not a glimpse of teeth. "Cards. I'll be anteing a white chip every round, Mr. Capone, if that takes the sting out."

"Yeah. Why not? And it's 'Al.' We're all friends here, right?"

Mizner was lighting up a cigarette, bummed from Runyon. "Al, I liked you the moment I saw you."

"Is that right?"

"Oh yes. You simply sparkle with larceny."

That made Rothstein laugh—he had an easy, infectious laugh

that swept up Masterson and Holliday, though Earp did not crack a smile, nor did Runyon.

"That's a compliment, Al," Rothstein said, still chuckling, displaying very white, perfect teeth that must have cost good money.

"Well, I hope so," Al said, forcing a smile.

"We're a civilized group," Mizner said, and blew a smoke ring. "We won't say anything bad about anyone else, until he leaves. . . . Ah, here's our charming waitress."

Al glanced up and didn't recognize the little Kewpie-doll brunette at first, in a blue satin pajamas-type outfit with red sash, carrying a round tray with assorted drinks; then he made her: Holliday's girl, the dish with the high pert breasts and the sweet little ass, whose praises he'd sung and got himself slashed for the trouble.

Earp said, "Everybody's here, so it's time to shuffle, cut and deal. Since I'm the only dealer, I'll be alternating the  ··t, left and right. Any objections?"

Nobody objected, and anyway Al was preoccupied. The brunette was delivering drinks and avoiding looking at him, and he was starting to feel a slow burn rising up his cheeks. Was Holliday insulting him, or trying to embarrass him, with her presence? Goading him?

Earp was dealing and Al had two cards already, but hadn't checked them out. He was trying to figure out why he was getting mad, and at the same time trying *not* to get mad, since Frankie wouldn't like that. . . .

Then she was standing, looming over him, having served everybody a drink (well, a cup of coffee to Runyon and a glass of milk to Rothstein) and finally, shyly, she met his eyes. "Sir? Would you like anything?"

*Was* she *goading him?*

"Scotch," Al muttered. "Straight."

Holliday, opposite, was leaning forward, smiling, though the smile had a telling tightness. "You remember Miss Douglas, don't you, Al? From the Harvard Inn?"

Al pictured himself pounding Holliday's face into a pulpy bloody mess with both fists; but instead, finally understanding what was expected of him, said, "I do. Uh, Miss Douglas, I apologize for my lack of couth, that there time."

"Yes, sir," she said shyly. "That's gentlemanly of you to say."

The flushed feeling left and he looked up at her, gave her his best boyish grin. "Not a good idea, a bartender sampling his own wares. I was feeling a little friendly, that night. Too friendly. Sorry, honey."

"Apology accepted," she said with a sweet tiny smile, and flounced off.

Johnny said, "Appreciate you doing that, Al. Takes a big man to admit he screwed up."

Al had a gander at his five cards. "Yeah. Well, she seems like a nice kid."

"And I hope you'll allow me to apologize to *you*. For going overboard in my reaction."

"Okay. Sure."

"Looks like it's healing nicely, though."

"Yeah." Al, having to work at not touching his scars, took a look at his cards. He had two tens and a bunch of crap.

Mizner, head tilted like a deaf guy, said, "Gives you character, Old Sport."

"What?"

"Like a dueling scar in days of yore. And you have three of them, which is three times as much character."

Al, not sure if his dick was being tugged by this odd duck, said, "Yeah. It's already a real selling point in my social circle."

Rothstein laughed at that, prompting laughter from everybody but Earp, even Al, who opened for fifty bucks. He picked up another ten and his triplets won the first pot.

An hour and several trays of drinks later, Al was winning, not big, but winning. Mizner and Runyon were both down, maybe a couple thousand each; and Rothstein was treading water, while Holliday won steadily and Earp and Masterson held their own.

Their hostess in the red sparkling gown would enter now and then, between rounds, and ask if anyone needed anything, fetching cigars at one point for Earp and Runyon, and a sardine sandwich for Rothstein, at about the two-hour point. The brunette in blue satin jammies, Miss Douglas, kept everybody's glass full—in Runyon's case, his coffee cup, Rothstein his milk, both guys apparently on the wagon—while Earp nursed one damned drink forever.

Holliday, about an hour in, had started asking for doubles; then at the two-and-a-half-hour point, requested Miss Douglas bring him two doubles at a time.

"Are you sure, Johnny?" she asked softly.

"Dix, I'm just trying to save you a trip. It's a relaxing evening with friends—don't worry your pretty little head."

At the three-hour point, a break for everybody to stretch their legs and heed nature's call revealed Holliday as a little unsteady on his feet. He'd been slurring his words for the last hour, and his play seemed reckless to Al; still, luck stuck with Holliday, who remained the big winner at the table.

But the goddamn guy was half cock-eyed, and Al overheard Earp taking the younger man aside and advising him to "ease up" on the booze.

Holliday swatted away the hand on his arm and said, "You're not my daddy. Just deal the cards, and leave me be."

When Holliday had gone off to use the john, Al wandered over to Earp, who was having a cigar near the front door. "That kid's damn near ossified," Al said.

"He is overdoing it," Earp admitted.

"Don't tell me he's going alky on you."

"Johnny's been fine ever since this place opened. But his wife died last year, and he hit the bottle hard, for a time."

"When that boy falls off the wagon, he takes a real tumble, don't he?"

Earp shrugged. "He may be nervous about you being here."

"Me? Why, we're all pals now."

Earp's eyes trained themselves on Al; hell, were Earp and Masterson brothers or something, with those same damn spooky blues?

"Don't con a con artist, Al. You and I both know any truce we forge is an uneasy one. Every morning, rest of your life, when you shave? You will look at what Johnny Holliday did to you. So forgetting is not in the cards."

Al shrugged. "I'm a big boy. I was out of line, that time, and anyway, I'm a businessman. And, as the man says, business makes strange bed fellas."

"Does indeed."

They were soon playing again, and Holliday kept on winning, though his eyes were half-lidded and he sat there, tie loose, weaving, like any second he might fall off his fucking chair. When the brunette brought him a single drink on her next trip, he snapped at her.

"I said 'two,' Dix! Can't you count?"

The little doll scurried out looking like she might bust out bawling.

"Take it easy, Johnny," Earp said.

"Deal. Just deal. Quit talking to me like I'm a goddamned fool!"

Mizner, about to sip his drink, said, "Why, Johnny, do you have your suspicions?"

Rothstein laughed at that, showing off his expensive teeth again, though Al didn't know what the guy had to laugh about. He must have been down six or seven thousand.

And, drunk or not, Holliday was winning. Al was winning, too, but the rows of chips across the table were towering, or they were until Holliday got so soused he couldn't stack them anymore.

Mizner was the first to toss in the cards, followed by Runyon fifteen minutes or so later. The two men did not depart, shifting to the sofa against the wall, where they were attended by Texas Guinan and Miss Douglas. Mizner drank bourbon and Runyon coffee and they ate sandwiches provided by the ladies and chatted very softly among themselves, Mizner doing most of the talking. Half an hour later, Masterson—down two thousand plus—joined them.

Al might have been suspicious of the way Holliday was winning, if he hadn't been winning himself; plus, the big loser was Rothstein, and he couldn't imagine Earp and Holliday running a crooked game to take down the most important man in their world.

Anyway, Earp was not fancy with the cards, and if the crusty old codger was a mechanic, Al could not spot it. The dealer continued to hold steady with his own stacks of chips, a little up, a little down.

By one a.m., Holliday seemed so smashed, he was barely staying awake. Without that incredible streak—he'd routinely had three of a kind, and more straights, flushes and full houses than God should ever grant—Holliday would have gone bust in any reasonable game. And got tossed out of most.

Al, up about seven thousand, yawned and said, "Been a lovely evening, gents, but I think it's time I cashed these in."

Earp nodded and said, "One more hand, Al? One more hand, everybody?"

This did not include Runyon and Mizner, the former watching and listening to the game, the latter asleep, sprawled over an arm of the couch. Texas was leaning against the open door, chatting with Masterson, who was drinking coffee, and Miss Douglas and her tray were gathering empty glasses.

Al nodded. "I'm okay with one more hand."

Rothstein said, "Actually, fellas, I'm down fifteen thousand. I wouldn't mind going a little longer and get a chance to catch up."

Barely understandable, Holliday slurred, "Hell, I just hit my stride. Let's keep at it."

"No," Earp said firmly, the deck tight in his right hand. "Mr. Rothstein, if you and Johnny want to play two-handed till the cows come home, be my guest. But this is my game, and we are playing one more hand in my game . . . and then cashing in the chips."

Rothstein said, with a polite nod, "It is your game, Mr. Earp. I bow to you."

"It's *my* house!" Holliday said, petulant. He sighed hugely. "Well, then, deal your last hand, will you, old man? And then we'll decide."

Earp, his face stony, dealt.

Al had a pair of aces, and opened for a hundred, and Rothstein raised him a hundred, and Holliday raised another hundred, in the kind of free spending that often accompanies the last deal of the night.

But Al's draw did not improve his hand, and he checked to Rothstein, who asked the dealer gently, "Since this is the last hand, is it permissible to extend the raise limit?"

"Raise whatever you want," Holliday said with a sneer.

Earp glanced at Al. "Mr. Capone?"

"I'm out, anyway," Al said, yawning again, tossing in his cards. "Let 'em do what they please."

Earp, who had stayed in through the first round of betting, nodded and also tossed in his cards. "Why don't we raise the limit to one thousand, Mr. Rothstein?"

"Fair enough," Rothstein said, and tossed in ten blue chips.

Barely had the blues clinked into the pot than Holliday tossed in ten more, and ten more. "See it, and raise another grand," he said unnecessarily.

Runyon had stirred Mizner to wakefulness, so he could get in on the little drama unfolding.

Rothstein wasn't laughing, but he was smiling with those unreal white choppers. His eyes were bright and alive and his skin was gray and dead.

In a cold tone he had not used at this table, Rothstein said, "Care to make it really interesting?"

Holliday snorted a derisive laugh. "You don't scare me, Arnie. You can't beat me. So why don't you just pack up and go find some doorway to hide in so you can buttonhole some poor bastard who owes you three dollars."

Rothstein's smile dissolved into a cold, blank mask. "I can't beat you, huh? What is it you have, Johnny boy? Royal flush?"

"Put in another thousand and see."

Eyes tight but flashing, Rothstein easily reached into his pants pocket and produced the biggest, fattest bankroll Al had ever seen.

Rothstein removed a rubber band from the bundle and began peeling off hundreds, counting as he went, "One . . . two . . . three. . . ."

It took a long time, a goddamn eternity . . . because Rothstein didn't stop till he got to one hundred.

*One hundred thousand dollars.*

Holliday was frowning; he almost looked like he might cry. "I don't have that kind of money. Not on me, I mean."

Rothstein glanced around him, gestured with one hand as he put away the rest of the bankroll with the other. "You have this place, don't you? And everybody says you have half the liquor in New York."

"My liquor isn't available," Johnny muttered.

Manhattan's mastermind sat forward and his eyes burned now, though his tone was reasonable as hell. "Then if you, say, lost this building to me . . . your club, your facilities . . . you'd still be in business. You could still supply me with liquor."

Earp said, "What's the bet, Rothstein?"

Rothstein flicked a nasty smile at the dealer. "No 'mister,' *Marshal* Earp? Johnny said I could bet him as much as I pleased. Well, I'm betting him one hundred thousand dollars against the deed to this brownstone, its contents to be included. It's a fair bet."

Runyon, who'd said very little tonight, said, "Johnny, I wouldn't. . . ."

Mizner, leaning forward, said, "Easy does it with Arnold, Johnny. He's a lovely man, but he'd steal a hot stove and come back for the smoke."

"It's a bet," Holliday said.

Earp sat forward. "Johnny! No. You're drunk, goddamnit."

Holliday's eyes and nostrils flared like a rearing horse. "You are *not* my *daddy!* You work for *me*, 'Marshal' Earp . . . and I take this bet."

"Fine," Rothstein said. "Good."

Masterson came over and put a hand on Holliday's shoulder, and said, "Don't, Johnny. I'm sure Mr. Rothstein will be reasonable if—"

"The hell I will," Rothstein snapped.

Holliday brushed Masterson's hand away and then grinned as he lay his cards down, all at once, fanned out, and Al suddenly understood the guy's confidence.

Four jacks. Queen kicker.

Al whistled, and even Runyon—on his feet, as was Mizner, on the periphery—smiled.

"Whoa," a grinning Masterson said, in the doorway with Texas again.

"That *is* a good hand," Rothstein said, expressionless.

Holliday's curled fingertips went out for all those chips and all that cash . . .

. . . but Rothstein gripped his opponent's nearest wrist and said, "You're as premature as you are immature."

Holliday frowned, still poised to rake in his winnings, and Rothstein lay his cards down one at a time.

King of Hearts.

King of Clubs.

King of Diamonds.

"And one more," Rothstein said, laying down . . .

. . . *the King of Spades.*

Stunned, Holliday got to his feet, staggering, his eyes filled with disbelief.

"You cheating bastard," Holliday snarled at Rothstein.

Rothstein held up his hands as if in surrender and quietly said, "I understand your disappointment."

"Everybody knows you're a goddamn cheat, Rothstein!"

Rothstein, slowly, carefully, rose, still with his palms forward, patting the air gently. "Normally I would take offense. But I understand you've been drinking, and a hand like this is, I admit, an unlikely one . . ."

"*Unlikely!*" Holliday leaned on the table with one hand and trembled all over as he sneered at Rothstein. "You think because of who you are, you can steal everything I've worked for? You think I'll walk away from this?"

From the doorway, Miss Douglas, pale as death, whispered, "Oh, Johnny . . . please don't do anything—"

Whether that was all she had to say, Al would never know. The waitress might have added "stupid" or "rash," but her boy friend had already done something that was both those things.

Holliday drew that same gleaming blade from a sheath under his left sleeve, steel winking and flashing, poised to slash Rothstein, but Al wasn't having any, not this time.

The .38 came out of his pocket and Al fired three times at Holliday, one at his head and one at his chest and one at his belly, and the last two found their mark, as Holliday clutched his heart while his other hand, still tight around the hilt of the knife, found his stomach and as Miss Douglas raised clenched fists to her cheeks and screamed bloody murder, Holliday took a sort of bow, blood spreading on his shirt in two bright slick scarlet patches, as he folded in two and dropped to the floor, with a dead-weight *thump*.

Al stood frozen, the .38 snout twirling a smoky question mark.

The little waitress was already at her fallen lover's side, cradling his head in her arms against her breasts, crying her eyes out, screaming, "Call a doctor!" again and again, not caring about the blood all over him and her now. Holliday's eyes were closed, his face slack, but Earp was moving in, kneeling there to check for a pulse in wrist and neck.

"No doctor, Dix," Earp said gravely, and shook his head.

Rothstein was at Al's side. Almost whispering, he said, "I owe you. You saved my life, and I won't forget it."

"He was gonna . . ."

"I know. But you have to get out of here." Now Rothstein really was whispering. "Everybody here knows you were defending my life, but these are not your friends, and with this many witnesses . . ."

Behind Rothstein were the bobbing heads of Mizner and Runyon.

". . . you can't risk it."

Al, his mind racing but not getting anywhere, said, "What should I do, Mr. Rothstein?"

"Get the hell out. Out of here, out of town . . . just *go*." Rothstein took the .38 from Al's slack fingertips. "I'll ditch this."

"I don't know if—"

"Go talk to your boss—Yale. Tell him what happened, and ask him what to do."

Al nodded and kept nodding. "I will. I will."

Then Earp was at Al's side and the old man gripped the young man's arm and squeezed. "Listen to him."

Al swallowed and said, "You saw what happened! You know I had no goddamn choice!"

"No? You couldn't have shot him in the shoulder? Listen, punk, it's time."

"Time?"

"You need to get out of Dodge."

And Al Capone hurried past the crying girl and her dead bloody boy friend and, getting his Borsalino handed him at the door by a grim Texas Guinan, got the hell out of the brownstone.

Even forgot to cash in his chips.

# Sixteen

FROM THE POKER ROOM WINDOW, PEERING BE-
tween blinds, Wyatt Earp watched young Al
Capone skedaddle down to the black Cadillac
parked across the way, and moments later, when
the hood and his vehicle were out of sight, Wyatt
signaled the "all clear."

Laughter—nervous, relieved, raucous, depend-
ing on its source—rang off the walls, and some
applause did, too, as Dixie helped a stone-sober
Johnny (who had put away a record amount of
lukewarm tea over these last hours) to his feet.
Johnny was grinning but looked almost as dead as
he was supposed to be, trembling with his face
haggard and of course his pastel shirt sporting
twin blotches of blood.

Or that is, of stage blood, as prepared
by Tex.

She was at Wyatt's side now, an arm around his waist, beaming and beautiful. "Amazing what a little Karo, Hershey's and red food coloring'll do."

Wyatt slipped an arm around her shoulder and gave her a squeeze. "Young Scarface said he wanted to see you put on a show, Tex. Well, he got his wish."

Little thin-rubber bladders of stage blood had been adhesive-taped to Johnny's chest, ready for him to prick with a small sharp spike on the back of a ring and with the tip of his knife blade, respectively.

Wyatt assumed, correctly, that Capone would shoot until Johnny dropped, and—missing with a head shot—would go for the body.

Bat, damn near giddy, came over and gave Tex a big kiss on the cheek. "Slick work, how you pulled the switch on that son of a bitch."

Basking in praise, Tex bowed and said modestly, "Thank your friend Runyon. If he hadn't been wise to Capone carrying a .38, how would we've known what caliber blanks to substitute?"

There had been a second set-up to fall back on, of course, if Capone brought some other pistol or even came unarmed, though Tex had been ready with several other calibers of blank cartridges, as well. The movie cowgirl knew her way around shooting irons.

Wyatt bussed Tex on the lips, then left her with Bat to go see how Johnny was doing. The younger man was standing there obliviously dripping fake red onto the floor, looking dragged-out but relieved, exchanging words and little kisses with the satin-clad waitress.

Wyatt put a hand on Johnny's shoulder—one of the few safe

places not to come back with a sticky red palm—and said, "Son, you have the makings of first-rate swindler."

"Thank you!"

"But I recommend dentistry."

Johnny nodded toward Dixie, whose pretty face sent contradictory signals as she smiled with eyes wet. "Did you know that Dix has secretarial training? Third in her class!"

"Perfect to work in your office, John." Then Wyatt turned to Dixie and touched the tip of her nose lightly. "Get him upstairs and cleaned up. You two have a train to catch."

The couple followed Wyatt's orders, though Dixie paused to remove Johnny's front shirt tails so he could cup it and curtail the mess.

A voice at Wyatt's side said: "We were wrong."

Wyatt turned and found the deadpan Runyon, lighting up his hundredth cigarette or so of the evening.

"How so?"

Runyon flicked a smile. "We all said little Dixie didn't have the talent God gave a termite. And maybe she can't sing or dance . . . but hell, you saw her, Wyatt. She can act."

Wyatt offered his hand to Runyon, who seemed surprised but then accepted the offer to shake. "Mr. Runyon, without you we couldn't have been able to stage this little show. Thank you."

"Melodrama's my specialty. Glad to help."

Runyon had not only agreed to be part of conning Capone, he'd suggested enlisting their mutual friend Mizner, who had been both a confidence man and cardsharp in his time. More to the point, Runyon had helped plead the cause when Earp presented the idea to Rothstein in a back booth at Reuben's just . . . my God, was it just yesterday?

Wyatt had revealed to Rothstein that Johnny's liquor was gone, destroyed, which put Johnny fatally on the spot with Capone. Would Rothstein be willing to buy Johnny's brownstone, nightclub and all, for a modest hundred grand . . .

Certainly!

. . . on *two* conditions? First, Rothstein would have to be a player, in several senses of the word, at the poker party; and second, after the scam went down, Rothstein must spread the story that Johnny had sold out everything to him, and disappeared.

Yale, of course, would know the "truth" that Rothstein was covering up: that Al Capone had killed Johnny. No matter what the kid said, Yale would likely make Capone lam it out of New York, probably to Chicago and under Little John Torrio's protective wing . . . that is, if the unreliable hothead didn't wind up dead in a ditch, courtesy of his unhappy boss.

Rothstein knew a bargain when he heard one.

"Anyway," the bright-eyed, gray-skinned mastermind had said over a plate of figs and glass of milk, "I don't mind keeping these Brooklyn crumbs in their place. And who doesn't like a good confidence game?"

With the exception of Johnny and Dix, who were upstairs changing, the entire cast assembled in the dining room where Tex served up sandwiches and coffee, an unlikely waitress in her spangly red gown.

Though they'd just spent hours pulling this scam—and Wyatt had never in all his gambler's days dealt more crooked hands of poker in a single night—everybody seemed wound up from the experience, really charged. Moments from the evening were re-enacted in anecdote form, as if they were all looking back on something that happened long ago.

"Well," Bat said, raising his coffee cup in a sort of toast, "any way you figure it, that's the last we'll ever hear of one Alphonse Capone."

Everybody was vocally agreeing with that . . . except Wyatt, who wasn't so sure. He did feel confident that Capone had been thoroughly bamboozled tonight, and that Johnny Holliday could safely re-emerge as Johnny Haroney somewhere out west, and open his dental practice with his lovely new young wife.

Before everyone left, Wyatt led them back to the poker lounge, where he returned their money and gave both Mizner and Runyon a bonus thousand.

"You have to respect money," Mizner said with a sideways smile, delicately inserting the stack of fifties into a front pocket of his tuxedo trousers. "It's the only stuff that can keep a cold cruel world from turning your name into 'Hey you.'"

The hundred grand Rothstein had "bet" tonight stayed on the table: this was Johnny's payoff for the brownstone, the deed of which had already been signed over to Rothstein.

Soon only Bat, Wyatt and Tex remained, but for the two kids upstairs.

Tex, tapping her spoon on her coffee cup lightly, did not look at Wyatt when she asked, "So you'll be going, too, then?"

"Yeah. Rothstein has his own ideas about this place. And without Johnny here . . ."

"Wouldn't be the same," she said. Her smile was wistful yet bitter. "Doc Holliday's boy. . . . How the hell much like his father *is* he?"

"*Just* like his father," Wyatt said.

Bat gave him an are-you-kidding look.

"If," Wyatt amplified, "life had dealt his old man a straight card or two."

"Johnny's healthy," Bat granted. "And he's got a good woman. Better than Big-Nosed Kate."

Wyatt wasn't sure about that, either; not that Dixie wouldn't make a good partner . . . but Kate did have her merits. Still, he let it stand . . . though it did occur to him Johnny's mother might owe him that five hundred, after all.

At the front door, Wyatt gave Tex a little kiss that she turned into something bigger. She seemed to mean it, and wanted him to have it, so he let her; wasn't half bad.

He walked her outside, where the sun had come up, and escorted her down to where a woman in a red sparkly gown could catch a cab to her apartment.

Before she got in, she paused and touched his face and, in the daylight, out of the dim light of a nightclub, she looked every year her age. Still, not half bad.

"We could've had something, Wyatt Earp."

"Seems to me," he said, "we did."

Then she was just a face in the rear window of a cab, gliding away into one more memory.

On the walk back Wyatt established to his own satisfaction that Frankie Yale had pulled his men from their watch of the club; in the aftermath of the warehouse shoot-out, Yale—who was likely under the impression the Irish White Handers were rallying against him—had apparently been too short-handed to keep up the surveillance.

That meant when Wyatt in his black Stetson and Bat in his jaunty black derby accompanied Johnny and Dix to Grand Central Terminal, the little party had scant to worry about, though of course both the two old gunfighters had revolvers in their coat pockets.

Johnny would have been hard to spot in his inconspicuous

brown business suit with a brown derby, and Dixie was just another pretty but unremarkable young woman in her simple dark blue frock with white trim with white cloche hat. They had only two suitcases, plus the briefcase of money, and the former they checked, the latter Johnny held on to.

At the gate Dixie gave Wyatt a kiss on the cheek, Bat, too; she told them both they were wonderful and they did not disagree.

Johnny and Wyatt shook hands.

"We never really did get a chance to talk about my father," Johnny said.

"Maybe next time."

"Funny thing is, being around you these weeks . . . I feel I do know better what he was like."

"You need to know what he was like," Wyatt said, and tipped his Stetson, "just look in the mirror."

Johnny liked hearing that, and he and Dixie waved as they went off and disappeared onto the steam-floating platform.

"Dunstan's?" Bat asked, as their footsteps echoed among the many others in the vast marble terminal.

"What, more food? Bartholomew, we just had sandwiches."

"I could use some eggs and bacon."

So they had breakfast together, and reminisced about old times, and recent times, too, and Bat promised he would come west someday soon, and Wyatt promised he would come east again.

Neither happened, of course, because a year or so later, more or less—at his desk at the *Telegraph*, chasing a deadline—Bat Masterson slumped over a half-written column and fell asleep forever.

And when Wyatt read about it—in a several-days'-old newspaper over a cup of Sadie's terrible coffee out at the Happy Days mine—it was way too late to head out from California for the funeral.

Not that it mattered.

Hadn't he and Bartholomew already bid each other a bang-up goodbye?

# Tip of the Black Hat

Despite its fanciful nature, this novel does have a basis in history beyond the famous names of Wyatt Earp, Bat Masterson and Al Capone. Like these three, the majority of characters here are real-life figures and appear under their own names, though a few major players are wholly fictional, notably Johnny Holliday and Dixie Douglas. For the sake of the narrative, the deck of history has occasionally been shuffled, with events taking place sooner or later than in reality; and, while I have attempted to maintain a reasonably clear picture of New York in the early months of Prohibition, at times research dating to the later twenties has come into play.

Many of the real events that underpin my fictionalized depictions are inconsistently portrayed by historians, such as when exactly Al Capone shifted from Brooklyn to Chicago, sometimes shown as early as 1918 and even as late as 1920, with the major Capone biographers in disagreement as to even the reason for that departure. When exactly Capone received the knife wounds that resulted in his famous scars remains an historical blur, although the circumstances most often reported are similar to those given in this novel. The beginnings of Texas Guinan's nightclub career are also all over the map, though in fairness it's unlikely her act was in as full-blown bloom so early during Prohibition.

I have endeavored not to use pop cultural references (song titles, movie stars, etc.) often associated with the Roaring Twenties because the likes of "Baby Face" and "Bye Bye Blackbird" and Clara Bow and Rudolph Valentino weren't on the scene yet. Nitpickers are discouraged, however, from addressing the 1920 of *Black Hats* as the 1920 of reality.

The notion for this novel grew out of the publication of two fine biographies, *Wyatt Earp: The Life Behind the Legend* (1997) by Casey Tefertiller and *Inventing Wyatt Earp: His Life and Many Legends* (1998) by Allen Barra. I noticed a fascinating fact in Tefertiller that was later confirmed by Barra: Wyatt Earp had been a private detective in Los Angeles in the first part of the twentieth century.

Then a few years ago, a writing student of mine, cartoonist Steven Lackey (to whom this novel is dedicated), approached me with an idea for a sequel to my novelization of the Hollywood film *Maverick* (1994), derived from the wonderful old James Garner TV show. Steve, not understanding I had no claim to the property, suggested I write a novel about Bret Maverick meeting a Brooklyn-era Al Capone in New York at the start of Prohibition— tommy guns and sixguns. I immediately thought of using Earp, who I knew had lived till 1929, and recalled also sportswriter Bat Masterson's concurrent presence in Manhattan.

I'd also like to acknowledge my longtime research associate, George Hagenauer, for New York reference, among other things. And I wish to thank writer Robert J. Randisi, who wrote a fine mystery about Bat Masterson (set about ten years prior to this novel) entitled *The Ham Reporter* (1986); I asked Bob for his blessing and he graciously granted it.

Wyatt Earp has interested me since childhood, when like so many Baby Boomer boys I watched Hugh O'Brian in the late 1950s television series *The Life and Legend of Wyatt Earp*, as well as Burt Lancaster as Wyatt (and Kirk Douglas as Doc) in the John Sturges film *Gunfight at the O.K. Corral* (1957). I was greatly impressed that the show and the film had been based on a real person's life, and my interest in historically based narrative probably begins there.

Of course, neither the series nor the film was particularly accurate, though the former was based on the official biography, *Wyatt Earp: Frontier Marshal* (1931) by Stuart Lake. Wyatt cooperated with Lake, much as several decades later sportswriter Oscar Fraley would do with Eliot Ness on the first major Capone book, *The Untouchables* (1957). Earp and Ness have much in common, both lawmen being subjects of entertaining if flawed image-building books spawning late '50s TV hits, which presented exaggerated versions of their heroics that would in turn lead to much over-zealous debunking.

Like the Fraley book on Ness, Lake's biography of Wyatt has been roundly dismissed over the years, though in both cases these landmark works are relatively accurate. In each case the writer, a professional looking to create an entertaining read, depended upon the memories of his aging subject, and organized and embellished the material into a coherent, compelling narrative.

As an overreaction to the O'Brian TV series (again, the Ness parallel maintains), a number of legend-busting books were published, notably the indefensible Franks Waters tome, *The Earp Brothers of Tombstone* (1960). Any other work on Earp—and Wyatt has inspired dozens—that draws from Waters is of little value to the scholar or even a novelist just trying to get Wyatt's character right.

Pro-Earp writer Glenn Boyer—author of numerous interesting books on Wyatt and related subjects—tried to right the Waters wrongs in *I Married Wyatt Earp* (1976), a purported nonfiction work derived from "the recollections of Josephine Sarah Marcus Earp." Unfortunately, this book has been demonstrated to be at least in part historical fiction (some of Boyer's later Wyatt Earp volumes are clearly labeled such).

So as I gathered approaching fifty books on Wyatt Earp, Doc Holliday, Tombstone and related subjects, I determined that for my purposes any work using as an unquestioned nonfiction source Lake, or Waters, or Boyer, was best avoided.

The Earp books that were of the most value, after Tefertiller and Barra, were Bob Boze Bell's *The Illustrated Life and Times of Wyatt Earp* (1993) and *The Illustrated Life and Times of Doc Holliday* (1994). With their vivid illustrations, rare photographs and countless interesting sidebars, these chronological breakdowns of the lives of the two notorious friends are entertaining and informative. Bell is the editor of *True West* magazine, numerous issues of which were another helpful source.

Also helpful was *Wyatt Earp: A Biography of the Legend Volume One* (2002) by Lee A. Silva, a massive, extensively researched work; unfortunately this installment only goes through Wyatt's Dodge City days. Other key references were *The Earp Decision* (1989), Jack DeMattos; *The Earp Papers: In a Brother's Image* (1994), Don Chaput; *The Earps Talk* (1980), edited by Alford E. Turner; *Gunfight at the O.K. Corral and Other Western Adventures* (1954), George Scullin; *The Real Wyatt Earp* (2000), Steve Gatto; and *Wyatt Earp: The Missing Years* (1998), Kenneth R. Cilch and Kenneth R. Cilch.

Despite the controversy surrounding his work, Glenn G. Boyer has played such a vital role in Earp research that I did draw upon his series of pamphlets, *Wyatt Earp—Family, Friends & Foes*, most specifically, *Who Was Big Nose Kate?* (1997). Of the Doc Holliday biographies, I leaned upon *Doc Holliday: A Family Portrait* (1998), Karen Holliday Tanner, which draws from Boyer.

I generally do not read other historical novels about a subject I'm contemplating; but I would be remiss not to mention the best Wyatt Earp book, the long out-of-print, and yet extremely influential, *Saint Johnson* (1930), by W.R. Burnett. Burnett, the most undervalued of great American crime writers, went to Tombstone and researched this unflinching study of the Earp/Clanton conflict, beating Stuart Lake to the punch. Many Earp films have derived from Burnett's work, including the first major one, *Law and Order* (1932) with Walter Huston as the Wyatt character.

As part of immersing myself in the subject, I watched every Wyatt Earp film available. The power of Wyatt's life and legend is borne out by how many really strong films he's inspired, in particular John Ford's *My Darling Clementine* (1946) with Henry Fonda as Wyatt; John Sturges's aforementioned *Gunfight at the O.K. Corral* and his vendetta sequel, *Hour of the Gun* (1967) with James Garner as Wyatt (Garner also played Earp in Blake Edwards's jokey *Sunset*, 1988); and the two competitive big-budget '90s films, George P. Cosmatos's *Tombstone* (1993) with Kurt Russell as Wyatt, and Lawrence Kasdan's *Wyatt Earp* (1994) with Kevin Costner as Wyatt. Film fans and Earp buffs often argue the merits of the latter two, but I find both worthwhile.

Bat Masterson was the hero of another Western TV favorite of the 1950s, with actor Gene Barry bringing the derby-sporting, cane-clubbing lawman to larger-than-life. The biography serving as basis for the series, *Bat Masterson* (1957) by Richard O'Connor, appears to take a legend-building Stuart Lake stance. Nonetheless, the book remains a valuable Masterson resource. A more scholarly yet very readable path was taken by Robert K. DeArment in his definitive *Bat Masterson: The Man and the Legend* (1979).

Masterson himself wrote a series of magazine articles about Earp and other Western figures, collected as *Famous Gun Fighters of the Western Frontier* (1908); an article written about Bat by his friend and editor, Alfred Henry Lewis, rounds out the collection of historical sketches. Unfortunately a difficult book to find in any edition, the 1982 Weatherford Press version, annotated by Jack DeMattos, is recommended. Bat's memory doesn't seem any better than Wyatt's, but the collection represents a rare semi-memoir by one of the West's most famous gunfighters (and one turned professional writer, at that).

I have read and written much about Al Capone over the years, but the major sources remain John Kobler's *Capone* (1971), Laurence Bergreen's *Capone* (1994), and Robert J. Schoenberg's *Mr. Capone* (1992). Background on Johnny Torrio and Frankie Yale was derived from *Johnny Torrio: First of the Gang Lords* (1970), Jack McPhaul; *Paddy Whacked: The Untold Story of the Irish American Gangster* (2005), T.J. English; and in particular *Under the Clock: The Inside Story of the Mafia's First 100 Years* (1988), William Balsamo & George Carpozi, Jr., which concentrates on Frankie Yale. For Arnold Rothstein I turned to *In the Reign of Rothstein* (1929), Donald Henderson Clake, and *Rothstein* (2003), David Pietrusza.

A key work on New York during Prohibition, *The Night Club Era* (1933) by *New York Herald-Tribune* city editor Stanley Walker, is a source used by virtually every modern book on the subject, and mine is no exception. Other vintage works consulted include *Incredible New York* (1951), Lloyd Morris; *New York* (1930), Paul Morand; *New York Nights* (1927), Stephen Graham; *Rand McNally New York Guide* (1922); *Valentine's City of New York* (1920), Henry Collins Brown; and *The WPA Guide to New York City* (1939). Two memoirs reflecting the era were useful: *Belle Out of Order* (1959), Belle Livingston; and *Blonde, Brunettes and Bullets* (1957), Nils T. Granlund. So was the unusual (and unsigned) tribute volume, *The Iron Gate—Jack & Charlie's "21"* (1950).

More recent works consulted on New York night life during Prohibition include *The Devil's Playground* (2004), James Traub; *Gangsters & Gold Diggers: Old New York, The Jazz Age, and the Birth of Broadway* (2003), Jerome Charyn; *New York Night: The Mystique and Its History* (2005), Mark Caldwell; *Nightclub Nights: Art, Legend and Style 1920–1960* (2001), Susan Waggoner; and *The Stork Club* (2000), Ralph Blumenthal.

For background on Coney Island I turned to *Coney Island: The People's Playground* (2002), Michael Immerso; *Coney Island: Lost and Found* (2002), Charles Denson; and *Good Old Coney Island* (1957), Edo McCullough.

Information on trains and train travel came from *All Aboard! The Railroad in American Life* (1996), George H. Douglas; *The American Railroad Passenger Car* (1978), John H. White, Jr.; *History of the Atchison, Topeka and Santa Fe Railway* (1974), Keith L. Bryant, Jr.; and *The History of the Atchison, Topeka & Santa Fe* (1988), Pamela Berkman.

To portray various secondary characters I sought inspiration and information from the following biographies: *Jack Dempsey: The Manassa Mauler* (1979), Randy Roberts; *A Flame of Pure Fire: Jack Dempsey and the Roaring '20s* (1999), Roger Kahn; *My*

*Life East and West* (1903), William H. Hart; *The Legendary Mizners* (1953), Alva Johnson; *Hello Sucker! The Story of Texas Guinan* (1989), Glenn Shirley; and *Texas Guinan: Queen of the Nightclubs* (1993), Louise Berliner.

Damon Runyon, though a minor player here, nonetheless casts a large shadow. I had only read a handful of his stories as an adolescent, and, seeking flavor for the world of this novel, I began to read about him, and by him. His stories were a revelation to me; he is dismissed as a comical/sentimental twist-ending specialist, which ignores the vividness of his first-person narration, the toughness of his view, and the darkness of his world. I came away from this project thinking Runyon deserves a place beside Dashiell Hammett, Raymond Chandler, and James M. Cain, only he's a better short story writer than any of them.

Books about Runyon that I read in whole or in part include *Broadway Boogie Woogie: Damon Runyon and the Making of New York City Culture* (2003); *Damon Runyon—A Life* (1991), Jimmy Breslin; *The Men Who Invented Broadway: Damon Runyon, Walter Winchell & Their World* (1981), John Mosedale; *Trials and Tribulations: The Best of His True-Crime Writing* (1946), Damon Runyon; and *The World of Damon Runyon* (1978), Tom Clark. Also helpful was *Winchell: Gossip, Power and the Culture of Celebrity* (1995), Neal Gabler.

Dozens of Internet sites answered questions on the fly on subjects ranging from milk delivery to Western lingo, as well as filled in blanks on individuals like Wilson Mizner and Texas Guinan, and locations including Coney Island and Times Square. I acknowledge and thank the mysterious, industrious individuals who put so much research at a writer's literal fingertips.

I would especially like to thank my editor, Sarah Durand, who responded enthusiastically to the idea of this novel from the outset, and whose hard work, guidance and patience has kept it (and me) on track. And I am, as always, grateful to my agent and friend, Dominick Abel.

Of course the last and biggest thanks must go to my wife, Barbara, who was always willing to interrupt her own writing to play in-house editor, on-call psychoanalyst, impromptu researcher, and reliable sounding board. She is truly queen of the cowgirls.

# About the Author

PATRICK CULHANE is the pseudonym of mystery writer Max Allan Collins, who has been called by both *Publisher's Weekly* and *Chicago Magazine* "the master of true-crime fiction." A frequent Mystery Writers of America "Edgar" nominee, and winner of an Anthony for nonfiction, he has earned an unprecedented fourteen Private Eye Writers of America "Shamus" nominations, winning twice for Best Novel.

His graphic novel *Road to Perdition* is the basis of the Academy Award–winning film starring Tom Hanks and Paul Newman, directed by Sam Mendes. His many comics credits include "Dick Tracy"; his own "Ms. Tree"; "Batman"; and "CSI: Crime Scene Investigation," based on the hit TV series for which he has also written a *USA Today*–bestselling series of novels.

An independent filmmaker in the Midwest, he has directed and/or written features appearing on HBO and Lifetime, and recently completed a film version of his play, *Eliot Ness: An Untouchable Life*. His other credits include film criticism, short fiction, songwriting, and movie/TV tie-in novels, including the *New York Times* bestseller *Saving Private Ryan*.

The author lives in Muscatine, Iowa, with his wife, writer Barbara; their son, Nathan, is currently taking postgraduate work in Japan.